THE SOUL MUST GO ON

A sequel to Soul's Choice

Kerri Davidson

Once again, this book is dedicated to my husband, Travis.
You are my biggest supporter in writing and in life.
I would be lost without you.

ACKNOWLEDGMENTS

Most heartfelt thanks go to:

My beta readers, Mark E. Gelinas Sr., Patricia Earnest Suter,
and Owen M. James.

My editor, Joanne Paulson.

My cover artist, Jamie Isfeld.

You all helped make this book shine.

Chapter 1

So, this is the afterlife. I can't say I'm impressed.

Where are the fluffy white clouds, the harps and gates? Alternatively, where are the burning pits of fire? And where is everyone else?

There's nothing here but swirly clouds of acidic green. Thick, suffocating clouds that taste like copper.

Okay, there's a bunch of little sparks of light darting about. Other people, I suppose. And there's a whack of glowing doorways dotting the gloom. I think I came out of one of those when I died.

Yes, sad but true. I'm dead. I don't want to talk about why.

So, if I'm dead, am I still Amy Clarke? Well, Amy Clarke-Grant.

Whatever. Am I still me? I feel like me, but there's nothing to me. I have no body, yet I can see, taste, hear, and smell. Hell, I can even feel.

I think. Maybe it's my imagination. Maybe this is all my imagination.

Except nothing has ever felt this real.

Strange. I'm laughing, but I can't hear it. What am I laughing at? Goodbye to dieting? Yeah, I had a problem with that. Not anymore. I'm nothing more than a spark now, just like those other things blinking around up here.

Crap. I'm still hungry, though.

This place is weird. Everything is weird. I shouldn't be here. I was only eighteen years old. Actually, if we're going to talk about things that shouldn't have happened . . .

No, not yet. That door right in front of me, that is absolutely the one I came out of. I have a feeling if I were to get closer to it, I'd be able to see things. The world I lived in. Maybe the people I left behind there.

Like I said, I'm not ready.

Exhausting, just floating here in the middle of nothing. I'm going to need to do something to keep my mind occupied.

I want to see my parents. My dad died not even a year ago, my mom the year before that. Where are they?

As I think the question, something tugs at me. Might as well follow this mystery pull. At least it's leading me away from my door.

Ick. Is there such a thing as motion sickness if you don't have a stomach? Sure feels like it. Can we not slow this down?

Neat. Apparently, I can.

Slower now, I'm heading toward the third door away from my own. Those blips of light right outside it, that white one and that pinkish one, those are my parents.

I pull to a stop, watching. They have no physical form, just colors. There's nothing to tell me who they are but a feeling. They haven't noticed me, which is fine. All of a sudden I'm not so sure I want to reunite with them anymore.

They abandoned me on Earth. Well, my mom was killed in a car accident. Not her fault. And my dad died of heart disease. Still . . .

Here they are, having a grand old time. I bet they're not thinking of me at all. They certainly hadn't been watching over me when I died.

Where'd they go?

I fly over to the doorway they vanished into, stopping just outside the threshold. Should I look in?

***

Well, holy shit. What a world. Definitely not Earth. It's mostly water, with one big continent shaped kind of like Africa.

And there are my parents, Jason and Amelia. They look just like they did the last time I saw them. They still have those colors inside them, but I can see their physical forms as they float down to the ground. Are they reincarnating?

They're getting farther away, their bodies dissolving into only colors again. Just as they're about to disappear altogether, Mom opens her eyes and looks right up at me.

Yeah, bet you didn't expect to see me here.

Dad opens his too. They both look shocked.

Well, they should be.

Goodbye again, folks. I wave and give them a sad little smile, before turning away and shooting off into the darkness.

I don't need them. I don't need anybody.

Chapter 2

Elizabeth Stapleton was a special child. Precocious, was what her parents called her at the age of four. Funny how she understood what that meant. She had yet to begin her education programs.

That wasn't the only thing she knew as she became aware of herself and her surroundings. Her physical brain was only beginning to develop, but there was a wealth of knowledge already in there, just waiting to burst out.

Her first words were nothing as simple as Mom, Dad, or juice. Her first word was Jason. Her first sentence was, "I want to go home," followed by, "I miss writing."

Confusing for Sydney and Marsha Stapleton, no doubt. But they chose to turn that confusion into pride and encourage her apparent love for learning.

Still, as her vocabulary grew, she spoke of the strangest things. Everyone commented on what a vivid imagination she had. What a creative mind she must possess, to assign colors and associated attributes to each person.

Mom was onyx. Shiny, smooth, and stern. Dad was royal blue. Gentle and calm, yet he could be fun. Oh, she had a color for them all. Friends, relatives, even the people at the supply depots.

As if that wasn't enough, she gave them outside colors too. Ones that changed depending upon their moods. And she was dead accurate – enough so to prompt the talk before she began her education programs.

True to her first words about wanting to write, little blond-haired, golden-eyed Lizzy was in her chambers tapping away on her flashpad the day her parents came to have the discussion.

"Lizzy, do you have a moment?"

"Of course, Mother," she replied.

She saved her work and swiveled around to face them.

They seated themselves on the settee opposite her.

"You're awfully orange today. Is something wrong?" Lizzy asked.

Her mother swallowed and looked at her father, who was also orange.

"Sort of. You know how we talked about special people, children with gifts?"

"Like imagination?"

"Yes. Our society is an open-minded one, and we're lucky to live in such an accepting time, however . . ."

"Is this about the colors?"

"Yes. Most people enjoy your talks about inner and outer auras. You are truly gifted with creativity, but sometimes it makes people uncomfortable."

"Because I know too much?"

"You are very intuitive, that's for sure," her father confirmed, growing oranger.

"I can stop talking about the colors."

Both outer auras settled into a pale orange. They must be pleased. But she knew they weren't finished yet.

"Do I have to stop talking about Jason and Amy, too?"

The orange flared.

"No. Imaginary friends are acceptable for someone your age, but perhaps you could find a way to keep the stories at home." Her mother peeked over Lizzy's shoulder, trying to see her flashpad.

Lizzy had darkened the glass after saving. Maybe they were right. Maybe people didn't need to know everything she did. The memories, or as her parents called them, illusions, were coming back faster and stronger every day.

"Sure. Is there anything else?"

Orange, orange, orange.

"You're aware of how advanced you are compared to other children your age."

It wasn't a question, but she responded, "I am."

"We thought you might like to begin therapy at the same time you embark on your education programs." Her mother was glowing orange now, picking at a loose thread on her jumpsuit.

"I think I would enjoy that," she said, beaming at them.

Their colors relaxed once again. Lizzy was certain hers would be a bit red if she could see it. She was irritated, but she was getting good at hiding it.

"Oh, well, great," her father said as they rose to leave. "You do understand we only want to set you on the path to a productive and enjoyable life, don't you?"

"I do. Thank you for the talk."

She turned back to her workstation and waited until they left before reactivating the flashpad.

She should have seen that one coming. People were indeed open to new thoughts, new ideas; creativity was encouraged. As a hobby. Oddities were tolerated. Crazy was okay until it ceased to be amusing.

Whoops, crazy wasn't a word used here. Note to self.

Lizzy returned to where she left off in her work. She was writing a diary of sorts.

She wasn't documenting this life; she was writing about her past life. About people, places, and experiences from Earth and the In Between. For this entry, she would be dealing with auras.

Who knew, maybe one day writing would be classified as a job. As of yet, there was no such profession. Some people wrote for fun, like herself, but they didn't get paid. Not like she used to when she was an author on the planet Earth.

Everyone has a main aura directly in their core which doesn't change a whole lot. Around that is a second aura that fluctuates sporadically depending on their moods.

My husband Jason's main aura, his very soul, was a pale red. Not quite pink, but gentle and soothing.

My daughter Amy's was practically black. I was never sure what to think of that.

I didn't get the chance to find out what color mine was, back when I was Amelia Clarke. I couldn't see my own. I still can't. Not even when I look in a mirror. I wonder if it's changed.

Oh, what the therapists would make of all the words she'd stored on this device over the past few months. She was actually looking forward to beginning therapy early and couldn't quite understand why her parents were so nervous about suggesting it.

Everyone here went to therapy. It was normal and mandatory, seen as a benefit instead of a weakness, as opposed to the last society she'd existed in. Most people didn't start until the age of nine or ten, but she wasn't about to complain. Maybe she would learn more about herself and why she was so special.

Or maybe not. She wasn't sure exactly how much she would be able to share with her therapist, never mind the rest of the world. According to the conversation she had with her parents, it was something she would need to watch.

But she had plenty of time to figure it out. She was still only four.

Chapter 3

Why am I so tired? I can't sleep. Believe me, I've tried. Whenever I go to close my eyes, nothing happens. I just hang here, continuing to see everything.

Maybe it's my old life following me, haunting me. I was tired right before I died. That's kind of why I died.

I hadn't realized I'd wandered back to my doorway. I was just traveling along aimlessly, or so I thought. Maybe it's time to take a look in there. I don't even know how long I've been dead. I'm not sure if I want to see my husband or the kids yet, but maybe I can look at other stuff.

I wonder if I can haunt people.

Woah, who's this?

A lemon-yellow spark is coming right at me. I know this spark. But I have no idea how.

She slows her approach as she gets closer. I find myself smiling. She feels like family, long-lost family. I think I love this person.

As she hovers uncertainly at a respectful distance, I sense someone else coming up behind me. I turn around and . . . Dad?

What in the world is he doing here? Well, not world; whatever this place is. But seriously, did he go ahead and die again already?

The pink dot is weaving its way toward me. He looks like he's drunk.

The yellow dot shoots past me, and I watch as they latch on to each other. It looks like she's dragging him to a spot away from the doorway to Earth.

I have no idea what's going on, how they know each other, or who she is to us.

I'm not sure I want to go over and join them. I can still see them. They're just sitting there. Are they talking? Can we talk to each other here?

I look back in the direction Dad came from, half expecting Mom to come strolling by. Nope.

Well, I'm not just going to stand here all day. What will it be? Dad and Mystery Pal, or Earth?

Maybe I will just stand here all day. It's not like my legs are going to get tired. It's not like I even know how long a day is. No sun or moon to tell me.

Hmm, I suppose my decision's been made. I'm drifting toward the door.

Why not?

***

Cripes. My head spins as my view is sucked into Dean's apartment. Well, I guess it had been my apartment too. We weren't married long before I kicked it.

Just long enough to have a couple of kids. Actually, not even. I was knocked up before we got married. Neither of us was even sure if the twins were his.

Weird. I don't think I've been dead all that long, although it's been long enough that I at least don't have to see my own corpse.

Dean and my cousin Stacey are in the very room I died in. The twins' nursery. There are tissues and tears, the boxes I never bothered to unpack when I moved are still stacked in the corner. The babies don't look much older than the three months they were when I left – not that I looked at them very often.

Why is everyone so colorful? They all have sparks inside them like the ones I see up here, but they also have another circle of color around their bodies. The outside ones are kinda wavy.

Senses overloaded, I resist the urge to pull away.

"You've got to stop that, Dean. It wasn't your fault."

"It was. I knew how depressed she was. I thought I was doing all I could, but I know now I wasn't. I should have done

more. I should have spent more time with her, instead of just the kids."

"Hey, I was here every day after school and on weekends helping out too. I saw how you were with all of them. She wouldn't let you in. She wouldn't let me in either, but neither of us gave up. You don't see me blaming myself, do you?"

"You were her cousin. I was her husband. It's different."

Eesh, their outside colors are making me sick. They keep flicking from one color to the next. I wonder if it's possible to have a seizure when you're dead. We'll find out.

They each pick up a baby as the twins start to cry simultaneously. Now there's a sound I definitely don't miss.

When I was alive, I was diagnosed with acute postpartum depression, and had a pailful of medicines for the condition. The doctor was certain I would be fine and eventually bond with my children.

I think it's safe to say I proved him wrong. I didn't want them to begin with. I'm still not sure why I went through with it. My dad had just died when I learned I was pregnant, and Dean was there all in love with me, not caring whether or not he was the father.

Looking at them now, I don't feel as much resentment toward them as I did when I was alive. The crying is still annoying, but some small part of me wants to reach out to them.

Darren and Diedre aren't identical twins, but their middle colors are. Not quite black, but a dark grey. There's not much to their outer ones, just a hazy golden mist hovering around them.

Hey kids, wanna tell me who your father is?

Maybe these colors are what people call auras. That would make sense. I'm just not sure why they need two of them.

Dean's inner aura is cream-colored, Stacey's a drab grey. What a pair they'd make. Both super nice, both super boring.

The babies stop crying together, as was their way, having been rocked to sleep.

"Do you think she meant to do it?" Dean asks in a whisper, gaze fixed on baby Darren.

"I don't know. We'll never know for sure. What do you think?"

"I love her so much. Why do I feel like I'm betraying her when my heart tells me to agree with the results of the investigation?"

"You can't tell your heart what to feel. Again, I truly don't know what happened, whether it was an accident or intentional, but it saddens me to know she'll be forever branded as the victim of suicide."

***

What a lousy pair of —

I can't even. I push myself away from the world so I can no longer see them.

Suicide. They ruled my death a suicide. I would love to get my hands on that investigation. Did no one look at the cocktail of pills that were prescribed to me? Surely that's what happened.

Yeah, I took a bunch of them right before I died. And a few sleeping pills. And I was drinking vodka. But I was tired. Stacey was supposed to be over within the hour that day, and I was getting ready to have a nap.

No one ever explained that the pills could kill me. It's not like I downed a bottle or anything.

I was just so goddamned tired.

Am I crying? Oh, how in the hell would I know? I'm pissed off, that's for sure.

Those two, my biggest supporters who claimed to love me, think I offed myself.

And now they're down there playing house with my kids.

I sit in the murk and stew. Rational thoughts creep into my fury, dowsing it.

Did I do it on purpose? On some level?

I don't want to think about it. Not yet. You guys enjoy yourselves with my babies, I shout at the opening with my imaginary voice. Go ahead and get married for all I care.

Turning away, I search out my dad and Mystery Pal. Yep, they're still sitting together over there. My dad's aura is brightening. Maybe he was hurt and she's helping him.

I'll figure them out later. Right now, I want my mother.

Chapter 4

Lizzy stepped up to the sensor and tapped her wrist on it.

"Name and identification number, please."

"Amelia – shit."

Good thing it was an automated system that didn't record the actual words. She was pretty sure most six-year-olds knew their own names. And they didn't swear.

Not the first time she'd done this, she waited through the ten-second cycle of silence before the program reset itself.

"That name and number is invalid. Please repeat the process and be sure to enunciate." Pause. "Name and identification number, please."

"Elizabeth Stapleton. 310TCOH7267."

The sound of a latch clicking was followed by the door sliding into the wall.

Lizzy entered the reception area and took a seat on the settee. The only one there, she activated her portable gopad and settled in to read.

She was right in the middle of a story by an author who reminded her of herself. The voice and style of writing was similar to what she remembered publishing in her old life. Or her imaginary life, as she was encouraged to believe.

The only difference was that this person wasn't getting paid. There were no physical copies of books. The writers weren't even called authors. The only occupations that had anything to do with writing were journalists and educators. Not a lot of creative reign to be found in those professions.

She really was trying to reconcile her memories as being a product of her imagination. It wasn't going well, but at least she was getting better at hiding it from others.

The door to the therapist's office whooshed open, and Lizzy sighed as she looked at her. The fact that she could see her lavender inner aura and took note of her brownish-green outer one, was not helping her believe in normal.

"Good day, Ms. Stapleton. Please come in."

"Thank you, Dr. Artaria."

Lizzy switched off her gopad and entered the doctor's office.

Just like all the other rooms in their building, it was plain. White, white, and white were the colors of choice everywhere.

There was no art in this world. No paintings. No one hung photos on their walls. There were only bits and pieces of computer-generated designs on obscure ethersites, created by unpaid artists for their own amusement. The sites did not get a lot of hits.

"I'm glad you showed up early. You're my last appointment for the day, and I'm not feeling the best."

Lizzy swallowed her "I know" comment. The woman's outer aura was screaming illness. She settled for offering her sympathies and hopes that she would feel better soon.

"Thank you. I'm sure it's just a bug."

Yep, that was Lizzy's guess too. No serious diseases or plagues to speak of on Celadon.

They both took their seats, and the doctor flipped through the screens on her flashpad.

"How was your weekend, Lizzy?"

"Productive. I completed all my extra education assignments, spent a lot of time at our horticulture station on the roof, and I attended a schoolmate's birthing commemoration."

Dr. Artaria pecked some notes on the flashpad.

Lizzy had a pretty good idea what they would be about. Using large words, overachiever, etc. At least the birthing commemoration should please her, no?

"How are you coming along with those dreams? Are the therapy waves helping at all?"

Awkward. The therapy waves were helping, but not in the way they were intended to. They were frequencies administered at night via one's earchip, designed to reduce the rate and vividness of disturbing dreams.

But Lizzy didn't consider her dreams to be unpleasant. In fact, she looked forward to them. Even though she was supposed to be trying, she didn't believe they were dreams at all. They were memories.

She'd been using the waves for weeks, and they were only making her recollections clearer. The one she had the night before was a breakthrough rediscovery, and she was dying to talk about it.

None of this was anything that would please Dr. Artaria. How to put a spin on it?

"The waves are helping, Doctor." Not a lie.

"Excellent. So, when is the last time you had a dream?"

"Last night. It was about how we entered the world."

A crooked eyebrow popped up over the flashpad.

"We?"

Whoops. An unnecessary overshare. Well, might as well finish.

"It was silly." Lie. "My husband Jason and I were floating down to be reincarnated together, and we saw our daughter appear in the doorway. She shouldn't have been there. She was still only a teenager on Earth and she'd just had twin babies of her own."

Both eyebrows were up in the air now. Okay, quick wrap-up.

"We tried to go back through the door, but I couldn't. I was too tired. I think Jason made it, though. It felt like we ripped apart."

"That's an interesting dream. All the same characters as usual, I see."

"Like I said, it was just silly . . ."

Eyebrows gone, the doctor returned to tapping on her pad.

Argh. When would she learn to just keep her mouth shut?

"Well, I think we should increase your waves. We'll start the new program tonight. All you'll need to do is update your earchip before you retire, all right?"

"All right."

"How are you enjoying the new education programs you were advanced to?"

"Oh, I adore them. I'm learning so much. I had no idea there were so many different job options to choose from. I can't wait until I'm old enough to leave the domes and start field training so I can decide which one I want to do."

Dr. Artaria's chuckle was one of amusement, but short. Lizzy knew she'd said the wrong things yet again. She knew before she said them.

"It will be quite a while before you're old enough for that. Always in such a rush, you are. How about your education mates? Have you made any new acquaintances?"

She was definitely going to fail this session. Unless . . .

"I have. I find I'm able to be more social amongst my older peers."

Not a lie, but the doctor's face reminded her to dumb down her words a touch.

"I mean, I think I wasn't making acquaintances because I wasn't fitting in. I am now. I have plans to attend the Ethereal Ceremony with a group of my education mates this week."

Dr. Artaria didn't need to know her parents had encouraged her to do this, promising her an entire afternoon of uninterrupted free time. Free time she was intending on using to work on her extracurricular studies and writing.

"That's great to hear, Lizzy. So, if you'll just go ahead and do that earchip update tonight, we'll see you again next week."

"Thank you, Doctor. I hope you feel better soon."

Dr. Artaria's face had taken on the same shade as her outer aura.

"Thanks. I'll set myself up with some healing waves as soon as I'm done here."

She continued tapping on her flashpad as Lizzy let herself out.

She raised her arm to open the second door leading to the corridor but paused with it halfway to the sensor. What an odd sensation.

"Amy?" she whispered, eyes on the ceiling.

Chapter 5

Um, confusing?

When I first peeked in, I expected to see that shiny world with domes encasing buildings bigger than you could imagine.

It wouldn't have surprised me if I saw my mom as a baby, beginning a new life.

But all I saw was some kid wearing my mom's soul.

No, it doesn't make any sense. I push myself farther away and try to figure out what I just saw.

I recognized Mom's color right away; that brilliant white light, that feeling. There was no mistaking it was her. But how did she get so old already?

Never mind that; she remembered us. She remembered me. She felt me when I reached out to her just before I left. I don't know how I did it, but she knew I was there.

I wonder if Dad knows about this? By the sound of things, he never even made it all the way in. Maybe that's why he's not doing so well.

More than a little part of me wants to just give up. I still feel like a kid myself. How am I supposed to even begin sorting all these messes out?

I've got that whole Earth disaster I left behind, and my mother's living in some sort of space world as a kid who remembers me and Dad. And Dad . . . well, he's off visiting with Mystery Pal.

Yeah, I'm going to need to take my time traveling back to them and my doorway. Not really a problem, since I'm still just as tired as I was before I died. More so.

Being dead isn't easy. And why in the hell am I hungry? There's no food here. No stomach to put it in. I have no head, yet I have a headache. What I wouldn't do for a cigarette . . .

I drag my ghost-ass back to where I can see my pink Dad and my yellow pal and halt, undecided again.

I kind of want to go back and look at Earth, but I don't want to see the kids, Dean, or Stacey. I want to see something else.

I already know I can't just flip through the world willy-nilly, but the last time I looked in, I felt there was someone else calling to me. I don't know who, but there was someone else.

They can wait, I decide. Give them a while, and maybe they'll all space-age too. Wouldn't that be convenient?

These two up here, they're not going anywhere. I might as well join them and see if I can figure out what they're up to.

I approach them slowly, but they see me coming. How do I know this? Did Mystery Pal's head perk up at the sight of me? Of course not; she's got no head. But her color brightened.

My apprehension lessens the closer I get. Times are tough, things are weird, but there's nothing to be afraid of here. These two souls love me.

It still feels odd, settling into the little circle. What am I supposed to do?

Hey, guys. First of all, how'd you get out, Dad? What's wrong with you? Oh, and Mystery Pal, who in the hell are you?

Nada. Great. All I'm getting is a bunch of vibes. They're probably sensing how confused I am.

Vibes, sensing, really? This is what it's going to be like up here?

Fine. I try to relax and clear my mind. This is going to take a while.

Mystery Pal moves to my side and connects with me. Don't ask. All I know is she's touching me and doing something. Something that's recharging me. It feels so good, I'm not going to question it. This must have been what she was doing with my dad.

Before long, she detaches herself, gives me a comforting nudge, and heads off into the green darkness.

It's just me and my dad now.

She had definitely been healing him. He looks a lot better. Like a shiny little apple instead of rotted salmon. But he's angry and confused.

Yeah, well, join the club.

I know he wants to yell at me. He probably is in his ghost-head, just like I was doing earlier. There was only one time he yelled at me right good during our lives on Earth. I deserved it then, and I turned my life around that very day.

For a while. As soon as he died and I found out I was pregnant, back down the hole I went. I didn't care about anything. Not Dean, not the babies, not myself. I was back to where I started as an overweight, socially-awkward teenage girl.

After my mom died when I was sixteen, but before my dad got sick and followed her, I really had a good life. All two years of it, more or less. I smile now at the brief interlude of happiness I worked so hard to earn.

Turns out, life had other plans in store for me. I wasn't strong enough to fight back.

Come to think of it, our whole Earth stint had been kind of a wash. Sure, I had a decent childhood at home. Great parents, but a crappy social life. In fact, I didn't have one at all until I made my changes in high school, starting over in a new city after we lost Mom.

But that was strike one. A car crash took her from me when she was only forty-one. Her own relatives didn't fare much better. Her father and one of her sisters were gone before her, her mother not long after.

It was less than a year later when Dad decided to up and have a few heart attacks and croak on me. The last time I saw his parents, Grandpa had just had a massive stroke and Grandma had gone bonkers.

What a joke. What had been the point of all that? Sure, I left behind a widowed husband and a couple of kids I don't even know –

Oh my gosh, Dad really is ghost-yelling at me. I hadn't been paying attention, and there are no words to hear, but he's definitely in the middle of chewing me out.

All of a sudden, I start to cry. Hard. This isn't what I need right now, Dad. I screwed everything up. I'm scared and I don't have any idea what I'm supposed to do next!

Jump into one of those doorways and start again? Would I get to remember stuff like Mom?

Or is there something else I'm supposed to be doing? I don't need a talking to right now. I need help.

He stops his ranting and moves closer to me. I accept the ghost-hug and hang on tight. The last time I did this, he was lying unconscious in a hospital bed, hooked up to a life support machine they were about to pull the plug on.

I laid there all day with him, Dean close by my side. I remember the warmth, the love.

I feel it now.

I stop crying and hug him back. You don't know how much I missed you, Dad.

He does.

Chapter 6

Lizzy sat in front of her flashpad, finger hovering over the update icon.

She didn't want to update the therapy waves. She wanted to dream. She wanted to remember more. Especially after feeling Amy in the doctor's office earlier.

What would the update actually do, though? The last one had only increased her recall. Unless the memories were just something that couldn't be stopped.

How long could she keep up this act of being normal? Or at least half-assed. Another expression not used here. Was she incurably insane? Destined to end up in The Ward in the basement of their city, with the handful of hopelessly delusional people? Were they even delusional at all? Maybe they were like her. Special.

Six-year-old Lizzy put her head in her hands and sighed the sigh of the ancient. Before today, she'd been content with dreaming and remembering. She may have been able to eventually believe she really was just making up imaginary stories and move on with her life.

Except this wasn't her life. Not really. Amy's presence had driven that point home. Deep.

She remembered a house. Not a compartment like she was living in now, a standalone building with colors and carpets, knickknacks and pictures. She remembered sitting and drinking a warm beverage with her husband at a table. The feeling she had when she drank it reminded her of the energy nectar here, but it wasn't as strong and it tasted different. What was the name of that bitter drink again?

She could see her teenage daughter walking by the table, rolling her eyes at something her father had said. She remembered feeling sorry for her. Amy was so overweight and uncomfortable back then. She remembered wishing there was more she could do to help her.

But then she could see her a few years older, skinny and confident. Beautiful.

That was after Lizzy died.

She remembered the car crash. She remembered dying.

It was too much. She tapped the update and deactivated the flashpad. The new waves were ready and would be delivered through her earchip when she fell asleep.

She pulled out her sleeping shelf and climbed on. Another tap on the wall with her wrist, and a rubbery blanket rolled out to cover her.

She wouldn't be sleeping for a while. She could use her wrist monitor to activate her sleep system which would deliver weaker waves to aid her into slumber, but she wasn't in a rush tonight.

Waves. The cure for almost everything around here. There were no surgeries. Not like the bloody, gory images that flashed through her head from Earth. No pills or needles. Just waves and lasers.

Waves were the most common treatment for everything from sleeplessness to general malaise. The different frequencies and strengths targeted specific areas of the brain or body. Lasers came into play where waves failed, and were used for major physical procedures.

Lizzy only experienced the lasers once for a dental procedure, but they were really no different from waves. They didn't feel like anything.

Lizzy still felt like a newcomer on Celadon. No one else she knew questioned waves and lasers. As far as she was aware, she was the only one to give them a second thought. Another thing everyone but she took for granted was the absence of crime.

Her Earth husband, Jason, would have a heck of a time finding employment here. He used to be a police officer, something they had no use for in this world. There was nothing to steal. There was no money; no trinkets or designer clothing.

Everyone had the same things in the same amounts. Everyone worked. Why had Earth been so different?

The only outcasts here were those incurable oddballs buried by society in what her old world would call the loony bin, The Ward. Even there, they were treated humanely and were supposedly happy. Not that she'd ever seen the place. There was still so much more she had yet to observe in this world.

Lizzy lived in building 4-80. Not so much a building, it was what people of Earth would classify as a city. The complex rose hundreds of storeys into the sky, housing thousands of families. It contained all the amenities – doctors' offices, schools, halls, the employment agency, supply depots that you just walked into and picked up what you needed. No need to pay, everything was tracked with the chips in their arms and via verbal identification. She really needed to stop screwing that up.

Lizzy had yet to leave 4-80, but she knew a lot about the world from the data stored on the ethernet. Only six years old, she had no need to leave the building, and certainly not the dome. No one did, unless they had an occupation that required them to take a transport pod out for work.

There were no vacations or sightseeing adventures. Just like with art and music, no one else seemed to be interested in these things. If you wanted to look at or learn about something, what more could you need than what was on the ethernet?

She could think of plenty of things.

Never mind the lack of artwork or photographs on the walls, the building didn't even have windows. What would one need to look outside for? The solar-simulating lights were all a person required.

The one time she'd dared to ask her educator about the lack of windows, her first mistake had of course been calling them windows. Rephrasing the question to glass in which one could peer through, like on the travel pods, she received a strange look and the simple explanation that such a thing would be unnecessary and distracting. The entire class had looked at her the same way. That was the end of such questions from her.

The dome Lizzy lived in was Dome 80. That was what Earth people would consider a country. The hundred or so buildings populating the dome were other self-contained cities.

Celadon had over a hundred of these domes spaced over the planet, and more were being constructed each year. The planet was made up of only one continent, but it was enormous, encompassing nearly half the globe. Lizzy had seen the image on the ethernet, and of course as she was entering the world to be reborn.

The planet, Celadon, still sounded strange when she spoke its name. More than once someone commented that she had a strange sort of accent. Inserting made-up words at random probably didn't help. Just another abnormality.

She understood the way everything worked here, and it made sense. The Earth world she remembered did not. How could people live that way? The hatred, the violence, the way they treated their planet?

Sure, her memories could all end up being dreams, a product of imagination gone wild.

Except for two things.

The colors. No one else could see them, and the outer auras were as good as mind-reading most days. They told her far more than a person's expression or words.

And then there was her heart. Her heart that remembered her family.

Kerri Davidson

Lizzy activated the sleep system and closed her eyes. A fat tear rolled down her cheek to fall on her white blanket.

Chapter 7

As my dad and I sit together, I notice he keeps drifting off. Each time he catches himself doing this, he flares up and scurries back to me. Is he feeling that pull? The one from Mom's world? I don't even know if he's seen her yet.

I should probably go with him to visit.

But I'm feeling a pull myself. From my old world. I need to go back there first.

I try nudging my dad like Mystery Pal had done to me, to assure him I'll be back. I think I might have smashed instead of nudged, but he gets it and I head off to my doorway.

Halfway there, Mystery Pal appears, blocking my path. I wait while she tries to communicate something of importance to me. If I didn't love her so much, I'd be right irritated.

Weird. I love her? I don't even know her. Yet I do. And that's the only word that comes close to describing what I feel. Am I gay now? How do I even know she's a girl?

Whoops. She can tell I wasn't paying attention. She's stopped her efforts to ghost-converse and moves to the side so I can continue on. What a patient soul. I try the nudging thing again, to let her know I'll give it another shot later. I think it worked; she only bounces off me a little. I might be catching on.

Back at my door, I prepare myself for the dizzying sensation of being mind-sucked into the world.

***

It's not so bad this time.

I'm pulled back to the same nursery. The babies are asleep now. Dean is sitting in what used to be my chair, reading a book. Oh geez, "Single Parenting for the Modern Dad."

In all honesty, he should really have gotten that book when I was still alive. I hadn't done much in the way of taking care of the kids. I did only the bare minimum on the rare occasions I was left home alone with them.

Dean was going to school at the local technical institute, training for a career as a plumber. In the evenings and on weekends, he worked as a stock boy at Walmart. I had worked there with him before everything went to pot. It's where we met.

Once the babies were born, as soon as he came through the door, day or night, he'd taken full charge of them. My cousin Stacey and Dean's parents came by daily to help out. Stacey must have been the one who found my body that day. Poor thing.

I study my husband as he sits and reads, trying to feel something besides pity for him. I really do love him, just not in a romantic way. I never did. He was my best friend, my rock, my constant champion. But a lot of it was one-sided. I know I'd done him a disservice by accepting his proposal of marriage.

I contemplate the babies. My children. Still nothing there, either. Just as in life, I have no urge to reach out to them now.

So, what was pulling me here? I can still feel a tug, something trying to redirect my vision. So I let it.

***

Crap.

My clingy, stalker ex-boyfriend Scott. Of all the people I'm able to see, why him?

He's lying on his bed, staring at the ceiling and smoking. Typical. He'd been a lazy bastard when I was dating him. The only thing not typical is the contented smile on his face. It does not match his disgusting inner aura in the slightest. It's a flamey, hellish red. His outer one is black.

I wonder if he still has a job. He used to work in construction, showing up whenever he felt like it. He was homeschooled and had given up on his Grade 10 last time I checked.

It looks like his parents let him move back home. He had a habit of getting kicked out after fighting with his alcoholic father.

Hmm, he has a new cell phone too. I remember kicking his ass and smashing his last one when he tried to manhandle me after I broke up with him.

There are some sheets of paper on the bed next to him. Maybe he's trying to finish his schooling after all. I have to squint to make them out.

One is a newspaper. Ew. My obituary. That could explain the smile. I also kicked him in the junk when we said our farewells.

Turning my attention to the printed sheets from an Internet search, my eyes and my heart stop at the title, "Court Proceedings to Obtain a Paternity Test."

Oh no, no. I flip back to the obituary I hadn't wanted to read. It's lengthy. Dammit, he knows about my kids. He obviously suspects they're his.

The first wave of motherly instinct rushes through me as I picture him coming anywhere near them. I'm going to need to look into that haunting business. I know my own mother reached out to me on more than one occasion after she died. Once, when I was in danger, she'd gone full-out poltergeist, shattering a lightbulb and blowing open doors.

I force myself to go back to Dean and my kids. He's still sitting there, thumbing through the book. His outer aura is dark blue, sad but peaceful. It won't be for long, not once Scott comes after them. I still have no idea if he's the father or not, so he can't either, but he'll sure as hell give it a try.

Scott came from a family who still had to count their nickels in order to purchase a meager supply of food for the month. The rest went to his father's drinking.

I, on the other hand, came from a wealthy family. My mother had been an author and my father a policeman, so they had a decent income. I lacked nothing growing up.

It was my grandparents, my father's parents, who were rich. Neither of them had to work a day in their lives, though they chose to. My grandfather, Randolph, had inheritances enough to see several generations of his family through while living in splendor.

I can't see them now, but they were not doing well the last time I did.

And guess who the sole beneficiary of everything they have is?

Me. Or my next of kin.

Dean gets up to check on the babies as they stir in their crib, and I just want to scream.

I'd been the shittiest mother ever, the rottenest wife. The one thing I could leave them with was financial security.

And now that bastard is going to try take that from them too.

Chapter 8

Celadon birthing commemorations were nothing like the celebrations Lizzy remembered from Earth. No singing, no cake, no gifts. There were no gifts to buy; they already had everything they required. Just people in white jumpsuits parading through to pay tribute to Lizzy and her mother.

They really put the emphasis on the mother here. After all, it was she who had gone through the atrocious task of having the fetus that was to be Lizzy sucked from her body and placed in an incubator.

It was Lizzy's seventh such commemoration here. Still better than the last one she had in her previous life. Her forty-first. The day she died.

Lizzy sat in the living area for most of the day, smiling and thanking each person who stopped by their living quarters to acknowledge her and express condolences to her mother. Boring.

By the time evening arrived and she was released from her obligations, it was all she could do not to sprint to her room and her waiting flashpad.

Her story was growing to epic-novel proportions. Too bad it would never be published, even if it were only on the ethernet for the occasional curiosity seeker to read for free. The words she was writing were for her eyes only.

The increase in her sleep wave therapies had worked just as she predicted. Each dream was becoming more detailed and vivid. All the memories were coming back faster, stronger. She wasn't just remembering them, she was reliving them.

The necessity of walking around pretending to be a seven-year-old kid was wearing on her, but she was getting used to it.

After that first wave boost, she bided her time, pretending it was working the way they wanted it to. She held it all inside, telling no one about her dreams. After a decent interval passed, she casually mentioned the dreams were back, and they were bothersome.

She was getting good at lying, too.

She was on her fourth frequency bump already and looking forward to the next.

Lizzy stared at the last words she had stored on her flashpad, fingertips hovering over it. She'd been in the middle of describing Jason. How they first met, their courtship, how in love she was with him. Something was preventing her from continuing.

Not new to writing, she recognized the block for what it was, and flipped to a new screen. Let it rest. Write about something else. Her birthing celebration.

No, not this one. She'd had enough mind-numbing boredom for the day.

If I'm good and careful, no one will read this until after my departure from this world. I may check in on you from the afterlife, so here's a question you can feel free to answer aloud for me: How are you all so happy here?

There's no art, no music, no colors. The only colors are outside, which is apparently off limits to everyone who doesn't need to go there for work. Fun. You don't even have windows to look out of.

Where are all the other creative souls? I know they're out there somewhere. I've seen snippets of their creations on the etherweb. Pictures, poems, and stories. Are they locked up in the basement with the other pot-stirrers?

Here's a cute tale to curl your happy little hairs. Let me tell you what giving birth was like in my last life.

You got sick and you got fat and you got miserable for nine-plus months in a row. You did not get a fetus sucked out of you after three months of cozy wave treatments, and have it put in an incubator to finish growing.

Oh, no. You suffered. And when the birthing day arrived, you screamed and you pushed and you wanted to die. Eventually, blood and mucus and a baby came shooting out of you. Or else they slit your guts open and pulled it out.

Yeah, and you were allowed to be cranky there. You were allowed to feel feelings that are not calm and rational and positive. For better or for worse? I'm thinking better.

A birthing celebration on Earth is a party. You've never heard of those either, have you? You sing, you dance, you eat things that are bad for you. Why? Because it feels good. You feel alive.

You get presents. Not your mother who went through the inconvenience of birthing you. You get special things, things that not everyone else has. Colored things. Useless, pretty things.

Your mother smiles and laughs, and watches you celebrate YOUR day because she loves you. I pray you do have love somewhere in this world. My own parents are nice people, but that's all they are.

Here's another fun thing we did on Earth. When you're old enough, you get to drink alcohol. Well, I guess you guys kind of have that here. The aged nectar for grownups. I wouldn't know what it's like. Apparently, I'm only seven. But from what I've seen, it's boring too. The grownups get slightly flushed faces or head off to rest early, but

Lizzy pushed her pad to the side. Even her writing was bland today. That was the only drawback of all the memories she'd recovered: this place was boring, and the more she recollected, the more detached she became from this life. She just wanted to go home.

Right from the beginning, she felt like she didn't belong here. Teased by the bits of information as they began to leak through, and spurred on as the recollections kept coming, she thought she could manage with her dreams to keep her entertained.

And there were always those colors, the auras she saw, to make her feel special.

But she wasn't feeling special today. Not in a good way.

Chapter 9

Mad as hell, I push myself away from the Earth doorway. I don't know when he joined me, but my dad's here.

I want to yell, demand he do something to help save my kids, blow up some lightbulbs like my mom did that time. I can't do anything but be angry.

At least he can sense that much. I can tell he didn't see what I saw, but he's trying to comfort me.

I'm not in the mood to be soothed.

I shoot off into the greenish blackness, away from Earth, away from Mom's new world, away from Dad and Mystery Pal. Away from it all.

I'm so pissed, I'm leaving a trail of red sparks behind me. The strangeness of it only aggravates me more. I'm sick to death of this supernatural shit.

I hadn't been athletic in life. Gym class in high school had been a literal nightmare for me. First off, they made you change your clothes in front of all the thin, pretty girls. Then, they made you run until you were ready to puke, whipped balls at you, and once we even had to do a cheerleading-style dance routine.

No, I didn't do well in that class. Skipping half of it probably didn't help grade-wise, but at least it hadn't counted toward our overall GPAs.

Which no longer matter. What was the point of any of that?

It was torture enough when I resigned myself to riding an old exercise bike every day, in order to lose all that weight in my senior year. Again, what a waste of time and effort.

Now here I am, putting on the ghost-miles, and it's the best feeling I've experienced up here so far. I'm not running; I'm flying away.

I don't know how far I've gone, but I'm suddenly out of steam. No worries about getting lost around here. The vastness is mind-boggling, actually incomprehensible, yet I can already feel a pull coming from the worlds and people I left behind.

Leave me alone!

I'm not ready to go back. I need some time to figure it all out. Really, I need to get away from that too.

Stubbornly securing myself in a random spot in the middle of nothing and nowhere, I sit and watch the strange flecks of light. Some zoom by, some dawdle along. I wonder what their stories are. How long have they been up here? Are they all humans?

These questions would be more suited for my mom to speculate on. Sure, I dabbled in writing when I was very young, and I was a voracious reader. But Mom was the author, the master of imagination.

She never knew, and I don't know why I never told her, but I read every one of her books front to back. Maybe I didn't want her to know because I was jealous. Or maybe there was simply something wrong with me. I spent my whole life feeling like something was missing, something important I could never quite put my finger on. Something that prevented me from ever really fitting in, from making those true and lasting connections on Earth.

So many doorways here. They're countless. I have no desire to look into the ones I've landed by. I don't need to see inside to know there's nothing in them for me.

I think I'm out of the area of the In Between I sort of belong in. Fine by me.

As I said, I've never genuinely belonged anywhere. At least not in this last life. Awkward kid turned messed up teen, I did have a solid year of success in the twelfth grade.

I lost more than eighty pounds, gained the self-confidence and motivation that had always eluded me. I had friends, a boyfriend, a job I enjoyed.

And then I screwed it all up. Scott turned out to be an asshole, so I dumped him. No regrets there.

But then Dad got sick and I fell apart. After he died, I turned to drinking and sleeping around, even though I had Dean waiting for me, loving me, trusting me.

He didn't deserve what I did to him. Yet he continued to love me.

When I found out I was pregnant, he insisted on marrying me. The likelihood of the babies being his was slim, but he didn't care. He loved us unconditionally.

I should have said no.

What's going to happen to him now? Scott will go after him. I'd bet my bottom dollar on that, not that I have any dollars here.

Dean won't care about the money, though he should. He needs every cent of what I left him. He's a single parent now, trying to complete his education and working in the evenings. His own parents aren't overly wealthy, but at least I know they'll be there to help him out.

The tears begin to fall as I picture the fallout Scott's actions are bound to cause.

Dean's name was on Darren's and Deidre's birth certificates. He claimed them as his own without any hesitation. Dean's parents naturally assumed these babies were their biological grandkids. No one knew the truth.

Actually, there is one person who at least knows that we didn't know the truth. Susan. Stacey's sister, and the cousin I'd done most of my drunken partying with. She was the first person I showed the pregnancy test to.

She was also the first to bail once I had the twins. She came over a couple of times to help out at the beginning, but you could tell she didn't want to be there. Hell, I didn't want to be there. It wasn't long before she disappeared entirely. Texts, emails, and all. Some friend.

Well, here I am again. Alone and messed up.

Is this the way it has to be? Or is it time to start thinking about someone other than myself?

I changed before. I became a brand-new person on Earth, albeit briefly. Maybe I can do it again. Maybe I can do it better.

And maybe I don't need to do it alone. That had always been my biggest downfall. I see it now. My whole Earth-life, I refused to let anyone in all the way. I counted on no one and nothing but myself. Let's see if we can work on that.

I allow myself to drift back to my family. Spread out over Earth, the In Between, and my mom's new world, they draw me in.

First step: Accept the fact I'll have to lean on them, allow them to help me make this transformation. I don't think I can do this one on my own.

Next step: Learn to do it wordlessly.

Chapter 10

Lizzy finished running the cleanser/smoother over her hair and reattached it to the wall. She flashed a dazzling smile at herself in the mirror and found it felt genuine.

She was still wearing the smile as she walked out to the eating area to join her parents for their midday meal. Their colors were nice and calm today. They'd noticed the difference in her ever since she stopped the dream therapy waves, claiming to be cured while actually seeking a cure.

That day, three years earlier, she'd been mad. Madder than she'd ever been. She didn't want to go on like that anymore. If it had been true, if she had this marvelous Earth family that was still out there somewhere loving and missing her, where in the hell were they?

Whoops. Hell is not a word. No religion here. The closest thing they had to anything spiritual was the annual Ethereal Ceremony, when they gathered to remember the dead. Half a day of that, and they moved on without them. Healthy.

"Care for some more food rations, Lizzy?" her mother asked.

"No, thank you. I'm adequately nourished. I have to get going to my cardiovascular session anyhow."

She sipped the remaining liquid out of her pouch and hopped up.

"You're in a hurry today. Is there a special someone waiting for you?" her dad inquired with a quirked brow.

"There might be," she chirped. She gave each of her parents the acceptable hand hug and headed out into the halls of the complex.

She felt so much better since turning her back on her imaginary life. She hadn't noticed how detached she was from everyone and everything here on Celadon until she gave up the waves and turned her nose to the illusions.

Just a year ago, she would have been comparing the cardiovascular session she was heading for to hamsters running in a wheel. She was pretty sure that's what she used to call them. The details were starting to get confused.

Yes, hamsters. A kind of animal that lived inside with humans. No way could that have been real. Animals living indoors? How filthy would that be?

Still, the image of the hamster wheel lingered in her mind as she made her way through the halls to the practice room that housed the community treadwheels.

The world she'd created in her head was a strange one, indeed. The people living on that imaginary planet were obese and sickly more often than not. Lazy, too. There wasn't much structure in the way of health and cardiovascular or muscle maintenance sessions. They kind of just did as they pleased.

At least here, the community cared enough to ensure their citizens remained in excellent physical condition. It would be downright irresponsible not to.

Daniel Masters was waiting for her just inside the doorway as she entered the practice room. The sight of him rooted Lizzy's feet to the ground, her pleasure sensors sending endorphins through her young body.

He was gorgeous. Truthfully, all the citizens of Celadon were good-looking. Only the best of the best were cooked up in those incubators. But Daniel was something else. He had jet-black hair and dazzling green eyes. Most people had blond or black hair, but the green eyes were something of an anomaly. The common colors were blue and gold.

Those eyes, she could gaze into them for –

She jumped forward as the buzzer sounded, indicating someone was blocking the entryway. Flustered, she looked away from him to hide her reddening cheeks.

"Did you get stuck?" he teased her.

"Yeah, my mind was . . . somewhere else."

Lame.

"Still thinking about those imaginary friends?"

If he hadn't added the wink at the end, she might have become defensive. Instead she laughed, remembering how they used to play "Jason and Amelia" together when they were younger, before she learned to stifle the stories.

"No, I left them behind when I grew up."

"Well, I can't say I don't miss playing, what was it you called it, 'house?' But I sure do like how you grew up." He made a show of inspecting her from head to toe, nodding his approval.

She laughed again and swatted at his arm. His muscular, perfect arm. He'd grown up nice himself. Now it was her turn to eyeball his six-foot-something powerful body as it towered over her five-foot-five slender one. Dressed in the same white workout garments as all the other attendees, she had to say he wore his the best.

The signal sounded and they climbed onto their walking machines.

Lizzy allowed the machine to scan her and set her pace for the next hour. Moderate today. She tried to keep her eyes straight ahead so Daniel wouldn't catch her staring at him.

They were encouraged to find life mates at a very young age. Ten was about the right time to home in on one. She hoped Daniel would be hers. He most likely would be, as she was already staking her claim. There wasn't a lot of flaky drama in this world.

Her world, she corrected herself. But even as she rectified her mistaken thought, her mind was wandering back to the other place. Something about Daniel usually set her off on a fantasy relapse. Maybe because they shared in the pretending when they were younger.

But his eyes, his hair . . .

Today they conjured up images of rain. A grassy park at nighttime with a funny little structure called a gazebo. She and Daniel were standing under the soft lighting in the rain. She was twirling around, laughing and catching the drops on her tongue.

No, not Daniel. It was Jason. The memory was one of the most vivid recollections she'd had in ages. She could smell the rain and closed her eyes, yearning to be back there.

She snapped her eyes open, pulling in her tongue that was waiting to catch the fake drops. No. It wasn't a memory. It wasn't real. This, she thumped her hand on the plastic machine, this was real.

That memory wasn't possible. She'd never seen or smelled rain before. Rain and snow existed, but only outside the domes. She'd never been outside the domes. The only thing they experienced in here were the artificial sunrises and sunsets programmed into their thirty-hour days. Really, all they did was brighten or dim the lights in the halls and public spaces.

She'd never witnessed an actual sunrise or sunset, having no windows to see out of, but somehow she knew what they looked like. Every time she'd been on the roof to work on the horticulture stations, it had been midday. She was probably just thinking of images she'd seen on the etherweb.

She peeked at Jason – Daniel – peripherally. His rust-colored inner aura was surrounded by a cheerful yellow today.

Yeah, there was no ignoring that eccentricity about herself. Wave therapy or no wave therapy, those colors never went away.

At least she didn't slip up as much as she used to, making comments about things she shouldn't know people were feeling. Most days, she was able to dismiss the auras altogether.

The thirty-hour days were one of the hardest realities to adapt to. Her mind always seemed to peter out six hours before everyone else's. And she'd been here for over ten years now.

No, not here. Alive. The only alive there was.

Argh. She liked Daniel. She wanted him to be her life mate. But if he kept triggering these hallucinations every time she saw him, she may need to reconsider.

Chapter 11

Hey guys, I'm back.

No, they don't hear my words, but they welcome me all the same as I join them in their spot.

It's a good spot, really. Just far enough from the Earth door to be peaceful, but not too far. I get the feeling this is something they've done before.

Still not ready to return to my world or take Dad to visit Mom, I turn my attention to Mystery Pal. She moves over and presses herself close to me.

I feel the replenishing vibes immediately, but there's something else there. It's like a hug, only deeper. I allow myself to bask in the sensation and look around at the other doors in my vicinity. Even from here, I can see enough to make counting them impossible.

So, what's going to happen to me, to us? Do we just pick one and jump in? How long are we supposed to wait? Will it hurt? I assume this is a reincarnation sort of deal.

Unsettling, yet not. It's nice to know there's more out there, that death isn't the end. But unless I do some sort of weird ripping thing like my parents did, I'm not going to be Amy anymore, am I? I won't remember her at all.

What was the point of being her in the first place?

Still focusing on the doors, I try to imagine how many lives I've lived before this, how many different people or things I've been.

My fake head whips around to Mystery Pal. This is how I know her. She's part of my lives. Not this last one, but she has been before. That feeling . . . I feel like we go together. We're a set. Well, we're supposed to be. Kind of like my mom and dad. I know my last life would have been better if she'd been there.

She nuzzles me and gives me an extra burst of energy. I smile back at her, hoping she can feel it. Wherever I end up next, she's coming with me. That's all I know for certain.

I'm okay with putting my attempts at trying to figure out this place on hold for now. Indefinitely, really. I don't believe it's all that figureoutable.

With my unknown connection as known as I need it to be, I leave Mystery Pal with my dad and head back to Earth.

***

Okay, this is actually cute.

Diedre and Darren, in their highchairs wearing birthday hats, are completely covered in chocolate cake. Their hands are full of it, as they continue to laugh and smear it all over themselves and each other.

Dean, his parents, and Stacey are sitting around the table laughing with the kids. Their outer auras are all similar. They still have that hint of mourning blue, but it's a lot lighter.

A banner on the wall reads, "Happy six months, Darren and Deidre!"

So, I've been gone for three. Hmm.

Why do I all of a sudden want to touch my children? I want to put my arms around them and hold them close to me.

When I was alive, I never voluntarily picked them up. I certainly never cuddled them.

I will myself to reach out, the way I did when I saw Mom, but nothing's happening. I'm about to try again when Aunt Robin, Mom's sister, enters the kitchen.

Her inner aura is a murky grey, kind of what I would have expected. She isn't exactly the most exciting person. But her outer aura is surprising. It's psychedelic. Her face tells the same story before she slaps a fake smile on it. I've never seen her so . . .

I don't know what she is. Happy, sad, worried, all of the above? When I'd known her in life, she'd been stuffy. When I got to know her better at the end, I found her to be caring but beaten down by her husband. Mostly unflappable.

She's definitely flapped about something today.

Which reminds me, I should check on Scott. I force myself to concentrate on him and pull away from the party.

Holy shit. I didn't have to go far. He's walking up the path to Dean's apartment building.

He's reading the tenant list. He raises his finger to press the buzzer.

No, no, no!

Sparks come shooting out of the keypad and he's flying backward off the steps. He comes skidding to a halt on his ass, looking around as if he expects to see someone.

Heh. That would be me you're looking for, you bastard.

He sits in the middle of the sidewalk shaking his head. Probably wondering whether to give it another try.

Eventually, he gets up and hobbles back to the building. He stands there inspecting the keypad without touching it. Like a monkey discovering tools, he picks up a stick. Dammit.

He pokes the number for Dean's apartment and is buzzed in without question. Party day; they must be expecting more guests. Or they're just that trusting. Shit.

Up the stairs he goes, alternating the papers between his hands to rub his arms and sides. Looks like he doesn't trust the elevator today.

On the third floor now, down the hall he goes.

Argh. I'm trying, but I can't do anything. Do I need to get angrier?

Now he's knocking on the door.

Aunt Robin is the one to answer it.

"May I help you?"

"I'm looking for Dean Grant."

"And who's calling?"

"Just send him out. He'll want to talk to me in private."

Aunt Robin frowns at him and shuts the door. I follow her back into the kitchen.

"There's a scruffy looking young man in the hall who says he wants to talk to you in private."

Dean puts down the cloth he was using to wipe up the chocolate disaster. Darren snatches it and puts it to use on his sister.

"Mysterious. I'll go see what he wants."

"Be careful, he looks strange."

"Yes ma'am." *Dean gives her a mock salute. Aw, I remember him doing that to me when we worked together. Before we were dating, before the babies, even before I met the asshole standing in the hall waiting to ruin his life.*

I can't watch. Yet, I do.

Dean recognizes him as soon as he opens the door. He steps out into the hallway, pulling the door closed behind him.

"What are you doing here?"

"Serving you papers," *Scott replies with an evil grin.*

Dean refuses to look at the papers Scott's holding out to him. Scott tries shoving them into his hand. Dean doesn't move, nor does he take his eyes off Scott's face. His own face is furious, almost scary. But his outer aura is trembling and kind of yellow. He's scared.

"I don't want your papers. Give me words."

Scott sighs and lowers the documents. "Fine. Those kids in there are mine, and I thought I'd let you know in person that I'll be suing you for custody of them."

"You're letting me know in person because you're a cheap, filthy weasel who can't afford a lawyer. These kids are not yours; they are mine. If you think I'm going to let you anywhere near them – "

"Okay, okay, just relax. I thought you might freak out like this. I'm willing to barter."

"Barter? Barter my kids? Are you insane?"

"No, I'm smart. You love the kids, fine. You want me to go away?" He pulls another paper out of his pocket. "Here's my offer."

This paper, Dean accepts. I can't see what it says.

"You have got to be kidding me."

"Take your time. Think about it. My number's on the bottom. Just don't take too long. I'm not a patient man."

Scott turns and leaves via the staircase again.

Dean leans against the wall in the hallway, examining the note in his trembling hands.

"Everything okay out here?" Stacey pokes her head out the door and Dean hides the paper behind his back.

"Yeah, just an old friend. I'll be right in."

I can't believe he managed to choke out the word friend. I also can't believe what I'm seeing on the paper he's holding.

Scott wants one hundred thousand dollars. Cash. Or else.

The rat bastard took the time to write out the dollar amount in both numbers and words. He hadn't even spelled thousand correctly.

I take off in a rage, unleashing my anger and frustration on him as he flees down the stairs.

Ouch. But cool.

Whatever I did caused the barrier between our worlds to flash with lightning, distorting my view. As the rippling settles, I see I've pulled a poltergeist move. Much as my mother had done when she was the ghost and I was alive, I shattered the lightbulb in the stairwell. Only instead of blowing doors open, I knocked him down the flight of stairs.

He doesn't stay down for long. This isn't his first run-in with an angry spirit. I'm pretty sure he's too stupid to realize exactly what happened, but he's not too stupid to get the hell out of there.

Chapter 12

"Name and identification number, please."

"Elizabeth Stapleton. 310TCOH7267."

The door slid open for Lizzy to enter the foyer. The next door opened before she had a chance to take a seat, inviting her to walk right into Dr. Artaria's office.

"Good morning, Lizzy. You're looking well."

"Thank you, Doctor. I feel great."

No lies today. She felt so much better since turning her back on her old life, real or imagined. She was actually living this one now, free from her haunted past or imagination. She still wasn't sure which it was, but she'd had enough of trying to figure it out.

If it had been a past life, well, it was over.

She'd also been successful at tuning out most of the colors. Auras, as she used to call them. She still saw them but had taught herself to ignore them.

As soon as she thought about it, she noticed the pretty pink glow hovering around Dr. Artaria. She immediately dismissed it, refusing to acknowledge it.

Sitting on the white sofa, she smoothed out her white jumpsuit and crossed her legs.

"I can't believe what a change I've seen in you over the last few years, Lizzy. I must say, I was quite concerned for a while. You're so much more relaxed now."

"You know what? I was concerned myself. I guess it was something I just needed to outgrow."

"So no more dreams?"

"Nope. Just regular ones. Beneficial ones."

"You've been taking the job simulation waves, I see."

"Yes. They're fantastic. Next year I get to start my career trials, and there are so many things I'm interested in. Too many, really. I have to start narrowing them down."

"Excellent. I'll be excited to see the list you end up with."

"I have it with me, but like I said, it's still too long. No way will they let me take on twenty trials."

Dr. Artaria's laugh was one of familiarity. "No, but I'm sure you'll get it down to the maximum five by next year."

"It seems impossible. Every time I scratch one off the list, I find a dozen more. I wish I could just clone myself and then we wouldn't have a problem."

She was only half joking. She'd turned thirteen last week. By this time next year, she would be out doing the actual trials. Maximum five, as Dr. Artaria reminded her. Even though she had her list narrowed down to the top twenty, it originally consisted of over a hundred.

Why couldn't they have more than one job? Why couldn't they at least try them all? Worst of all, what if she ended up picking the wrong one? They only had a year after the trials began to decide. Once you made your choice, that was your job for life. And life was long here. The average lifespan was 230 years; some people lived to 250. And most citizens worked right to the end.

A far cry from Earth where you were free to work many jobs, pursue all your interests and dreams. But for some reason, there didn't seem to be enough jobs for everyone. They had a thing called unemployment. And whether you worked or not, you didn't get the same amount of food and other necessities as everyone else. Some people didn't get any.

Then there was retirement. That had been the end goal on Earth. Put your time in, then quit and sit around doing nothing. Or even weirder, finally start doing everything you wanted to do when you were younger. It didn't matter if it was a useful job, or one you enjoyed. You just had to do something and then totter off to begin dying.

No, Earth wasn't real. Mental slap.

"Cloning is still far off in the future. But is that one of the fields you're interested in?"

"Not really. I find science in general to be boring. As a career, I mean. I'm still interested in it for my independent learning. I've stored hundreds of ether-classes on my flashpad, but most of the scientific ones are flora and fauna-based. Oh, and animals, but that's one of the field training options I'm definitely keeping."

The look on Dr. Artaria's face told her she'd shared too much, yet again. Oversharing was one habit she hadn't been able to shake. Another was her thirst for knowledge. She wanted to know everything about this – her – world. At least she'd given up on creative writing as a hobby. That one was always guaranteed to raise all the wrong eyebrows.

"Remember, you won't have as much time for all these extra things once you've settled on your career and life mate. You do intend on having a family, no?"

Finally, a question she had an answer for. The correct answer, at that.

"Oh, I do! And I already know who my life mate will be."

Dr. Artaria's face and aura lit up. Concentrate on the face, Lizzy.

"That's terrific news. Why didn't you tell me?"

"He only officially asked me this week. Two nights ago, to be exact. His name is Daniel Masters and he's oh so dreamy."

"Dreamy?"

"Sorry. I like him a lot."

"Well, I'm pleased to hear this. I wish the two of you many years of happiness and productivity. You'll wed at seventeen, then?"

"We will. And we're planning on having just the one child. We have no special requests."

"Excellent. I'm thrilled that everything is working out for you. You've come a long way from the days of imaginary friends and seeing mysterious rainbows lurking about. Now, is there anything else you require or would like to talk about today?"

Lizzy averted her eyes from the mysterious rainbow lurking around the doctor and plastered on a fake smile.

"Nope, I'm all set for waves. Thanks, Dr. Artaria."

"Anytime. Actually, same time next week?"

"That will be fine. Thanks again."

She rose and strolled from the room, even though she had the sudden urge to run. Not just from the office, but from the building.

Once she was back in the hall, mixed in with the other white-suited citizens, she relaxed.

She had to stop beating herself up. She'd done an excellent job of squashing her eccentricities today, as she had for the last three years. Every little slip should not send her spiraling. She just needed to keep on improving.

Besides, she did have a great life to look forward to. Before she knew it, she'd have a career, a life mate, and a child of their own.

It wasn't so bad here after all.

Chapter 13

Poltergeisting takes a lot out of you.

Mystery Pal and Dad must have noticed the commotion I was causing. I'd gone back to check on Dean, and was about to go chasing after Scott again, when they up and yanked me right out. How disorienting.

I was so enraged, I tried to fight them off to continue my hellraising. I suspect I may have given them a jolt or two in my jacked-up state. If I did, they didn't complain. They only continued to drag me away.

I'm a lot stronger here than I was on Earth. I didn't make it easy on them during the scuffle as they hauled me back to our spot.

By the time we arrived, I was completely spent. Now I sit and wait as they try to heal me.

I'm not helping with this process, either. Their energies feel like they're just bouncing off me. Even though I'm exhausted, I'm still all worked up, spouting steam-like waves all over the place.

I can't help it. How dare he do that to my husband? How dare he threaten Dean and our kids that way? Whether Scott's the biological father or not, and we still don't know, that creep has no interest in babies. He just wants money.

If I wasn't so mad, I would laugh at how clueless he is. Sure, my grandparents have money. But Dean doesn't. How in the hell does he expect him to fork over a hundred grand in cash?

When we were dating, Scott was always on me to quit my job so I could spend more time with him. He couldn't understand why I was working in retail after school when my dad was rich and bought me whatever I wanted. I corrected him time and time again; my dad wasn't rich, my grandparents were. Besides, I liked my job.

Brains were never his strong suit.

So far as I'd seen in life and now from here, he doesn't have a strong suit. He's an evil manipulative idiot who –
Oh, shit.

My companions have yet to notice, but we've got company. He's not here yet, but a light-purple speck is floating our way. It's Grandpa Clarke.

I pull myself away and try pointing at him. It doesn't work. They move closer to me, probably thinking I'm just having another fit, and try to continue their work. I grab hold of Dad and turn him around so he can see. This does work.

Dad's happy and sad at the same time. Happy to see him, of course. But sad because he's obviously dead. Dad floats off to welcome his own father to the afterlife.

Mystery Pal and I stay behind to watch the reunion. I feel her own joy and sorrow mirroring ours. But the sympathies aren't just those of a pal, the emotions come from somewhere deeper.

How do you know us?

No way could she have heard the words, but all of a sudden I have her full attention. I don't get any words from her, either. Just another jolt of love.

I suppose the why of it all isn't important. I might as well ask my dad why he's my dad. It doesn't matter. All I know is Mystery Pal is a part of my past, my present, and my future.

And that's all I need to know.

I still think she is what was missing from my last life. Throughout the whole thing, I always knew deep down inside that something wasn't right. I wasn't complete. I think the next go round will be a lot better if she comes along.

She will. Whatever happened last time, will not be repeated so soon. I doubt we'll be letting each other stray far until it's time . . .

No, it's still too soon to be thinking about what's next. Now is good for the moment.

With a warm heart, I welcome Grandpa as he and Dad join us in our circle. I can tell he wants to get back to the door already. Of course, he'll want to see Grandma.

She must be absolutely devastated. She was such a strong woman. So patient, so kind, so unshakeable. Until everyone started dying.

She'd gone to pieces after Dad died. The last time I saw her was shortly after Grandpa had his stroke. She wasn't even talking anymore at that point.

The four of us do sit and share our energies for a decent interval. My own memories of Grandpa on Earth play through my mind.

We didn't live close to them when I was growing up. Our annual visits were always rushed, packed full of activities, and then there was Mom's side of the family to see as well.

But Grandpa Clarke had been one of my favorite relatives, mostly because he worked so hard and didn't overdo the cute kid stuff. He worked long hours from his office in their grand home as an investment banker, and I never saw him out of a suit until the very end.

After Dad and I moved closer to them, I got to know him better. He and Grandma were both incredibly patient and forgiving as I went through my nasty selfish phase . . . part one.

They helped me as I made my changes and a better life for myself. Even after I screwed it all up again, resorting to my old ways and thoughtless treatment of them, they stood by me.

Orphaned at seventeen, I refused to stay with them or Aunt Robin any longer. Despite their misgivings, I turned a cold shoulder to them all and moved in with Dean. Then back to my own apartment, then . . . well, you know what happened after that.

I told them they could call the cops, take away my access to the bank accounts. I didn't care anymore.

And I wasn't sure whether to be pleased or disappointed when they didn't do either of those things. I got my way. I know they still cared, but again, look where I ended up.

Busy day around here. Grandpa's already finished with the reunion and has indeed returned to the Earth door. Just like he was in life, he doesn't piss around.

He wants to be close to his soulmate and he'll sit there until she emerges from that doorway.

There'll probably be another scrap when he needs to be dragged away for energy replenishment.

I'm finished with the healing for today. And Dad's taking a page from Grandpa's book. He's ready to go see Mom, and I should go with him. He's waited long enough.

It looks like Mystery Pal is going to stay and Grandpa-sit. I'm a little uneasy about going so far without her, but that's probably because I just got her back. She'll be here when we return.

It's my fault Dad was pulled from that world. My fault he wasn't born again alongside Mom.

So, sorry, Dean and kids, you're on your own for a bit. I'm taking my dad on a trip.

And believe me, Scott, I'll be back for you.

Chapter 14

Lizzy settled her travel pod on the ground and donned her helmet. She activated the hatch and got out, her feet sinking deep into the long grass.

She reveled in the sunlight for a moment, wanting to take off the helmet and breathe in the fresh air. It wasn't that there was a lack of oxygen outside the domes; it was just the opposite. There was too much oxygen. The air was simply too rich for humans.

But it wasn't too thick for the animals she'd come to study. They, like the gorgeous lands around them, flourished in the outside environment.

She finished her five sessions of field training tryouts when she was fifteen and had settled on Animals. Yes, that was her occupation. She wasn't a zoologist or an ethologist; those were Earth words. She was an Animal Employee, working for the Department of Animals.

Lizzy gave her encased head a shake. No Earth words. Earth wasn't real. It hadn't been for a long time. It was only when she left the domes and communed with nature that her imagination reared its persistent head. Well, not only, but it was stronger out here.

Sixteen and a half years old, it was her first week being out on her own after completing the supervised training. Her duties were simple enough that half a year was more than sufficient to learn it all. She simply observed, scanned animals that had chips implanted in them, and transferred data to be sorted later.

No need for her to touch the animals – that was the job of someone in another branch of the department. Of course, she did touch them. They were irresistible.

As much as she struggled with the idea of making a career decision at sixteen, one she would be stuck with for the next couple of centuries, she was certain she picked the right one. There was no way it would ever become boring. Even though the job itself was mindless, just being outside the domes surrounded by nature and all its beauty was rewarding enough.

A Class 3 - Category 11 approached her and nuzzled her hand. Okay, on Earth it was a deer. She was vigilant in keeping the imaginary terms to herself and hadn't slipped up in her reports or around coworkers yet. In fact, she'd more than half convinced herself she was actually inventing nicknames for the creatures. Just like she made up Earth all those years ago.

She gently scratched behind the creature's ears and scanned it.

Yes, another oddity. One that hadn't appeared until after she was off her training, thank goodness.

All animals, big and small, flocked to her. What they sensed or saw in her, she didn't know. She didn't care to know, so long as it wasn't drawn to anyone's attention. The last thing she needed was to provide them with another abnormality to add to their lists.

But she enjoyed her relationship with the animals so much she didn't care about the additional secret she was required to keep. She loved them all.

Their colors were easier to ignore than humans', too. They only had a central aura instead of two. The simplicity of it was refreshing. Not that she spent much time looking at the colors anymore.

Okay, maybe some days, but this was her world out here. It was as free as she was going to get, and she was determined to enjoy every minute of it as appropriately as possible.

A cloud moved across the sun and a light drizzle began to fall. She couldn't resist. Screw the appropriateness. The smell of rain was her favorite. She removed her helmet and let it hang by her side as she breathed in the freshness. A small dalliance wouldn't do any harm. Besides, she could breathe just fine. It wasn't her first time taking her head covering off.

It was at that exact moment when Belle chose to arrive.

Lizzy let the helmet fall to the ground, all worries about being normal gone now. She was back on Earth and it was real. This was Belle, her parakeet from that life. The one that died and broke her heart. The one who welcomed her to the afterlife and perched on her nonexistent shoulder until she made her decision to fly off into this world, breaking her heart all over again.

Belle took her old spot now and pecked gently at her hair just as she had in the other life.

But she wasn't a parakeet anymore, she was a parrot. A two-foot tall parrot was sitting on Lizzy's shoulder, cuddling with her.

She wasn't crazy. But crazy was a word. Deer, parakeet, and parrot were words too. Earth was real. It always had been.

Belle dug her claws firmly into her shoulder, as if to reinforce the point. As much as she loved this soul, it wasn't helping.

Knowing she would see her again, Lizzy brushed the bird off her shoulder and walked back to her pod.

Once inside, she sat without activating the vehicle. She stared straight ahead, seeing nothing at all.

Why? She wanted to yell the word aloud. She wanted an answer from the universe, and she wanted it now. Her eyes flicked to the sensor board which would recognize her voice and be activated if she spoke.

Instead of yelling, she thumped her head on the back of the seat and bit her tongue. Hard. Hard enough to draw blood.

It tasted good.

Why was this happening to her? She'd been doing so well for so many years.

Okay, not so well. It had been a constant battle trying to keep the memories stifled, pretending not to see colors, doing her damnedest to fit in.

How was she supposed to reconcile these two lives? How was she supposed to live a life here, when she was still living her last one?

Her family, her real family, was out there somewhere.

Where in the hell were they? Watching over her? Running around the In Between doing who knew what?

Fighting the urge to call out their names, she activated her pod and tapped in the sequence to return her to the dome. It wasn't until she arrived at the docking station that she remembered she left her helmet out in the grass.

Great. Another thing she'd have to try explaining. Not today. Today she had some writing to do.

Chapter 15

Cool. Mom's driving a spaceship. No, not a spaceship, just something that looks like one. She flies right through the bubble and into some sort of parking garage. She looks pissed.

I wonder what Dad's thinking right now. I hadn't known how to communicate what I knew to him, how to prepare him to see his wife as a four-year-old girl.

Apparently, there was no need to. Time is definitely moving along faster in this world. She looks like a grown woman already. Maybe about my age.

She's in a hurry as she navigates the endless white corridors, filled with busy-looking people also dressed in white. She gets to her apartment and swipes her arm over a sensor, swooshing the door open.

A man and a woman who must be her parents are sitting at what might be a really plain kitchen table. They greet her as she enters. She acknowledges them brusquely and heads for her room.

I've only been here once before, but it's creepy how everything is such a stark white. No pictures, no random objects lying around, no dirt. It's all so sterile looking.

And that glass pad on the desk she's sitting at now is obviously a computer or something, but it's see-through. No keyboard. Just a thing.

She's tapping away furiously on it, her lips moving as she works. I focus on the screen and can make out most of the words. They're flowing out fast.

The language is English, but they have strange words for some things. They also have funny accents when they speak, although Mom doesn't really have one.

Hey, she's writing about us! Dad sees this too. I feel his heart leap.

Just when I had myself convinced it was all a dream or it didn't matter, there she was. Belle, my parakeet from Earth. She came flying to me right out of the blue, as if no time had passed since we were together.

There's no denying everything was real. Everything is real. My family is real.

Where are they? Why did they leave me here? I'm sixteen years old, and I haven't felt them around since I was four. It can't be because they don't care. I know they still love me. I still love them. I always will.

She pauses and frowns at the screen.

Now that I think about it, when I was a ghost up there in the In Between, time had been a bit wonky in some of the worlds I peered into. Especially this one. Years would pass here, when only days or months would pass up there or on Earth.

So they will probably be back. It makes sense they would have other things to do before checking in on me. Especially considering the circumstances I left Jason in.

But what am I supposed to do? I've started living my life here. I have my career, I have my life mate picked out.

Ouch. I feel Dad's pain.

Can I get out of here without dying? Of course not.

She stops writing again and swivels around to face the mostly empty white room.
"Jason, what do I do? I can't expect you to wait for me for centuries. Well, centuries for me, at least. I can't pretend to live here. If I stay, I'll have to really live here. I'll have to get married to someone else. I'll have to make another life while loving you and wanting nothing more than to join you."

She has to live here for centuries? We're all crying now as I feel Dad reach out to her. Mom continues to cry, but she's laughing at the same time. She puts her hand on her shoulder where Dad must be holding her.

"I knew you were real. I knew you'd come back. I knew all along."

He releases her and presses against me. She shakes her head and pulls a cloth from her pocket. Oh, weird. They have hankies in this futuristic space world.

"I'm supposed to be getting married soon. Well, wedded, as they say here. He's a real nice guy. He reminds me of you. That's probably what drew me to him in the first place. And that's probably not fair to him."

Dad's doing something. The fabric between our worlds is shimmering. It's blinding, really. I have to look away.

I turn back when I hear her sigh. The light is gone and she's still dabbing at her face with the cloth, though she's stopped crying.

"Please take care of Amy, my love. I'll do what I need to do here. After all, if I learned anything during my last life and my time up there, it's that there's a reason for everything. A reason I'm not meant to understand."

I want to let her know I'm okay. Well, sort of okay. I must have done something because she looks up and smiles again.

"You're together," she breathes.

Fortified, she gets up and brushes herself off, tucking the hanky back into her pocket.

"I don't know how, but I'll do my best to live this life, and trust in the fact that we'll all meet again one day."

Dad and I huddle together. I think we know what she's going to say next.

"You'll never be far from my thoughts, but if I'm going to do this, you can't stay with me. Not all the time. It's so strange to think of everything that lies in front of me here, everything I have to do . . . alone.

"I promise I'll come to you as soon as I can. I promise I'll find you."

Dad's shaking. He knows what she's saying is true, but even my heart is breaking for them.

"I'm sorry I couldn't make it out with you."

Dad's reached out again. She pats her own arm and smiles up at us.

"I'll love you for always."

I take hold of Dad and pull him back. All the way.

***

We float over to a quiet little spot and sit there, sharing our energies and our sorrows. How are we supposed to go on after hearing that? Mom's right there inside that doorway beside us and we're not meant to see her again?

The most disturbing part is knowing how long she'll have to be there. She has an entire life to live, a big one. The next time we stop by, what will she look like? What will she be like? Will she really remember us? Would it be better if she didn't?

Geez, Dad. You should have just stayed with her. I'm sorry I messed everything up.

I can tell he's forcing himself to perk up as he feels my remorse. He's trying to assure me it's not my fault.

Yeah, I'm pretty sure it is.

But he reminds me why he's here, why he's not where he should be with his wife. He takes the lead as we head back to the Earth door.

It's time to do what we're supposed to be doing, just like Mom is. Only, she seems to have her journey figured out. I have no idea what lies in store for the two of us.

Chapter 16

The good news: Lizzy was now certain she was not insane.

The bad news: She was pretty sure the rest of this world would not agree.

Just as she was getting her life together, this life, Belle showed up and dragged her back into what she'd convinced herself were fantasies. Jason and Amy arriving on the very same day as she was having her tantrum about it only cemented the truth.

The truth. Her latest and greatest struggle.

From the day she committed herself to this life and said farewell-for-now to her family, she'd waffled back and forth about what to tell Daniel.

Nothing, was the easiest answer. Everything was absurd.

While he remembered playing make-believe with these characters when they were young and adored her quirkiness, there was no way he would adore the facts.

How could she even expect him to believe her?

The biggest question of all . . . how could she marry him, enter the unbreakable bond of being wedded, while keeping some or all of the truth from him?

Yes, just as it was for careers, the act of wedding was for life on Celadon. There were no exceptions. Once the ceremony was performed, your chips were synched and that was that. There were no divorces. There were no separations, at least not any that were spoken of.

Lizzy had heard of couples that had affairs. A lot of them. People lived together, had children, but strayed. If they wedded out of love or for some other reason, whether or not that reasoning remained, they did.

It was disturbing, but these unfaithful people all seemed to be as happy as everyone else here. It was simply the way things worked. These dalliances weren't well hidden, nor did they need to be. Wedded to one, sharing your day-to-day life and home with them; committed to another, enjoying all the fun stuff together. This was an acceptable way of living.

It wouldn't be like that for Lizzy. She couldn't imagine carrying on in such a way. It was bad enough her heart already belonged to a ghost.

That was why she'd been torn for the last six months, and even as she stood in the ceremony hall with her mate-to-be.

She was still uncertain, to a degree. But only on the inside.

Her decision had been made.

The service was quick and to the point, as were most things on Celadon. Efficient, too. There were eight couples who were all wedded at the same time.

Mr. and Mrs. Daniel Masters followed the others to the chip formatting area, and the deal was sealed.

She'd told him nothing.

As they headed off to settle into their new quarters together, she found herself surprisingly at peace with her decision.

Jason – no, Daniel – looked so happy. And she would spend her life here continuing to make him happier.

She would also keep her old life alive. But that was only for herself. No one else needed to know.

She would go back to writing. She would tell the story of her previous life. She would talk to her family through the words she wrote. She would never forget.

In the meantime, wedding ceremony complete, it was time to go to work. No honeymoons here.

There was very little to do in the way of setting up their new home. It came with everything installed, just like all the other living quarters. No pictures, gadgets, or sentimental items to pack and move here. Flashpad data came from their chips; no need to pack that either. It was firmly embedded in their wrists and ears, ready to be plopped into a new terminal.

Looking around the place, Lizzy held in her sigh of disappointment. It might as well have been her old living quarters. The only thing missing were her parents. Her commitment to this world and its ways was tested further, as she wondered if they even noticed she was gone. They hadn't attended the wedding ceremony. No one's parents did.

Why would they? It was purely functional, not something to be celebrated. More like an appointment at the bank or doctor's office on Earth.

The thing that frustrated her the most was she didn't miss them at all. Normal in Celadon, it didn't feel normal to her. Where was the love? The two of them might love each other, but why not her? They'd done a great job of raising her, if you only looked at it on the surface. They worried about her, looked out for her best interests and future. They even had a few laughs together. But where was the bond?

When Lizzy and Daniel had their own child, things would be different. How could they not be? It wasn't like Lizzy hadn't been stomping all over the line of normal throughout her Celadonian life. Might as well carry on with it. Maybe Daniel would learn some of her Earth ways by simply being exposed to them.

Minimally. And carefully. And not entirely.

After a walkthrough of their living quarters and a quick peck on the cheek, Lizzy and her new husband wished each other a lovely half-day of work and headed off to their jobs.

Everything would work out, Lizzy assured herself as she accessed her travel pod. She was here for a reason, and she shouldn't expect to know what it was.

She was making a checklist in her head when she landed and sought out Belle.

Step one: Live life here with Celadonian husband.
Step two: Have a child, another soul to love.
Step three: Make the best of it all and enjoy your work.
Step four: Go home.

Chapter 17

Mystery Pal and Grandpa are hovering in our spot when we return. She must have taken him there to replenish. He's actually trying to creep away right now. She snatches him back. Good for her.

After the trip we just made, there's no avoiding some recovery time of our own. Grouped together, we keep up a flow of energies and my mind wanders.

Just look at this place. This In Between. Random souls skittering to and fro, popping in and out of doors. And I thought Earth life had been confusing. This is unfathomable. Factor in Mom, her new life and world . . . let's just say my brain needs as much of a timeout as my soul.

Yet no one but Mystery Pal seems content to sit here for long. The three of us are still being drawn to that doorway. Grandpa wants to see his wife, no doubt. Dad is supposed to be helping me take care of all my unfinished business. I need to figure out what in the hell my unfinished business is.

My ghost-headache returns as we set out for the doorway. Grandpa gets there first and settles in to watch over Grandma. Mystery Pal and Dad trail behind as I pull up to the portal.

***

"I'm telling you, you need to let your parents see this."

Stacey sits next to Dean on the loveseat with her arms crossed. Scott's blackmail letter is lying on the coffee table in front of them.

"No. I'll figure something out."

"You can't afford a lawyer on your own, not a good one. And you know this creep will be back."

"He can't afford one either."

"Sure he can. There are free lawyers all over the place. It's not going to matter how respectable they are if he does turn out to be the father."

"I am their father," Dean spits out, his face and aura reddening.

Stacey places a hand on his leg. My nonexistent eyebrows quirk. This is new.

"Of course you are. You've been there for them since day one. We're not going to let anyone take them from you. Why won't you let your parents help? You know they love those kids just as much as you do."

"Exactly. Their grandkids. They don't need to know about the questionable genetics. I'm not going to put them through that."

"It may not be up to you. This guy will take care of it for you if you don't."

Dean picks up the letter and runs his fingers over it, as if touching it will provide him with an answer.

"I still have another week to decide. This says I have until the first of the month."

"Decide what? Oh, Dean you can't possibly be thinking of giving him the money?"

"Of course not." He drops the letter back onto the table. "I don't have that much money. But maybe if I just give him some . . ."

Stacey flies to her feet and throws her hands in the air. It looks like she's about to pull her hair out.

"Are you listening to yourself? He's not going away. You start paying him now and he'll only keep coming back for more. You need a lawyer, you need the police, you cannot do this on your own."

"I thought we were in this together."

Again, since when? What is going on here? Is my cousin seriously hitting on my husband?

I turn my attention from the living room to the nursery. The babies are fast asleep, oblivious to the drama going on in the other room.

They look so sweet. I can't believe they're mine. Well, were mine. I also can't believe I didn't see this when I was alive.

These adorable, innocent souls. Pieces of me. Physically and spiritually. I can feel it now.

I reach through the veil and place my hand on theirs, which are entwined as they nap. Oh, their eyes open. They don't cry. They're not scared. They know I'm here and they love me.

I can't let go. It feels like magic. It is magic.

I do release them when my sobbing becomes uncontrollable. Dad and Mystery Pal are pressed close on either side of me.

I missed out on so much.

For the first time, I allow myself to wonder, "What if?"

What would have happened if I'd lived? Would I have been able to turn my life around yet again? Would I have grown up and learned to love Dean as a husband, instead of just a provider and sometimes friend?

Would I have gotten over the depression and realized the gift I'd been given in these two children? Would I have been a good mother?

I watch them fall back asleep and realize I'll never know. Those ships have all sailed.

Well, dead or not, I'm here now, and I'm going to do my damnedest to be the mother I wasn't in life.

I'm about to go Scott-hunting when there's a knock on the apartment door. Good grief, is it him again?

No, it's Aunt Robin. She's bringing some terrible news. So says her face and her outer aura.

While Dean shows her into the living room, Stacey runs ahead to grab the note from the table and slips it into a drawer. He smiles his silent thank you.

"Sorry to bother you so late. Stacey, I didn't realize you would be here."

Is that disapproval in her voice? Great, it's not just me then.

"It's not late, Robin. What's wrong?"

"Is it Dad again?"

Uncle Ian? What's going on with him now? I can't say I care all that much. He was a perfectly dastardly man from what I remember.

"No, it's Martha. She's passed away."

Grandma?

***

Sure enough, I pull myself away from Earth and there she is. Sitting right next to us.

She and Grandpa are so close they're almost indistinguishable. Especially since their auras are an identical color.

Oh, they're still so much in love after all these years, after who knows how many lives they've lived together. I wanted that. I needed that. I never found that.

Crap. If they're both here . . .

There's about to be a lot of money flying around down there.

Chapter 18

Lizzy spent the morning of her nineteenth birthday at work. They were encouraged to take the day off, but she loved her job. The fresh air, the animals, Belle. She was getting better at remembering to bring her helmet back with her, tired of making up fantastical tales of mysterious helmet malfunctions.

She was also getting good at living two lives.

It had been more than three years since she committed herself to living this life and sharing it with Daniel. But of course, she didn't share everything.

The only way she could reconcile her past and her present was through writing. Every free private moment she got, that's what she did. She wrote both about, and to, her other family. Who knew when they may stop by?

That morning before work, she began making a particularly important entry that combined both lives. Something exciting was happening here, something she wanted to share.

Lizzy consented to taking half the day off since she did have an appointment in the afternoon. She was also itching to add some more words to her story before Daniel arrived home and her birthing commemoration began.

She rushed through the main living area of their quarters and to their chamber door, stopping short as the door slid open.

Daniel was already home. He was sitting on the sleeping platform, staring at the floor. He didn't look up as she entered.

"Daniel? What's wrong? Are you ill?"

Lizzy took a step toward him and froze as she noticed her flashpad was lit up. She must have forgotten to deactivate it when she left that morning. Normally, it would shut down if another person tried to access it. But she and Daniel had shared chips since they'd been wedded . . .

She turned her attention back to him. He was looking at her now, with red eyes and a clenched jaw.

"You read it?"

He opened his mouth to speak and shut it.

She got it. If he'd read only a small portion of it, he was bound to feel betrayed.

"I'm so sorry. I didn't want you to find out like this."

"It's been years, Lizzy. I think you didn't want me to find out at all."

It was her turn to be at a loss for words.

"Do you really believe the stuff you wrote, or is it just a story?" A flicker of hope flashed across his face with the words.

She wasted no time extinguishing it.

"It's all real."

He lowered his head in his hands.

"Daniel, I wanted to tell you, but I didn't know how. I finally came to the conclusion that it would be better, kinder to you, if I just kept it to myself."

"Kinder to me? Don't do me any favors, please."

"Do you think I'm insane?"

"Do you think you're insane?"

"I wasn't sure before. But ever since that day with Belle, and then when they came – "

"No need for a recap. I've already read that part."

"I said I was sorry."

"Me too."

"What are you sorry for, marrying me?"

"To be honest, yes, that thought did cross my mind. But then I remembered why I married you. I love you Lizzy, I always will. But I think we love each other in different ways. I could never imagine myself with someone else. Not before you, not after you."

"But that's where you're wrong. You have been with someone else before. You've lived other lives. I know this to be true."

"I thought the one thing you knew for certain was that you could never know anything for certain at all."

"Oh my God, did you read every single word? Have you been home all day?"

Lizzy was trying hard not to be irritated. Sure, she'd been keeping things from him, but they were her things. He'd invaded her privacy.

"Yes, I came back shortly after you left. I wanted to prepare a special sort of celebration, just for the two of us. Silly me, I wanted to make a party similar to the imaginary ones you used to talk about. Back when I thought they were imaginary."

"God, I feel awful."

"And what is God? Lizzy, you've been doing a super job of fooling us all here, but I think you're slipping. I used to assume you were just quirky, making up words of your own for fun. But I see now I was wrong."

"I don't know what to say. Of course, we'll need to talk about it – "

"No. We don't need to talk about it. Not ever. Just make it go away."

"I can't and I won't. And believe me when I tell you how sorry I am, but I'm only sorry about keeping it from you, not the fact that it's true."

"Well, I don't want to hear it."

"I'll leave it up to you. I realize I was wrong to hide it, and I'll tell you whatever you want to know, whenever you decide you want to hear it. But there is something I need to tell you today."

"I told you, I'm not interested in your other husband or your other family."

"This isn't about any of that. I'm pregnant. We're going to have our own baby."

"Are you – when did you – "

"I just got back from the clinic, where they confirmed it and assigned me my first dose of waves."

"Are you happy?"

"Of course I'm happy. I do love you, Daniel. And I'm sorry I have two lives, but this is the one I'm living now. The one with you. Surely you read that much into the story?"

"I can't remember everything I read, just the highlights. I keep picturing you and him together in your other life."

"So you believe it's true?"

He looked so tired as he raised his head to meet her eyes, so old.

"So help me, I do. I've known you all my life, Lizzy. I just can't help but wonder if that's enough."

She bent down and took his hand. "It is. I promise you, Daniel. Each life is lived for a reason. Everything that happens here matters, it carries over. I know it's strange that I've retained my memories of the last one, but it doesn't make this, it doesn't make us, any less important. Please be happy with me. We're going to be parents."

Just like that, it hit him. He jumped up and set her on the sleeping platform in his place. "Oh, we are! We really are! Are you okay? How do you feel? Do you know what it is yet?"

"It's a boy."

"Wow. Okay, so what do I do?"

She had to laugh. "Nothing. We just wait until the suctioning, and then sit back and watch him grow in an incubator. I feel fine, but they're starting me on the waves to make sure I stay that way. I've got to say I won't miss the morning sickness and the – "

"Different in that last life, wasn't it?" His excitement dulled but didn't disappear entirely.

"Yes, very different. For one thing, I didn't have you."

She'd chosen the right words. His smile and his aura lit up the room.

Chapter 19

I do not remember Grandma being this clingy in our Earth lives. She's latched onto Dad now and keeps hopping back and forth between him and Grandpa, frantic in her expressions of love.

Hello, remember me, your grandkid? Nothing.

Mystery Pal is also feeling left out and sidles closer to me.

She tugs on me as if she wants to go somewhere. Good idea. They look like they need a bit of time alone to settle Granny.

Mystery Pal and I drift along through the green darkness. I don't wonder where we're going. It's just nice to do something other than fret about everyone and everything else for a change.

I've given up on trying to figure out who she is. The closest I've come is accepting she's my other half. The missing piece of my last life, of my very soul. I don't question if she's a boy or a girl, if she's a romantic sort of soulmate or just the thing that completes me.

It doesn't matter. I'm thankful we've found each other. This is what's getting me through whatever it is I'm getting through. Dad really could have stayed with Mom. But how was he to know?

She slows down as we approach a door I hadn't taken note of before, even though we passed it on the way to Mom's. Now that we've stopped, I get a strange feeling there's something in there for me. For us?

She guides me to the doorway, allowing me to make the decision whether to look inside.

I'll give it a go.

***

What happened? Did we just loop around? This is Earth.

My vision is being pulled into an apartment building. I think it's in Canada. It zoomed in a bit too quickly to tell for sure, but it's definitely North America. It's a big city. Maybe Toronto?

Oh, weird. That girl looks just like me. Well, maybe if I'd lived to be forty, which is about the age she appears to be. Her inner aura is a flashy silver, but I recognize it as well.

Just like with Mystery Pal, I have no clue as to how I know this person, but I do. Alternate-Me has a nice place! It's the penthouse suite of a massive building. I didn't see much of it before I was brought into her private dressing area. She's sitting at a long vanity, the surface of which is covered with makeup, perfumes, jewelry, and magazines.

I swear this is my twin. My old, rich twin.

The door opens and a man enters. I recognize his soul as well. It's an interesting sort of grey. Fluid-like, it reminds me of mercury. He's gorgeous.

The woman catches his reflection in the mirror and smiles coyly at him. He strolls over and sweeps her into his arms. Passionate kissing ensues.

Oh no, are they about to do it? No way am I watching this.

***

Okay, I can't hear it, but Mystery Pal is definitely laughing at me. Yeah, I have to join in. Seriously though, I'm not a porn fan.

What was that? It was definitely Earth, but a different Earth? A different time?

And who was that? The woman reminded me of myself, but she couldn't be me, could she? No, she wasn't me, I'm me. A relative?

Mystery Pal leads me away from the doorway. She can't hear or answer my questions, but she knows they're there.

Okay, listen up, Pal. I concentrate on putting all my efforts into focusing on one thought. Why did you show me that?

She stops and we linger in the middle of nowhere. Specks of other souls drift past us, up to their own ghostly business. I ignore them, the doorways, the murky green.

I repeat.

Why did you show me that?

Ugh. Not the answer I was looking for. All I'm getting is something along the lines of "be patient."

But there's an underlying sense of doubt I'm getting from her now. Is she sorry she showed me this? Maybe it was too soon?

I think we both agree to let it go for now. I'm sure we'll end up back here again for whatever reason, but in the meantime, I've got Real-Earth stuff to tend to.

Grandma's settled down by the time we get back. Well, fancy that. She's noticed I'm here. Her hug reminds me of the hugs she used to give back on Earth, before she cracked when Dad died, and I immediately forgive the oversight.

Hmm, that felt like a goodbye hug.

Where on earth could she be going?

Oh, Earth. She and Grandpa are going back to Earth. Mystery Pal hovers nearby, as Dad and I move closer to the doorway they're about to go through.

Their colors disappear from our sight. We go right up to the portal and I can see them drifting down through the clouds. There they are, Grandma and Grandpa in their human forms. They're holding hands and smiling up at us.

Just like Mom and Dad had been in the middle of doing when I interrupted them, my grandparents are melting back into their lavender auras. This time, I watch until they vanish completely.

I pull away before my view can be directed anywhere else.

Dad and Mystery Pal are already on their way to our spot.

I take my time in following them. He needs a minute with his thoughts, and so do I.

I think he's going to hang out here until Mom joins us, then they'll probably figure out where to go next. Unless she brings her new guy along with her. Weird, weird, weird.

But what about me? I want to stay until I find out what's going on with my husband and kids. But then what? Where do I go?

And there she is again, right by my side. Mystery Pal. She'll know what to do when the time comes.

Chapter 20

"Hey there, Henry," Daniel cooed at the liquid-filled incubator.

Lizzy stood next to him, eyeing her baby, not quite sure what to think.

It wasn't a baby; it wasn't even the size of her hand. And it looked like an alien. It only had the outlines of a nose and mouth, its eyes just little black orbs visible through its transparent skin.

For her, the most disturbing part was the fact it didn't have an aura. Not an inner nor an outer one. It looked like it was a living thing, but it had no soul. Not one that she could see.

No, she wasn't feeling very motherly about him yet. It wasn't even visually apparent it was a him, still attached to the umbilical cord that had been hooked up to the incubator instead of her.

Daniel put his arm around her and pulled her closer to him.

"I'm so proud of you, Lizzy. Just look at what we've created, what you've done!"

What had she done? Not much of anything. That morning, she'd lain down on the medical table and been administered numbing waves. She didn't see or feel anything, as the three-month-old fetus was suctioned out of her and placed in the bucket.

An hour later, she was standing there looking at it.

As odd as it was, she couldn't help making comparisons to the last time she'd given birth. Back when she was Amelia, living on Earth.

Amy had been an accident. The news of that pregnancy did not bring any joy; it brought on months of deliberation between her and Jason. Neither one of them wanted children. In the end, their decision was made by indecision.

They ran out of time and had no choice but to welcome Amy into the world.

She'd carried that baby for close to the full term and gone through all the pain and humiliating atrocities that went along with childbirth.

On Earth, she suffered from postpartum depression. She felt no connection, no love for her child, until she was two years old. It took the better part of four years before her daughter finally won her heart.

This baby, Lizzy had been excited about. She'd been looking forward to welcoming the little boy into their lives ever since the day she found out she was pregnant. She was hoping the child would bring her and Daniel closer, by adding that missing element of love and family to their lives. She had truly expected to finally feel real love for the first time on this planet.

Now, here she stood, staring at this little creature with an emotion bordering on disgust. No, not bordering; she couldn't look at it anymore and had to turn away. Was she just not cut out for motherhood, or was it the past life thing interfering again?

"Are you okay? Are you sure you don't want to sit down? The technicians advised you to stay off your feet for the rest of the day."

That warranted a laugh. There was nothing wrong with her. It hadn't hurt at all, and the numbing waves had already worn off. All she wanted to do was go to work. But that would be pushing it, even for her.

"I'm fine. Just tired."

Not a complete lie. She was tired. Deep in her soul, she was tired.

Tired of living this dual existence. Tired of trying to fit into a place that was, like her baby, still alien to her. Tired of thinking of the centuries she had to spend here before she could return to her other family. Tired of trying to figure out where Daniel, and now this Henry kid, fit into the grand design.

"Actually, I'm really tired. I think I will lie down. I'd rather go home and do it, though. More comfortable," she added when she saw the look on his face.

Since the day he discovered her stories and accepted that at the very least she believed they were real, he'd been different.

Well, of course he'd been different. It was a load to have piled on him. And yet, he accepted it. The best he could.

She'd been different too. They came to a semi-truce after hours of discussion, agreeing they would find a way to deal with the fact she carried her previous life with her while living this one. Still, it was awkward.

She continued to write her story, the letters to her last family that would never be read. She didn't hide the fact she was doing this from Daniel, yet every time he walked in on her while writing, she instinctively darkened the flashpad.

She did love Daniel, but continued to slip up and start talking about her past. As soon as she caught herself, she stopped in mid-sentence. But the damage was done with the first words.

Daniel, doing his best to support an unsupportable situation, would get irritated and insist she finish what she'd begun to say. She would, wrapping it up quickly and keeping most of the details to herself.

So yes, the rift had formed. But she still believed it was something they could work on. Hell, it's wasn't like they didn't have the time.

Another thing he had yet to understand was how much she enjoyed spending time alone. She needed time by herself. Just because she wanted to head off to work early or go home without him, it didn't automatically mean she was going to write or spend time with her beloved Belle.

Not always, anyhow.

It was difficult for people living in this hive-like world to comprehend why someone would want to be alone – why they would desire to have something that was theirs, only theirs, such as her writing had been to her on Earth.

Even if she didn't have her secrets to keep, she needed that space.

And today, she just needed to get away from that Henry in the container.

Chapter 21

Grandma, Grandpa, Scott, my kids, Dean, Mystery Pal, Mom, that other Earth I saw, all flicker through my mind in a maddening cycle.

As had been my inclination when things got crazy-tough in life, I have the overwhelming urge to run away. I could go off on a jaunt through the murk, I suppose. But there would be no escaping the thoughts.

One thing's for sure: I don't have the patience to sit here sharing energies any longer. I'm full.

I don't bother inviting anyone to come along as I scurry off to my Earth door, but they do.

***

There are my kids. They're at Dean's parents' house today. Oh, the sun's shining in through the big picture window in the sitting room. I miss the sun. I miss everything. Food, cigarettes, drinks, and yes, these children are growing on me.

I do think I would have bounced back from my depression, if given the chance, and learned to love them right quick. I love them now.

I'd never been one to make a fuss over other people's kids. In fact, I avoided them at all costs. I found nothing appealing about the neediness, the crying, the smelliness.

But at this moment I would give anything, absolutely anything, to lean in and smell the sweet scents of my children. I'd also do anything to protect them.

I take a mental snapshot of them squirming around in the playpen together and head off with the intention of checking on Scott.

Instead, I end up in another apartment. I've never seen this place before. It's small, but modern. Dean, Stacey, and Aunt Robin are sitting together at the island in the kitchen.

Looking around the room, I notice pictures of Susan, Stacey, my mom, my mom's parents and sister. What's the connecting factor here?

Aunt Robin. I look closer at her hand, her left hand. It's bare. Oh my God, she must have left Uncle Ian. Well, hooray for her.

Uncle Ian had been, and probably still is, a vile human being. He was an over-the-top religious fanatic who disassembled the Bible and used the words to suit his own needs. He didn't really believe in any of it; he was just a monster. I actually wouldn't mind being able to see him, now that I can see auras. His must be ghastly.

My attention goes from Aunt Robin's hand to the paper she's holding in it. The note from Scott.

"You should have shown me this sooner, Dean."

"I know. I was hoping he'd just go away. He can't seriously want these children."

"Who knows? From what you've told me, they may very well be his. What else do you know about him?"

"Not much. I only saw him a handful of times. Amy was dating him just before her father got sick and we got together. He'd stop by work to pick her up sometimes. Well, really to catch a ride with her. He's not the most talkative guy, and Amy and I didn't speak about him after they broke up."

"So what makes you think he wouldn't want his own children, should they turn out to be his?"

"They are not his. They are mine." *Dean's aura is threatening to blow.*

Stacey moves her chair closer and puts her arm around him. Yeah, there's something going on there.

"We're talking about biologically. Dean, you need to understand the seriousness of the situation. No one is questioning who loves them more. It's all about the legalities now."

His aura settles and he leans into her. Hmm.

"I know. I'm sorry, I'm just scared."

"You should be. It's a big deal," Aunt Robin persists. "What do you know about him, Stacey?"

"Amy didn't tell me much about this guy either. Susan might be the one to ask. She was friends with him before he and Amy got together. All I know is he'd been kicked out of the house by his alcoholic father before they broke up. He doesn't have a steady job or even a high school diploma."

"We need to find out what Susan knows and get a private investigator on him. It would have been helpful to have started this a week ago, but there's no changing that now."

"Are they expensive? I can borrow some money from my parents without needing to tell them what it's for."

"It doesn't matter. I can take care of it. But my advice is to tell your parents what's going on. You don't want them to find out the other way."

Dean looks to the ceiling, like right at me. He's not seeing me, though. How could he, with Stacey pawing at him like that?

"You're right. I just never wanted to have to tell them."

"Trust me, they need to hear it from you. And soon. You haven't talked to this character since he dropped the note?"

"No. I haven't done anything but worry."

"Okay. Don't communicate with him again. Don't call, don't talk to him if he calls you. The same goes for if he shows up. That's another reason why you need to tell your parents. If they're looking after the kids when he decides to come knocking again, they need to know. Not only for the sake of truth, but for their safety. There's no telling what he may do."

Dean turns to Stacey and takes her hand.

"You'll come with me?"

"Absolutely."

Seriously! I've been dead for three months and – whoops.

"Ouch!"

Stacey and Dean's exclamations are simultaneous. I don't know what happened. I can't see through the rippling barrier.

When it clears, they're both rubbing their arms where they'd been touching.

Not anymore, they're not.

"What happened?" *Aunt Robin asks, eyes wide.*

"I don't know, static shock?" *Dean mutters, as he and Stacey eyeball each other accusingly.*

Heh.

"I saw the spark from here. I don't even have carpet in this place. But, back to this. According to the letter," *she pushes it from her as if it were diseased,* "you have until tomorrow until he does 'or else.' "

Why am I sitting here watching them? We need a private detective? Well, we've got one.

Leaving the three of them to fuss about what they're going to do next, I sniff out Scott.

Uh, oh. He is indeed back at home, sitting with his father in the filthy living room. They're both drinking.

When we were dating, the one and only thing he had going for him was the fact that he didn't drink. He didn't even like to be around alcohol because of what he'd seen it do to his father.

Now here he is, guzzling whiskey with the man.

"So you're going back tomorrow then?" *his father slurs.*

"Yep. I know he's just gonna pay me to get rid of me."

"He'd better. Or we'll sue him."

"He'll pay. They pretend they don't have money, but I know different," *Scott boasts.*

The semi-jovial mood darkens along with his father's aura.

"You better know what you're doing. The last damn thing we need is more kids around here."

"I'm your only kid."

"Yeah, and you cost us plenty enough. It's about time you started paying us back."

Scott's outer aura mimics his father's stormy grey cloud.

"I worked and helped out."

"Well, you're not working anymore, are you?"

"I'm working on this. I don't want the damn kids. I'm just going to scare him to get the money."

"What if he doesn't care? I swear, if you try bringing those kids here – "

"I'm not going to do that! What would I want with her babies anyhow?"

Scott and his father are both standing now. It looks like they're getting ready to exchange blows.

I've seen enough. I hope they take each other out.

Back to Aunt Robin's. She's on the phone. Sounds like she's talking to the private investigator. Dean and Stacey are cuddling again.

"Do you think we should keep the kids somewhere else for a few days? Maybe here or at your parents'?"

"I think here would be better. I really want to keep my parents out of it as much as possible. I know I have to tell them; I just need to figure out how. And I don't want them getting in the middle of it."

He puts his arms around Stacey and presses his forehead against hers.

"Sorry, I didn't mean that your mom should be involved either. It's just, she already knows."

"It's okay. I know what you meant."

Yeah, they're about to kiss.

Back to my kids. Their grandparents have them out of the playpen and are sitting at opposite ends of the room, cheering them on as they make their first attempts at crawling.

This is where I need to be. I laugh along with them as my son and daughter wiggle around and roll over. No, there won't be any crawling just yet. But this is good enough for me.

Chapter 22

Lizzy dropped Henry off at the Care Center, gave him a perfunctory peck on his shriveled little head, and fled to her travel pod. Early for work, she tapped her foot, watching the minutes tick by before she could sign in and start her day.

Rules, rules, rules. Another thing she would never fully be able to accept about this place was how regulated everything was. She could hear the tick, tick, tick in her head all day long as she went from assigned task to assigned task.

Wake up at the same time, take in nourishment at the same time (and the nourishment was not all that varied or tasty). Work, exercise, even free time was scheduled.

Yet everyone was so happy. At least on the face of it, the vast majority of the population was perfectly content. And look at the crime statistics. There were none. They didn't even use the word crime. If someone overstepped the boundaries too far and too often, they were called variances. They were counseled, given waves. If that didn't work, that's what The Ward in the basement was for. Even there, they boasted happiness.

Lizzy had never been to The Ward, but she'd seen virtual tours on the ethernet. It didn't look all that different than life up above. White halls, white rooms, white jumpsuited-people. The doors to their rooms were wide open. Unlike Earth jails or sanitariums, there were no bars to keep them in. The people in the clip Lizzy watched were sitting around a white eating platform, smiling and partaking of the same nourishment packs that everyone else did.

Strict routines or not, Lizzy wasn't exactly miserable with her life on Celadon. Just torn.

They'd brought Henry home from the incubator a week ago. A few days before that, she thought she saw the spark of an aura in him. She decided it was her imagination until it began to bloom into a soft red hue.

By the time they left with him in Daniel's arms, there was no denying it. His aura was the exact same color as Jason's.

How she wanted to share this with him. She didn't need a therapist to tell her that would be wrong. She should want to share it with Daniel.

But she didn't. She didn't talk about Henry's aura, or anyone's auras, anymore. She didn't talk about her other life. She didn't talk to him a lot at all.

And she avoided Henry every chance she got. Just looking at him made her want to go flying out of this world and back to Jason. Well, she couldn't fly out of the world, but she could fly.

Finally. Time for work. She was the first worker in her pod, and the first pod out of the launching doors. Not abnormal for her.

She guided the pod to her favorite rainforest, eager to spend the day with Belle. She had to be careful how often she worked in the same area. They were supposed to spread their days over the entire region their dome managed, and she did. But today was definitely a Belle day.

Sure enough, as soon as she hopped out of her pod and removed the bothersome helmet, there she was, flying her way.

Careful to drop the helmet inside the pod so as not to forget it again, she ran toward her beloved bird.

Once the beak kisses had been received and Belle was perched on her shoulder, Lizzy wandered about scanning and playing with the other animals. She'd entered and transferred most of her daily data quota before midday.

She decided to take a break, settling in the shade of a tree to have a nourishment pack. The day was warm, the sun shining strong.

Oh, that smell. The air. Yes, it was thick. But over the years, she'd found there really was no need for the helmet once you got used to it. Her scans at the medic center had yet to show any anomalies.

Belle nipped playfully at the nourishment pack, but there was no danger of losing any of it to her. Why on earth would she want to eat this synthetic stuff when she had a rainforest of tasty delights all around?

Why on Earth . . .

From the first time she set eyes on this world, through the doorway from the In Between, she'd been drawn to it. She had the opportunity to see the entire globe. It looked a lot like Earth, except there was only one big continent in the middle of all the water.

She remembered how it glistened. So fresh and clean and new looking, the sun shining so brightly.

Not for the first time, she wondered if it actually was Earth, just in a far different age. Before or after her last life? She couldn't begin to guess.

As strange as it was, it made more sense to think of it as an alternate dimension to Earth.

There were so many similarities. They spoke basically the same language, they were still humans, and they used the same names. There were Jasons and Amys here, just as there were on Earth.

The air was what really got to her. Even through the denseness, it smelled the same. Perhaps a bit fresher, but the rain, the snow, the warm summer breeze . . .

Another mind-boggler to keep her thoughts occupied during her stay. No, not stay. She wasn't a visitor. She was supposed to be living a life here. And she was.

But she had to admit, she was doing a terrible job of it lately. The distance between her, Daniel, and Henry was only growing.

"What can I do, Belle? How do I get back on track? I was doing so well right before Daniel read my writings."

Belle just croaked her parrot croak and continued to peck at the shiny white nourishment pack.

"And what about you? How many lives have you lived? This can't be your first one since you left me. Eons have passed here from the time I saw you enter the world. What keeps bringing you back? You can't remember me, yet here we sit."

Good thing there was no one around to listen to her chattering to a bird. Still, she needed to watch herself.

No, she didn't believe Belle remembered the details of their past together, but she did believe they were bonded. They were destined to travel the same circles together for all of eternity. She'd come to believe this during her stay in the afterlife, where she assumed Jason and Amy still resided.

The bird was yet another part of her soul family. But where did Daniel, and now Henry, fit in to all of this?

A definite thinker. How different would things be if she had come into this world as she should have – clean, and untainted with memories of her past. What if Jason had made it through with her?

Maybe not such a good thing to think about. Because of course, she and Jason would be together.

And there would be no Henry.

Chapter 23

I ended up voluntarily spending the whole day with my children.

I watched as Dean's parents fed them, bathed them, and did all the things I wanted so badly to be doing. I reached out more than once and was rewarded with smiles and fuzzy feelings each time I did.

It's after dark when Dean and Stacey show up to get the kids. My kids. Can he not do anything without her? Does she not have anything better to do herself? Isn't she supposed to be going to university?

She sure doesn't have her nose perma-buried in a book anymore, like she did when I was alive.

Eileen and David remark on how cheery their grandkids were today, and Stacey runs over to scoop them both into her arms.

Okay, she is my cousin, so that makes her their second cousin? Not their mother, though. I'm their mother. And that's my husband standing in the doorway, watching her hug my babies, with a smile on his face that makes me want to die all over again.

As much as I took him for granted when I was alive, as much as I was repeatedly unfaithful and detached, I remember him looking at me like that. With pure adoration.

My husband is definitely in love with my cousin.

No, he's not my husband anymore. He's a widower.

I want to hug my children, but I don't feel like crossing soul-paths with Stacey just now. I blow my kisses their way and pull back.

***

Watching and cuddling is exhausting, but so worth it. I'd been in a great mood until the lovebirds showed up to remind me I don't belong there anymore.

Dad and Mystery Pal have already returned to our spot. I drag myself over to join them. Mystery Pal immediately showers me with love and replenishing energies, which I'm grateful for; but something's up with Dad.

He's got that twitchy, distracted thing going on. Geez, he wants to go see Mom again. He keeps floating off in that direction, before catching himself and returning just like last time. Did he not get the part where she told us to leave her alone?

Unless . . . I wonder how much time has passed there. Maybe she's ready to join us. I don't even want to see what my children's guardians are doing tonight, so I detach myself from Mystery Pal and send the invitation to Dad by drifting ever so slightly in the direction of Mom's world.

Yep. Dad rushes over, and right past me. I guess we're going to see Mom.

I try to keep up with him, checking behind me to see if Mystery Pal is coming. She's not there.

Maybe she has her own ghostly business to tend to. Certain she'll be around when we get back, I continue to chase after Dad. He's really moving and I'm still tired from my day.

I know where he's going, so I allow myself to slow down and lose sight of him.

I don't like traveling in the opposite direction of my kids anymore. God, how unfair is that? When I was alive, you couldn't pay me to sit in the same room with them unless it was absolutely necessary. Now I can't even take a jaunt while they sleep?

Well, Doctor, it appears you were correct. I did eventually bond with my children and learn to love them. Too bad I'm a ghost, though.

My thoughts only grow more bitter as I pass the door Mystery Pal had shown me. Unfair, unfair, unfair. All of it. I've got Ghost Dad and Space Mom to tend to, and my kids are either in loads of trouble back on Earth or are about to be stolen by my cousin. So why in the hell am I still thinking about this other damn place? It's pulling on me just like everything else in this friggin' In Between.

I'm fit to be tied here. What was the point of Dad ripping himself out of his next life with Mom? Was he supposed to be saving me from something, or had he just made a foolish mistake?

A foolish mistake like I made. No one told me I wasn't supposed to drink with all that medicine. No one cared when I needed them to. No one tried to help me.

No. I stop dead in my tracks. That's not true. None of it.

I hadn't wanted to think of it. I still don't. But here, all alone in the middle of nowhere and nothing, the memories of my last days on Earth are floating to the surface. And they won't take no for an answer any longer.

Whether anyone told me or not, I knew liquor and pills didn't mix. Even if I hadn't, it was written right there on all the prescription bottles in big block letters. DO NOT TAKE WITH ALCOHOL.

And I wasn't alone. I chose to sulk in the dark and ignore everyone's attempts to help me. My mom and dad were gone, but there were plenty of people that cared about me. Dean, Stacey, Dean's parents, my grandparents, Aunt Robin. They were all there. All the time.

And they didn't just take care of the babies for me. They tried to lift my spirits as well, bring me back into the land of the living.

But I didn't want to go back.

I did know what I was doing.

I made my decision.

The insurance company hadn't been wrong at all.

That day. Stacey was supposed to be over within the hour when I took my antidepressants. It wasn't time for them, but I took them anyhow. I also took sleeping pills.

Prescription strength sleeping pills. I didn't take one or two. I took six.

Things were already getting hazy when I dug out one of my hidden vodka bottles.

I wasn't thinking about what was going to happen, but I knew.

I knew, and I wasn't thinking of anyone but myself.

I wasn't thinking about my children. I wasn't thinking about Stacey, who would surely be the one to come across what was left of me. I wasn't thinking about Dean. Just me.

I'm unable to move, immobilized and alone in the dark.

Alone. Well, this is what I wanted, right?

No. My entire soul vibrates as I sob. I didn't want this. I made a mistake and there's nothing I can do to fix it. How am I supposed to live with myself?

And just like that, I stop shaking. No more tears.

What I did was unforgiveable. Unchangeable. I don't have to live with anything. I'm not alive. But I do need to find a way to exist with myself and what I did.

I need to start by taking responsibility for it. Done.

A cold calm comes over me as I realize forgiveness is not to be mine, not to be sought. It's time to start thinking about other people, other souls. The worlds do not revolve around me.

It's going to take time. And I'm going to need help. But one thing that's become clear to me is that the soul must go on.

Whether it wants to or not.

Chapter 24

The weekend always seemed to arrive too soon for Lizzy's taste. Three days away from work was not her idea of a good time.

Today was different. She sprinted from her cardiovascular session, eager to get to her living quarters to spend time with Daniel and Henry.

The kid was growing on her. He was looking more and more like Jason every day. Well, Daniel too, since they were so similar in appearance. Henry had his first birthing commemoration the week before. She took the day off work without hesitation or complaint, surprising herself as well as everyone in the department.

Henry was a loving child, full of smiles and laughter. He'd already taken his first steps and spoken his first words. A bright one much like herself, his first word wasn't Mom or Dad. His first word was Lizzy. She couldn't wait to see what he'd do next.

And then there was his aura. If she didn't know better, it was Jason reincarnated. Of course, she did know better, but she sure did love the kid.

In her last life, it had taken much longer to warm up to Amy. There were times when she felt guilty about her quicker attachment to Henry. But different life, different ways. She would never forget her precious daughter, nor would she ever stop loving her.

There was one more thing she was ashamed of. Just one little thing that dampened the excitement and joy of her life with Henry and Daniel.

Henry had indeed brought Lizzy and Daniel closer together. They spent more time with each other, talked more, actually enjoyed being around one another as they watched their boy grow. All their other problems had been brushed aside, seemingly set on disappearing.

Seemingly.

She couldn't help it. She'd called out to Jason. More than once. She couldn't imagine not sharing this joy with her soulmate.

Weird? Probably and definitely. It wasn't his son, it wasn't his life. But yet, she couldn't hold herself back.

The worst part about it? He never came. She never sensed his presence.

She felt abandoned, betrayed, angry. Why? She was the one who told him to go away while she lived this life. It had been her decision, her request.

Lizzy's new goal was to let it go. At least for the day. He was right not to come, she reminded herself. It was best for them all.

Daniel and Henry were playing on the floor in the living area when she let herself into their quarters. Henry was watching his father stack the standard set of white playing cubes every child received.

How could they even see the white blocks properly on the white flooring? Why, why, why were they so stingy with the colors here? Would it kill someone to break out a can of paint every now and then?

Pushing the unpopular thoughts aside, Lizzy set down her daypack and joined the boys on the floor. No carpet here, either, but the flooring was just as comfortable. Rubber-like and durable, easy to clean.

Not that she had to clean anything. Everyone's quarters were routinely taken care of by the maintenance workers.

Same, same, same. Same colors, same nourishment staples, same standard of living for all. Money was another thing, another word that didn't exist.

She had to remind herself daily to be very careful about what words she was teaching her bright little boy.

Speaking of reminders, she was supposed to be enjoying the day with her family. This family. Not head-bitching about the days of old.

Lizzy crawled past Henry, who had yet to notice her arrival, pretending she was about to knock over the tower Daniel was placing the last cube on. Monster-style, she growled and waved her arms about. Daniel played along, cowering from the impending doom.

"Lizzy!" Henry exclaimed with sheer delight.

He had no fear. What was there to fear in a world like this?

"Mom," Daniel corrected.

"Close enough."

Lizzy swooped down on her son, smothering him with kisses.

"How was your exercise period?"

"Invigorating, but I couldn't wait to get back to spend the day with my favorite guys."

And then it happened.

"Jason?"

"What did you just say?" Daniel demanded.

"Uh . . ."

What *had* she just said? She'd forgotten about everything else as soon as she felt the presence.

"You said Jason."

"No. I, um . . ."

Focus, Lizzy.

"I'm sorry, I don't know why I would have said that."

Lies. He was there. He still was.

Daniel got up off the floor, brushing the non-existent dirt from his jumpsuit.

"Daniel, I really was – I am looking forward to spending the day with you two. Please don't be mad."

"I'll be fine."

"You don't look fine."

"Okay, I'm not. But I will be. Let me walk it off. I'm going to see if I can get into my therapy session a bit early. We can enjoy the rest of our day when I get back."

"All right. I really am sorry about that."

Little Henry had lost all interest in the white cubes and was watching their exchange intently.

"It'll be fine. Just like it always is."

He gave them both a kiss on the tops of their heads and left.

Lizzy and Henry were left sitting on the floor, alone in the living area. The boy was just staring at her, sensing the strangeness, waiting to see what she would do next.

What *was* she going to do? They weren't really alone at all. Jason was there. He finally came back. Was she just supposed to ignore him?

Mustering up a cheery smile and voice, she disassembled the stack of blocks and encouraged Henry to try remaking the tower.

"Now it's your turn. Do it like Dad did."

He studied her with the eyes of a child much older than one, before picking up a block and sucking on it.

She kept her own eyes on Henry as she spoke to the ceiling in the smallest of whispers, "Jason. I'm sorry. I shouldn't have called you."

The infant rolled over onto his back and dropped the brick. His feet were the new objects of his attention as he tried to get one up to his mouth. He wasn't interested in his mother whispering to herself any longer.

Still, she had to keep it brief.

"I couldn't help it. I wanted you to see my son. This is Henry."

Careful to hide her tears from the boy, she turned her face away and dabbed at the flow.

Jason could see. And he was happy for them. Not jealous, not disinterested. She could feel the love flow through her as he sent his congratulations from above.

Oh, how she'd missed him.

"I was angry when you didn't come at first. I had no right to be. This is all just – "

Henry was staring at her again. She flopped down on the floor and fiddled with the bricks until they recaptured his interest.

"Mom will be right back. She just needs to get some hydro packs."

In the eating area, she wiped the remaining tears from her face and took out the hydro packs.

"Thanks for coming. You know I love you, but I can't and I won't call you again while I'm here. You probably understand better than I do."

She placed her hand on the shoulder he'd touched, wishing she could reach back up to him. Settling on sending her love with a smile, she returned to the living area to be with her son.

Chapter 25

Well, this is not what I needed to see.

Dad's still mooning over the scene of his wife rolling around on the floor with some other guy's baby. This is what we had to come rushing over for?

Congratulations, Mom. Enjoy your kid. Hopefully, it turns out better than your last one did.

I give Dad a bump, hoping to hurry this along. He's supposed to be helping me, not hanging around here.

I have no desire to watch the rest of that.

I'm good and fuming by the time he tears himself away and comes to sit with me where I retreated to wait.

Is he seriously wondering what I'm mad about?

Me, Dad! Me! When was the last time anyone truly cared about me? Mom's off enjoying her brand-new son, Dean and Stacey are having a jolly good time with my kids, and I don't know what in the hell I'm supposed to be doing here. Never mind here. Anywhere. I never have!

He hovers beside me, unsure.

I'll give him a break. I'm not behaving rationally. How is he supposed to know what happened to me in the middle of my trip? How could he imagine I just came to terms with having committed suicide? He can't even know I did. He must think I'm just jealous of the new kid.

Well, I guess that's part of it.

Tired of being mad, I concentrate on the epiphany and resultant resolution I made on the trip.

It's time to grow up.

I give my dad a friendlier bump. Even though he seemed happy with what he saw, it must be hurting him a little.

Yes, I can feel it now. But despite the fact I can tell he wants to go back to Mom, once again he's the first to start out on the return trip to Earth.

He pauses to allow me to catch up. It's a lot nicer traveling with a companion. Really, everything is better when you're not alone. Life, the afterlife, it's all the same. In times of trouble or in times of joy, what a difference having another soul to share them with makes.

Dad and I automatically veer toward our spot to recoup instead of heading straight for the Earth door. We're getting to be pros at this.

Mystery Pal shows up as we settle in, and all is back to normal. Well, as normal as it gets around here. We'll see how long this lasts.

As we sit and share our energies, my thoughts linger on how important it is to share your experiences with others. How essential it is to have someone, anyone, to exist with.

The afterlife is turning out to be the best teacher I ever had. What had I done during my Earth life? As a child, I kept to myself, rejecting any and all offers of close connections or even fleeting friendships. I was convinced I was too fat, ugly, and socially inept, and that was why I had no companions.

But the truth was, I hadn't tried. A few failed awkward attempts and nasty looks were all it took for me to give up completely.

I kept a certain distance from my parents, too. Always on guard, whenever they said a kind word or encouraged me to try something new, I interpreted it as criticism or pity.

After Mom died, the summer before my senior year, I did try. Hard. And I succeeded. I lost all that weight, made friends, really started living.

I guess I forgot to love myself in the process. As soon as things started going sour, I pushed away every last person that cared for me, starting with Dean. I didn't have to push my own children away. I never even got to know them.

For the longest time, I blamed my mom and dad for leaving me too soon. I was bitter and angry, and felt like I had nothing to lose.

It wasn't their fault. There's no one to blame for any of this, not even myself. I need to let that go.

And surprise, surprise, it turns out I did have plenty to lose. No changing that now.

Before I can fully embrace any sort of new beginning, I need to clean up the mess I left behind on Earth. I'm not sure what I can actually do from up here; it's not likely I'll be able to eradicate blackmail, or better yet the blackmailer himself. But the least I can do is watch over them for a while. No more running.

Dad and Mystery Pal are with me at the doorway as I brace myself for what I'm about to see.

***

Yep, right to my kids I go.

In life, I used to dread seeing them because I resented them so.

In death, I'm punched in the gut because of the love and guilt I feel.

It's a good pain though, one I refuse to push away.

Today they're at Aunt Robin's new place, napping in the playpen. She's in the kitchen fixing a sandwich and humming to herself.

Even with the looming threat of court cases and blackmail, she looks so much happier than the last time I saw her in life. Uncle Ian sure had done his damnedest to crush her spirit. His hold had been so tight, I'm amazed she actually had the courage to leave him. No way would he have been the catalyst for their separation. It would not look good to the church, to say the least.

Her outer aura shimmers with lights of every color, and another regret surfaces.

I treated her horribly after the death of my father. She and my grandparents had bent over backward to be there for me, console me, guide me.

And how had I rewarded them? By telling them all off, and basically running away to move in with Dean.

They continued to love me as I proceeded to decimate my life. I was still only seventeen when I took to partying and sleeping around. Only seventeen when I got knocked up. And I was barely eighteen when I married Dean and gave birth.

In my mind, my life was over. Looking back, there was so much to live for. So many people that cared about me. I could have done anything I wanted, pursued any goal as a career or even just a hobby. I could have traveled; money wasn't an issue.

And most of all, I could have loved these beautiful souls. My children, whom I never took the time to so much as look at properly when I was alive. I'd never held them for the purpose of hugging them. I only sat with one or both in my arms to feed them, refusing to look at their faces.

I leave Aunt Robin in the kitchen and go to them now. I rub their little arms as they smile in their sleep.

I wish I could give you more. I wish I could come back. I can't, and I'm sorry. I hope your lives are good.

I pull back. I shouldn't be doing this. They probably don't remember me. They certainly won't remember me when they grow up. No need to be haunting them now.

I wonder what people will say about me when my kids are old enough to ask. Will they tell them the truth, or will they cover up the ugly details? What will happen if they eventually find out on their own?

Surely they'll have questions. And if asshat there decides to go through with court proceedings, there will be plenty of documents to feed their curiosity.

Speaking of the devil, it's time to pay him a visit.

Chapter 26

It was late when Lizzy, Daniel, and six-year-old Henry arrived back at their living quarters. They'd spent the day visiting relatives. Of course, it wasn't possible to stop in on all of them, that's what happens when you live for centuries. But Lizzy believed it was important to at least try connecting with their parents and grandparents.

Socializing, such as they had tried to do that day, was not really part of Celadon's culture. Apart from birthing commemorations, it was rare for someone, even family, to drop by. There were no dinner parties, no movie nights. Hell, there weren't even proper movies. People just scanned through their technological devices if they wanted to view content. Most of the doors they knocked on were opened by confused people who had no idea what to do with them.

Lizzy's own parents had been the worst. She called ahead to let them know they would be coming over. She was still talking to them via her earchip, trying to explain why, when they arrived at their living quarters. They actually stood outside the door for five minutes while her parents continued to ask questions before they would open it.

Not one person at any of the places they stopped thought to offer them a hydro pack or even a seat. As the day went on, they simply began seating themselves and talking about Henry.

Daniel had been supportive of Lizzy's "experiment" when they set out. Halfway through, the blank look on his face told her he'd checked out mentally. By the end of the tour, he was done. They were all done. No need to discuss future expeditions of the sort. It had been an epic failure.

At least they had Henry. Lizzy vowed never to become so distant from him once he was grown with a life of his own. Smart as a whip, just as she'd been at his age, they were already suggesting he be moved ahead in his education programs. Beginning therapy early had also been recommended, but not for the same reasons as hers.

Henry didn't see colors or have imaginary friends, a relief to both Lizzy and Daniel. Retaining past life memories and the ability to see auras wasn't something that was likely to be passed along genetically, but still.

Henry was the light of their lives. He was the happiest child she'd seen on this planet, content to be alone or around others. He was the center of attention everywhere he went. It just came naturally to him.

Apart from his intelligence and unbelievable good looks, his charisma was almost palpable. His hair mirrored Jason's – correction, Daniel's – hair, jet-black and shiny smooth. His golden eyes were brighter than even Lizzy's, which people had remarked on all her life. His straight white teeth were dazzling, outshining the other bland whiteness around him.

His aura was the most beautiful of all. His inner aura had blossomed into a full-out rose color. His outer one changed constantly from one brilliant color to the next. It never failed to lift Lizzy's spirits, as well as those around him who couldn't see it. They didn't have to see it to feel its joy.

An entire day of being hauled from living quarters to living quarters, receiving nothing but awkward hand hugs, left Henry wearing the closest thing to a scowl Lizzy had seen on him so far.

It didn't last long. His weariness vanished as he ran off to his chamber to work on his education project before their evening nourishment.

"He's just like me at that age," Lizzy marveled.

"What do you mean?" Daniel asked.

"Not what you're thinking," she answered, sensing the tone.

They'd been doing so well for so long. Still, the slightest mention of her childhood or past experiences always threatened to lead them into the more dangerous territory of past lives.

"I was referring to my love for learning. Most kids, whether they're six or sixteen, do not rush off to their flashpads on a Saturday night."

"Oh, sorry. It was a long day."

"Tell me about it."

Happy to be back in the safety zone, Lizzy took out the nourishment packs and inserted them into the warming vessel. She was used to biting her tongue at this point. No musing aloud about how she didn't miss cooking like it had been on Earth. No grumbling about the lack of variety. She allowed the thoughts to breeze through her mind, barely acknowledging them herself.

"I'm going to take off, but I'll be back before the meal," Daniel announced.

"What do you have? I thought we had a clear schedule today."

"It's not an appointment. I received a request to meet with a client."

"Oh, okay. We can reheat it if you're late."

"I shouldn't be. But if I am, you can go ahead and eat without me."

With that, he was gone. No old-married-person peck on the cheek, not even a see ya' later. Lizzy stared at the door long after it secured itself behind him.

Although she had settled into a routine of looking forward to the weekends and the time they spent together, Daniel seemed to be drifting in the opposite direction.

He wasn't as concerned with her slipups as he used to be. He didn't hover over her constantly, as was his habit after he first read her writing. Was it a false sense of security she'd been left with? Was it possible that instead of trusting her, he just didn't care anymore?

Years of practice had taught her to tune out everyone's aura but for Henry's. Apart from the fact she was trying to be normal, it really did seem like an invasion of privacy. It wasn't hard to condition herself to ignore this part of her life. The memories of her family and previous life were what she struggled with the most. Jason and Amy were never far from her thoughts, but she hadn't actively called out to them for years.

Tuning out is not the same as not seeing, though. As she continued to stand and stare at the door her husband had left through, she could see an imprint of the memory left behind. His outer aura had been green. Deceptive. Guilty?

Lizzy turned away, suddenly furious at the lack of cooking tasks or housework. She needed something to keep her busy, something to take her mind off her suspicions.

Aura-reading was not the same as mind-reading, but the signs were all there. He'd been distracted, not as attentive. He worked a lot of odd, late hours. A client meeting? He worked in dome maintenance.

How could she have been so blind? Why was she only putting the pieces of the puzzle together now? And how was what he may be off doing really all that different from what she'd been doing since the day they met?

Try as she might, and as much as she loved Daniel, her heart belonged to Jason. She believed it always would.

But she sent him away. She wasn't running out at night to meet him, to kiss him, to . . .

Risk her life here.

Furious now, she reset the temperature on the warming vessel, slamming the door as it had never been slammed before. It needed nothing more than a nudge to seal itself. Her intention had been to speed up the warming process so she and Henry could eat earlier. She had no desire to speak with Daniel tonight.

Instead, the broken door on the appliance sent out a maintenance signal and they would have to wait. Not for long. Someone would be knocking on her door shortly to patch it up with their lasers or whatnot.

Just long enough to let her sit and stew about what her husband was up to. Long enough for her thoughts to drift out of this world and across the In Between, to her other husband and child.

Chapter 27

Uh, oh.

This is not the place I was hoping to find Scott. He's in a lawyer's office.

My God, is he wearing a suit? What an idiot. If he wanted to put on a show for someone, he should have saved the fancy clothes for someone other than this ambulance chaser.

And seriously, tweed? Did he stop by the Salvation Army on his way here?

"Mr. Orchard, your case is strong. You say you are certain these children are your own?"

"One hundred percent, sir."

You lying son of a bitch.

"And they have no other living relatives?"

"Not a one, that I'm aware of."

Hello, Cousin Stacey is pretending to be their mommy right now.

"And when you approached Mr. Grant, he refused to let you see them?"

"Yep." *Scott's smile screams of ignorant pride.*

What is he doing? Does he think this seedy lawyer (who didn't even bother to stop for tweed himself) is going to award him his sought-after hundred thousand dollars?

"We certainly have the grounds to order the paternity test. I'll have the papers served straightaway. After the parentage has been proven, we'll proceed to the custody hearing."

"Who pays for the test?"

The lawyer peers over the rim of his glasses at Scott. "Well, you will of course. But you've assured me you are financially stable. Surely it's worth the cost. You do realize that with children come great responsibilities? And should you emerge successful, there will be a lot more bills to follow."

Maybe he isn't such a dud after all.

"Uh, yeah. I'm financially stable. But these kids come with money of their own. Millions of dollars. I don't see why I should have to pay to prove these people are lying."

The lawyer sets the papers on his desk and sits considering his client. Scott shifts uncomfortably in his seat.

"Mr. Orchard, I must say there are a few inconsistencies in your story. If you lie to me, you're not only wasting my time, but you'll be opening yourself to potential countersuits and perjury should this go to trial."

Scott opens his mouth to rebut, but the man cuts him off.

"I want to say two things, and I want you to listen carefully. No, no words. Just nods."

Scott nods, his aura burning with confusion and frustration.

"You had better not be going after these children because of their inheritances. You need to be damn sure you're capable of caring for them and your motives are pure. I would happily be on the opposing side of the lawsuit that comes after you, if that is not the case.

"The second thing is, it's just not possible to be one hundred percent certain these children are yours. Off the record, I don't believe you have a clue. Back on the record, I will have the papers served to Mr. Grant later this week.

"I urge you to seriously think this through. If you decide you no longer want to proceed, please call me immediately.

"Do us all a favor and take a good look at yourself. Think about these children. Whether they are yours or not, we want what's best for them, correct?"

Scott nods and continues to stare at the man, whose sigh comes from the depths of his well of patience which is surely being run dry.

"You may speak now."

"Oh, yeah. I do."

The lawyer doesn't bother to ask which statement he was agreeing with. He simply nods at the door to indicate they're finished for the day.

Scott jumps to his feet, stupidly pleased with himself, and leaves.

So do I.

Back to my kids.

Aunt Robin has them up in their highchairs. Dean and Stacey look as if they've just arrived. They greet my babies with kisses before seating themselves at the table.

Aunt Robin brings over bowls of pudding, so Stacey and Dean can each take charge of feeding a twin.

"Scott showed up at my work today," Dean announces as he spoons the pudding into Darren's mouth.

"You didn't give him any money?" Aunt Robin is quick to ask.

"No. I took your advice. I've got to tell you, it was still tempting. I'm sure he would have gone away for at least a while over a hundred dollars."

"Yeah, for a while," Stacey reminds him. "We need him to be gone forever."

"You know he'd keep coming back for more," Aunt Robin affirms.

Dean puts down the spoon, which Darren promptly grabs.

"You all seem to be more concerned about money than what happens if he does sue for custody. What if the paternity test comes out in his favor? What if he takes my children from me?"

"Dean." Stacey gets the spoon from Darren and hands it back to him. "That's not going to happen."

"You're willing to bet my children's lives on that?"

Aunt Robin hands Stacey a cloth to wipe Darren's face where he's smeared the chocolate pudding.

"No one's betting anything. This problem isn't going to go away on its own. And it needs to go away. The worst thing you could do is give him money and drag it out. You will have a lawyer of your own, a competent lawyer. And I think it's safe to say all three of us will do whatever we need to do, to ensure this man is out of your lives forever."

"But what if he's the biological father?"

"Then it will be more difficult. But, from what you've told me, he's only looking for a paycheck. We have a private investigator on him, and we'll use what we need to, if and when we need to use it. Don't forget, whatever happens, these babies have biological family here as well."

Aunt Robin taps Dean on the hand holding the spoon.

"Just take care of your children. I know it's hard to wait, but that's all you can do for the time being."

"And don't talk to him again if he comes around," Stacey adds, her heart in her eyes. "Look at your son, Dean. He needs you."

Dean focuses on Darren, who's reaching for the spoon in search of more pudding. Not a care in the world except for that. Dean's eyes tear up as he returns to feeding him.

"I don't know if I'm good enough. I work, I go to school. I just want more for them. I want them to have a normal childhood. I want them to have a mother."

Tears are streaming down his face now, but he smiles through them as he continues to spoon the sweet dessert into Darren's mouth.

I'm right here, Dean. I'm so sorry I left.

***

It's Dad who yanks me out. Mystery Pal helps him drag me away from the doorway. I force myself to relax and allow them to pull me to our spot.

I hadn't realized I was getting so worked up. The last thing I need to do is accidentally set off some ghostly phenomenon to further upset them.

117

My sorrow and rage are not settling even though I'm being flooded with loving, supportive vibes.

This is all my damn fault and I can't fix it.

Our spot is not where I need to be right now. Neither is Earth.

I pull away to head off on my own. Away from Earth, away from Mom's world, away from everything. I can feel Dad and Mystery Pal start to follow, but I blast back as much of an "I don't want you to come!" vibe as I can muster.

Now's not the time to worry about pushing people away. I'll be back. I just need a break.

Alone.

Chapter 28

Lizzy sat in the eating area, tapping her foot on the rubbery floor. He was late again. She checked her gopad to see if she'd missed a notification. Nothing. Their chips were connected. How hard would it be to send a message directly to her ear?

Daniel's tardiness wasn't out of the ordinary. He dragged himself in well after dark at least a couple of nights per week. She was only irritated because she'd fed Henry early and put him to bed, in order to have the talk with her husband.

Yes, the talk. There was little doubt left in her mind that he was having an affair. All the signs were there. Secret gopad notifications he hid when she entered the room, whispered voice communications, the late nights. If lipstick existed in this world, she was certain she'd find it on the collar of his white jumpsuit.

It would be simple enough to investigate by going through his notifications and communications, using the shared-chip advantage. He wasn't always careful about securing his devices. But she needed to hear it from him. And then she needed to figure out what to do.

Since divorce wasn't an option, she would have to find a way to deal with it. She didn't want a divorce anyway. What would that accomplish, other than traumatizing Henry?

She'd done enough marrying for this lifetime and had no interest in an affair of her own. She just wanted the truth, and a solution to the problem.

The likelihood of having a rational discussion was diminishing with each minute that ticked by. Each tick brought her closer to breaking her resolution and calling out to Jason, or even Amy. If she wasn't going to talk to Daniel, she was going to talk to someone.

The only friendships she had in this world were connections to other parents with whom she had nothing to discuss but parenting and the like. They were not riveting conversations.

If she were to call on any of her extended family, those would be longer interrogations consisting of nothing but questions as to why she was calling. She'd attempted a few of them in the past and had learned her lesson.

It wasn't like she could talk about her suspicions anyhow. You didn't speak publicly of affairs on Celadon. Having an affair was fine, but announcing it was taboo.

Lizzy had no one to have a heart-to-heart with, no shoulder to cry on.

She used to have Daniel.

The door slid open, and in he came with the dreamiest look on his face. He may very well have been arriving home from a day at the spa, if there were such a thing here. He was that relaxed.

He swiped the pad by the door to activate the light. Twice. The first time he deactivated it because he hadn't noticed it was already on. His pleased stupor was replaced by panic as his eyes focused on her sitting there.

"Lizzy, I must have forgotten to signal you. You didn't have to wait up. I hope you already ate because I grabbed something at the job site."

"I'm sure you did grab something."

This was already going badly. He turned from her and strode into the living area, but not before she saw his reddening cheeks. And there was no hiding the slithering green aura surrounding him. Guilt, guilt, guilt.

She followed him into the living area, where he was sitting perched on the edge of the settee. He wasn't using his gopad or comms, he was just sitting and waiting.

She sat on the other side of the room, on a separate settee, and said nothing. He obviously knew the time had come. She'd waited this long; she could wait a bit longer for him to come up with the right words.

"So, you know then?"

"I know nothing. I suspect things, but I don't know anything for certain." The anger was draining out of her, she was just sad and tired. "I would appreciate it if you would tell me."

His previously pink cheeks drained of all color. He looked like he was going to throw up. Then he looked like he was going to cry. Then he looked just as tired as she was. He rubbed his eyes hard before looking into hers.

"I'm sorry. You know I love you, and I do believe you love me in your own way . . ."

"Is this about Jason and Amy?"

His cringe was answer enough.

"Daniel, they're not here. They haven't been here for a long time. I told them to go away so I could live my life with you."

"Of course they're not here. How could they be here? They're dead, are they not? This is what I'm talking about. I believe you remember your past life and see colors and all that, but you continue to speak about them like they're still around.

"You may think you've sent them away, or have committed to this life, our life. But you can't tell me a day goes by where you aren't thinking of them or writing about them." He jerked his head at the door to their chamber where her flashpad resided, his expression one of disgust.

Lizzy couldn't hold his stare any longer. She dropped her eyes to the ground.

"You know my situation, and I'm doing what I can to deal with it. That's not what this conversation is supposed to be about. I asked you a question. All right, I suppose I didn't. Who is she?"

"You don't know her."

"That wasn't what I asked."

His sigh was more of a groan. "Her name is Anna, and we do work together."

"Is she married?"

"She is."

"How long has this been going on?"

"I don't know, just over a year?"

Out of patience, she snapped her head back up. "Are you asking or telling me?"

"It – I – it's hard to say . . ."

"Never mind. Final question. Are you going to continue to see her?"

It was his turn to look away.

"Are you going to continue to write about them?"

And there it was. Lizzy stood and looked long and hard at the man she'd married, the man she'd loved, the man she had a son with.

"I am."

Confident she'd answered for the both of them, she went to their chamber door and tapped her wrist against the pad to open it.

"Good night, Daniel."

Chapter 29

I don't know how far I've gone, but it's as far as I've ever strayed from my Earth door and I'm not yet ready to stop.

The doorways are looking stranger, and they're not so door-shaped anymore. All the others I'd seen near my own were rectangular, with a light something like dim sunlight shining out of them.

These ones are warped, fuzzy. They're not black inside, but they're so dark it's close. I can only see the grey illumination of the nearly-invisible ones out of my peripheral vision. Look right at them, and they're gone.

No eyeballs, but I have peripheral vision. Of course I do.

Out of gas, I pull over to rest. Yeah, I think I've gone far enough. It feels weird over here. Unwelcoming.

I'll head back soon. In the meantime, I'm sure I've at least put enough distance between myself, and everything and everyone back there, to get somewhat of a grip on things.

Away from all that, I'm having a hard time remembering what I'm supposed to be doing. What am I supposed to be getting a grip on? I've been calling myself a ghost, a spirit, a soul, but I think I'm really a phantom.

Am I even real anymore? Phantom strikes me as the most accurate word to describe what I am, if you think of what phantom pains are on Earth.

Someone loses an arm or a leg. The limb is gone forever, but they still feel it. It can hurt them.

Ew. Another soul brushes by me. It's not the first time it's happened, but this one feels wrong, kind of slimy. I'm definitely not in Kansas anymore.

As I sit and wait for my batteries to recharge, I notice the souls look different here too. Like the doors, they're also darker, shiftier. Hmm, maybe this is the In Between version of hell. Maybe you get to choose dark versus light. Maybe I deserve to be over here on the dark side. Maybe I should stay here.

Really, I can't imagine what I can do for my husband and children back on Earth, apart from haunting and possibly traumatizing them. They don't need me anymore. My cousin and aunt have taken my place, and I have to admit they're doing a better job of everything than I did. Cripes, the pizza delivery guy could have stepped in and shown me up.

Besides, after what I did, do I even deserve to head back to the light?

My sights are locked on the misshapen door in front of where I'm hovering. This one isn't quite as dark as all the others. I ignore all the voices in my phantom head and decide to take a peek inside. Why not?

***

Oh, bad idea. Very, very bad idea.

I want out. I can't move. It's sucking me in.

I changed my mind! Let me go!

I have no idea who I'm yelling at, but no one is listening.

I stop my flailing and concentrate on pulling back. I can't make it all the way out, but I'm no longer moving forward.

Damn, maybe Uncle Ian wasn't so crazy after all. This looks exactly like the hell fires he used to preach about.

The terrain is rocky and barren, a dull lifeless grey. A dim red haze hovers over the horizon, as if the sun is about to rise.

Shadowy creatures limp across the surface, solid black and cartoon-like in their appearance. It's hard to tell if they're supposed to be people or dragons or something else. They have no auras.

That sun isn't coming up, either. The red light dances like Earth's Northern Lights gone terribly wrong, casting flickering shadows on the ground that meld with the black silhouettes of the sinister beings.

I'm drawn to one particular figure in the way I was drawn to the woman in the world Mystery Pal showed me. This thing reminds me of myself.

I watch as it struggles to catch up to another shadow-beast. It stumbles and falls to the ground. Unable to get up, it digs its claws into the rock and continues to crawl.

Why am I crying? Why did I come here? Let me out!

The creature I'd centered on looks up. Not solid black anymore; two glowing red orbs appear in the area where a face might be. It's looking right at me. It wants something from me. Hell, for all I know, it wants to eat me.

The thing it was chasing, before I drew its attention to me, stops and turns around. The tables have turned, and it's creature number two's turn to seek out its follower.

Look out!

My cry goes unheard as the shadow pounces on the soulless version of myself. Its own screams are horrifying enough to spur me on, giving me that last drop of phantom adrenaline needed to yank myself out of Hell.

***

I feel so dirty. I try shaking the filth off as I propel myself away from the portal. Whatever had been trying to suck me in is still pulling on me.

Drained of energy from tearing myself out of there, I'm now the one who's limping through the In Between, desperate to put as much distance as I can between myself and that doorway.

This is the stuff nightmares are made of. My soul tingles with dread as I risk a look back.

Hysteria threatens to take control. One of the shadowy figures is trying to pull itself out of the hole. It's nothing but a shapeless head so far, but no way am I sticking around to see the rest.

With every last drop of whatever it is I have in me, I dig deep and push myself toward home.

Refusing to look back or to the side, I focus on the image of my children. My husband. My dad. My mom. Mystery Pal.

The odd-looking doorways and listless souls are still there in my damned peripheral vision, but they're becoming less strange and a little brighter as I pick up speed.

Darren. Diedre. Dean. Dad!

I can't see him yet, but I can feel him. Sure enough, here he comes, answering my ghostly call. Mystery Pal is right there beside him. They grab on as soon as they reach me and I go limp, allowing them to tow me the rest of the way.

I'm sure they're wondering what in the hell I'm blubbering about as they drag me along. One thing's for sure, I don't think they'll be keen on letting me go very far on my own anytime soon.

No complaints here.

Chapter 30

Lizzy rapped on the door to the former den – Daniel's room since the night their in-house split-up had been decided upon.

"I'll be right out."

She turned back to the living area without acknowledging him. There would be plenty of time for fake niceties later at the Education Completion Ceremony.

Yes, her little boy was not so little anymore. He was about to embark on his field training. Within the year, he would be choosing his career.

Lizzy and Henry were closer than most mothers and sons. Every pair that she knew of, to be exact. Society just wasn't designed for strong parental bonds. You were born, you attended your education programs, you went to field training, you picked a life mate and a career. The end.

Lizzy had been true to her word. She and Henry hadn't drifted apart like she did with her own parents, like everyone else did. She couldn't remember the last time she'd seen or spoken to her mother and father.

Her mother attended her last birthing commemoration, but sitting in the living area in silence all day as people came by to commiserate with her hardly counted as quality time. The last time she saw her father was probably during that ill-fated attempt to go out visiting family almost a decade ago.

Sure, she loved them, kind of. But there wasn't really a place in her life for them. Growing up, it was the same way. She knew they cared about her and wanted the best for her, but she followed the path that was set out for her with minimal involvement from them. They did their due diligence in setting her on said path, but that was all.

She and Henry were different. They enjoyed spending time together. Over the years, they'd spent countless hours just talking late into the night. They had an equally above-average intellect and shared many of the same interests.

She was careful not to over-overstep the closeness boundaries. The last thing she wanted to do was handicap him with a blatant oddity, but he was one of the most enjoyable aspects of her life. It was going to be a big adjustment for her when he finally left the proverbial nest.

Henry had yet to choose a life mate, something his therapist was concerned about. Lizzy wasn't. There was still plenty of time, and she more than suspected she knew who it would be; a sweet young girl who lived only two doors down from them. Though she tried to keep aura observations to a minimum, it was impossible not to notice how both of their auras lit up when they crossed paths. The effect was blinding.

The one thing she and Henry didn't have in common was her love for nature. He wasn't interested in the outdoors, nor working outside of the domes at all. She'd taken him out once in preparation for making his list of jobs to consider for field training. She didn't have to look at his aura to know how he felt about the experience. The bland expression on his face was sufficient.

He ended up narrowing his job list down to two fields. Dome maintenance, like his father, and The Ward. Keeper of The Ward was the closest thing to law enforcement they had on Celadon. A Keeper of The Ward's job was tending to the troubled and undesirable people down below. It looked like he would end up following in the footsteps of one of her husbands.

"Mother!" Henry appeared in the living area and swept her up in his strong arms. "Today's the day!"

"Yes. I'm so proud of you, my boy. Tomorrow, your life really begins."

"I can't wait. This Education Completion Ceremony is going to be boring, though."

"I know. What ceremony or commemoration here isn't?"

Henry lowered his voice as he eyed the door to his father's room.

"When will you let me read more about the other worlds?"

Lizzy's eyes went to the closed door as well. She still wasn't certain it had been the right thing to do when she started sharing her stories with Henry. She knew very well what Daniel would think of it.

She had no doubt Henry would keep their secret, but deep down inside she couldn't help wondering if it may somehow harm him. She never came right out and told him they were anything but fiction, but he must at least suspect she believed they were more than that. He was too clever not to.

"Soon. For now, let's concentrate on your success and get ready for tomorrow. You're sure you don't mind me tagging along to the basement with you?"

"Of course not. I know how intrigued you are with the complex. They can call me momma's boy all day long if they like."

"Do people call you that?"

"No, I'm just kidding. I don't think that's a commonly used term around here." He winked at the Earth reference she'd missed. "Besides, if they did, I'd only feel sorry for them for not having such a terrific mother as I."

"You're quite the sweet-talker, aren't you?"

Daniel's door slid open and he entered the living area.

"My son, a sweet-talker? Well, we know who he must have gotten that from, don't we?"

Oh, awkward. Daniel and Henry did not share the same relationship Lizzy and Henry did. They were closer than most fathers and sons, but only marginally, and only thanks to Lizzy's early efforts.

As far as Daniel knew, they were keeping up the happily married act and Henry was buying it. Lizzy never badmouthed his father to him, but he was well aware of Daniel's infidelity. Daniel having his own room would have been enough of a tipoff for most kids. But it would also have been impossible to spend as much time together as she and Henry did, talking about life, love, and everything in between, without the subject coming up.

Still, it was the way a lot of marriages turned out here, and Henry didn't seem to harbor any animosity toward his father. It probably helped that it was clear how little it bothered Lizzy now. She didn't care to spend time with her husband, but they put on false faces for the world just like everyone else in their situation. She had no desire to be his wife in anything but name any longer. Her initial feelings of jealousy and betrayal had eroded over the last decade.

"She was joking, Dad. I could never be as charming as you."

"Ah, I wouldn't be so sure about that. I've seen how Lynette looks at you," Lizzy teased.

Aha! A blush. She knew it. She was really only trying to take the focus off her failed marriage when she said it, but this was a double score.

"We'll see," was all Henry said.

"Who's Lynette?" Daniel asked.

"Just a girl," Henry replied. "Let's go, we don't want to miss the excitement."

"Of course, it's a big day for you!"

Henry and Lizzy shared a smirk, as Daniel led the way to the snooze-fest.

Chapter 31

I think I've been sitting here with my dad for days. Mystery Pal comes and goes, but Dad and I don't move.

I know I should get back to Earth and check on things there, but I'm having a hard time seeing the point of it. It's exhausting and painful. I don't know what I'm supposed to be doing there. And what happens if I unwittingly reach out or freak out while I'm spying on things that maybe aren't any of my business? I could hurt someone. Not just scare them. I could physically damage my family.

My family. Why now? Why do I think of them as my family and love them so much when it's too late?

I can't sit here forever, though. Literally, I don't think I have that option. It's the strangest feeling, as if I'm being pulled at from all sides. Something is telling me, in not so many words, I'm going to have to make a decision soon.

I think I'm supposed to be reincarnated. And I think I may have some say as to where that occurs. Grandma and Grandpa slid happily back into Earth. I don't think that's where I'll be going. I think Mystery Pal and I will be off to someplace else. Maybe through the door she showed me that looked like Earth, with the woman that looked like me in it.

But it's not quite time yet. When it is, I know Mystery Pal will be able to guide us to the proper place. She may be the only reason I don't expect to end up in one of those hell worlds. Dad means well and I love him, but he'll end up back with Mom soon enough.

I wonder if Mystery Pal is my soulmate. They say everyone has one. Maybe that's what went so wrong in my last life. Maybe she's what I was missing.

She seems to have been here for a long time. Apparently, she met my dad before she met me. She seems so much older than me. Maybe that's just because I still feel like a kid, having left my last life all too soon.

131

As tired as I am from that last excursion, I should tend to my Earth business. There's a strong pull still coming from there. Whether or not I know what my business is, I need to follow it.

Dad and I float off, as I allow the tug to reel me in. I wonder why he follows me every time. I don't think he's able to see what I see; he can only feel my reactions. Maybe he's watching his own parents, or maybe he's just waiting for me. That is why he abandoned his last rebirth, after all.

Okay, deep breath. What awaits me today?

*** *

Eesh. Nothing good. Dean is at his parents' house, and there isn't a dry eye in the room. Speaking of rooms, I can feel Darren and Diedre in the next one. As much as I want to go see them, I can't look away from this.

"So, never mind the fact you lied to us about being the father of these children, but now you have a druggie blackmailing and stalking you?"

"David, you'll wake the babies. Please, sit down." Eileen tugs at his shirt from her perch on the loveseat.

He sits, but doesn't take his eyes off his son pacing the floor on the opposite side of the room.

"Dad, you've got to understand. I loved Amy, and I love our children. They very well could be mine, but it doesn't matter. You can't tell me you'd love them any less, whatever the case may be."

"Of course not, but you're really screwing up here. We were willing to overlook what we thought was the fact you got a girl pregnant and married so young. We loved her too and wish we could have helped her."

"Dean, I think what your father's trying to say is that you need to make sure the children are protected."

"I'm doing my best."

"By giving this guy money? You should have come to us. You need a lawyer. A good one, now, since you've already given him something to use against you."

"I have a lawyer. I have lots of lawyers. Stacey's mother has been helping and she's the one who hired the private investigator to begin with. He's already dug up plenty on this guy. We'll do whatever it takes to protect the kids."

Hey, since when are we calling Aunt Robin "Stacey's mother" instead of "Amy's aunt?" I've only been dead three months, pal.

"So, let me get this straight. This guy shows up over two months ago, and tells you he wants a hundred thousand dollars or he's going to come after the kids?"

Whoops. That detour to hell must have taken longer than I thought. I guess I've been dead for five months now. Still, it hasn't even been half a year.

"Yes. He gave me a week to come up with it, but I didn't."

"Then he shows up again and demands less money?"

"He caught me by surprise. I thought it was over. I wanted to say no – I know I should have said no – but I had all that money after the wills were sorted out. I really did hope he might just take it and disappear."

I'm confused. Not about the money – my grandparents' money would have gone straight to him – but I thought Scott was supposed to be serving papers. Why come back asking for less money?

"So, you give him a thousand dollars, and surprise, surprise, he's come back for more."

"I didn't give him anything else. I knew it was wrong to give it to him in the first place. He was furious, but he left. If he comes back, the lawyers said to call the police and then them."

"You should leave the kids here until this is resolved," his mother suggests. *"You're welcome to stay here as well. This guy sounds dangerous."*

"Thanks. We've been staying with Stacey's mother, and will probably continue to do so. I agree, I'd rather he find me at work."

"You know he's not going to give up."

"No, I don't know that. I don't know anything, but I'm doing my best."

"You should have told us sooner."

"I heard you the first time! And you know what? If this hadn't happened, I never would have told you I didn't know whether or not they were biologically my children, your grandchildren. It doesn't make any difference. I wanted to protect them and Amy. People make mistakes.

"I only told you now, because if this actually does end up going to court like the lawyers think it will, it's going to be big news. No more keeping anything from anyone. I mean, a custody dispute, motherless twins, millions of dollars up for grabs. That's front-page news."

"What's the plan if he pursues legal action?"

"The lawyers want to bury him in paperwork. On the off chance he gets the paternity order and is proven to be the biological father, we fight it out in court."

"Do you think you would win?" his mother asks in a whisper.

"I do. Biological father or not, he's unfit. He's a drunk, he has no education or employment. He doesn't even have a permanent residence.

"Besides, Stacey's their blood relative. We'll be married by the time it ever goes to trial."

Chapter 32

Lizzy couldn't remember the last time she'd willingly taken the day off work, but she hadn't given it a second thought on this occasion. No way was she going to miss out on this.

Henry and five other teens were lined up in a hall in the basement of the building, waiting to sign in for the tour of the facility known as The Ward.

Sure enough, Lizzy was the only parent tagging along, but she didn't care. Finally, she was going to get to see inside the one place in this world that housed the oddballs, the nonconformists; people like her. She just knew she was going to come across a fellow creative in there, a kindred soul. They had to be keeping them somewhere.

Every city had a similar facility to store such people in. They were all incredibly small considering the size of the population, and all located in basements. Lizzy didn't see the point of even having basements in the complexes. It wasn't like there were any windows above ground for someone to bust out of.

The people that ran The Ward claimed there was no violence. There had never been an escape attempt; everyone was happy, happy, happy.

Even from the hall, The Ward already looked different than in the clips Lizzy had seen on the ethernet. The hall wasn't as wide, and the woman who came up behind them with the official employee tag did not look friendly at all. She looked like she came straight out of an Earth jail.

Her skin and jumpsuit were as white and smooth as everyone else's; her black hair and gold eyes not out of the ordinary. But her face was hard. Her skin looked as if it were made of the same rubber as the floors; the color of her eyes was as dark as the expression on her face.

A sidelong glance from Henry made Lizzy realize she was bouncing up and down with excitement. Planting her feet firmly in place, her apologetic smile was more of a grimace. She needed to watch herself or she'd end up a resident of The Ward instead of a tourist.

"Welcome to The Ward. I'm Maria, and I'll be in charge of your introduction to field training here. Keeper of The Ward is an occupation that is not for the faint of heart. You've probably seen the general informational clips on the ethernet, but Keepers are the reason everything is so well-run and maintained. Today you will receive a basic tour of the facility. Should you choose to continue on in your pursuit of the profession, I look forward to getting to know you better and working closely with you."

She eyed each trainee and Lizzy thoroughly.

"It's nice to see we have a parent with us. I don't believe I've ever encountered this before. I commend you for your support."

Lizzy nodded in reply, not wanting to risk saying the wrong thing before she even got inside. She wasn't sure what to say anyway. The commendation sounded less than genuine.

"Chip-swipe through the first set of doors and I'll see you inside."

Maria entered first. Lizzy was last in line as the trainees followed her one by one.

"Proximity error."

"Mom, you have to back up."

"Sorry."

Every door in the building was the same. Each person had to individually swipe, and in some cases provide their name and identification number. But this door apparently needed its space as well. Reading the sign above the sensor, she stepped back five paces as per the instructions, and waited ten seconds after Henry disappeared before approaching it again.

"Name and identification number, please."

"Amelia – shit!"

She needed to get a grip. Just as she predicted, she was already screwing up from the hallway. She wasn't all that afraid of getting the boot, but she didn't want to bring Henry down with her. This could be his life career.

Maybe she should just turn around and go back to her own job. Hopefully, this door was like the rest in not monitoring or recording her words.

"That name and number is invalid. Please repeat the process and be sure to enunciate." Pause. "Proximity error."

Oh, for – "It's still me you stupid . . ."

Back five paces, wait ten seconds. Move forward.

"Name and identification number, please."

"Elizabeth Masters. 310TCOH7267." The damn thing had better work this time, or she was going to really start with the enunciating.

The door slid open and she released the breath she'd been holding. She stepped through the portal, jumping as it snapped shut behind her. Things were a lot different down here. She decided to keep her mouth shut, and just nod and smile as much as possible.

"Thank you for joining us, Mrs. Masters. A little problem with the sensor?" Maria asked.

The woman was smiling, but it was a condescending sneer more than anything else. If there had been any doubt about her feelings toward Lizzy, a quick focus on her aura was enough to settle those suspicions. She was not pleased to meet her at all.

Perfect opportunity to nod and smile. Maybe dial down the smile a bit. It felt forced and toothy.

Maria did watch her grinning head bob up and down for longer than she cared, but soon she was off, leading the group to the next hurdle. A door-shaped frame in the middle of the hall awaited them, set just before the second set of doors.

"This is the contraband detector. I'm sure you've all familiarized yourselves with what is and is not allowed inside, so I don't expect any problems here."

Of course, she was looking at Lizzy throughout the entire speech. Lizzy didn't nod, but she kept the smile fixed on her face. It was starting to hurt.

"After walking through the contraband detector, we'll repeat the swiping process at the next set of doors and hopefully see you all on the other side."

Oh, this was going to be a long day. Fingers crossed she'd survive it.

"Is there something wrong with your hand Mrs. Masters?"

Heh. No finger crossing on Celadon. She hadn't realized she actually crossed them.

"No, ma'am. They're just a little stiff." She straightened her fingers and held them out for inspection. "I'll get some waves later on today."

"All right then, I'll just run the check on the detector and then we'll begin."

Lizzy reattached her grin. She might actually need the damn waves after this. Not for her fingers. For her face.

Chapter 33

Dad tries again to rouse me from the spot I've holed up in. Not our spot, but close to it. I shuffle farther away and resume my pouting.

No, I don't need ghost hugs or energy shares. I need a human. I need to be a human. One who can talk and yell. I'm sick of this place. I'm sick of everyone and everything in it.

Dad leaves to join Mystery Pal in our old spot.

Yeah, I can feel you both watching me. Why don't you go do something else? I'm going to be a while yet. Can't hear me? Shocker.

They must have felt something repellent coming from me. Mystery Pal zooms off on one of her mystery trips and Dad actually drifts away too. I wonder if he's going to see Mom. I don't really care. At least I got one thing I wanted. To be left alone.

Well, since it's vacant . . .

I move myself over to our familiar spot. I don't know what it is about this place. It's the closest thing to home I have right now. And even though I don't want anyone physically around me for a bit, traces of them remain here. Not just Dad and Mystery Pal, but Mom and other energies I can't identify linger as well.

It's comforting. Here, I'm able to relax and regroup.

No more pouting, but I try my best to do nothing but sit and watch the other souls fly by. Each time my thoughts drift back to Dean and Stacey, I swat them over to something else.

This time they land on Scott. Why hadn't he served those papers? What is he going to do next?

An unexpected and definitely unwelcome notion interrupts, flipping my wonderings back to the other two. How long has this been going on? Were Dean and Stacey together before I died?

Yo, brain, get back to Scott.

Better yet, let's go see what he's up to.

Good idea? Bad idea? I don't care. All alone, I pull up to my doorway and think of Scott. Only Scott.

***

Of course I don't land on him. That would be too easy. Instead, I'm treated to the heart-warming scene of my son speaking his first words.

Good one, Universe.

"Did you hear that? He definitely said, 'Mom.' "

Stacey turns her head away from Dean and the infants crawling on the floor. Is she crying?

"They're too young to talk yet. They've only started crawling."

"What are you crying for?"

"I'm not their mother," she sobs.

Dean scoots over and draws her close so she can bury her face in his chest. I remember doing that. It always made me feel perfectly safe.

"You will be. They're still so young. That's all they're going to know."

"They should know about their real mother. She deserves to be remembered. Her children will need to know what happened one day. We can't hide the truth from them, nor should we. Besides, mental health is something that should be talked about more, and you know it. She was sad, she was sick, and I don't think she wanted to do what she did. It's all too much. I think we're rushing into this marriage."

"I don't. I do agree they should know Amy, and there's no way we'll ever forget her, but she's gone."

No, I'm not. I just wish I was.

"What do you think they'll say when they're old enough to understand? What will they think of me?"

"They'll think of you as the woman who loved them and raised them, and who hopefully loves me . . ."

"You know I love you. But I don't want to get married just because of some court case."

"That's not why I proposed to you."

I try peeking at her finger. What would he have proposed to her with? Surely not his grandmother's ring, which he used to propose to me. She sits up straight and I can see. Nope, it's a new ring. Quite the rock, no doubt financed by my grandparents' money. I wonder what he did with the other one.

"Stacey, I'd want to marry you just as soon, court case or no court case. We don't even know if there's going to be one."

"Then why the rush? Look at how your last marriage turned out."

"Tragically. But I don't regret marrying her. If I hadn't rushed into that one, as you say, I wouldn't have had the time I did with her. I wouldn't have these two."

Stacey smiles as Darren takes notice of them and comes crawling their way. Of course, Diedre is right behind him.

"Maybe I just worry too much about what people will think."

"Mom!"

No mistaking that one. Stacey and Dean both cry happy tears as she scoops up Darren and he grabs Diedre.

"Mom?"

Their tears turn to outright laughter. Despite everything, I'm laughing too. Of course, Diedre would refuse to be left behind. Mimicking her brother's first word, she's just labeled Dean as her new mother.

I blow my babies my ghost-kisses and take off to do what I came here to do.

***

Scott is in his parents' living room with his mother. Wow, that's quite the shiner he's sporting. He flicks the ashes from his cigarette onto the carpet. He does not look happy, and there's a suitcase sitting next to his chair.

Where are we off to, pal?

"You need to leave before he comes back."

I'd never met his mother when we were dating, but she's exactly how he described her. Tiny, weathered, and barely audible when she speaks.

"I'll be gone. I'll bring you more money when I get it, but I'll have to find a way to do it when he's not around."

"I wish you'd just leave those kids alone. Even if they are yours, do you really think you could raise them properly on your own? I know you don't want to bring them into this sort of life."

"I could raise them just fine with all the money they come with."

"So, it is all about the money?"

Scott gets up and grabs his suitcase.

"Think what you like. You can go ahead and believe I'm as evil as Dad if you want. I don't care anymore. I never had a chance to be decent. Well, maybe this is my chance. Maybe I can have a family of my own and give them something better than this shithole."

His mother isn't fazed. She's probably used to being spoken to in this way.

"Just be careful," she whispers after him, as he yanks open the front door and storms out.

Chapter 34

They'd been through two detectors and three sets of doors already. Lizzy was getting claustrophobic. How in the world were they going to get out of the place?

"I see we're all still here. Fantastic. Now, we'll just go through some things you should be aware of before we do our final sign-in."

Thank God.

"As you know, we don't have too many troublesome citizens here, but we do have some. The most problematic patients are secured in a separate wing. You won't be seeing them today. As we tour the facility, you'll come across residents that are free to roam as they please."

Lizzy wasn't feeling so free herself in this third alcove. A look from Henry told her she'd taken to bouncing on her heels again. She glued her feet to the floor and fixed her eyes on Maria.

"These people may approach you and attempt to engage in conversation. Feel free to respond to them, but please do not encourage any odd behavior. If you are overwhelmed, or would like a patient to be removed, just let us know and they will be dealt with. You are in no danger here, but we want you to feel comfortable."

Good luck with that.

"The main reception area is on the other side of this last door. It's also used as a recreation space, so you'll be coming face to face with both staff and residents as soon as we enter. The residents have been advised a tour is coming through, but you'll find most of them have difficulty retaining information."

Was she sneering? How unprofessional.

"The Ward does not get many personal visitors coming through, and these tours are normally only held twice a year. Keep that in mind when observing and interacting with the patients. I also urge you to gauge your level of comfort initially and throughout the day. I don't need to remind you that a career is for life, but this is one of the harder ones when it comes to determining whether or not it's for you.

"Most trainees struggle with emotions," another sneer, "as they encounter people such as they have never been exposed to before.

"We will have a session at the end of the walk-through in which we discuss all the positions available at The Ward. They range from maintenance, security, and administration to Keepers and Keeper's Aides. I understand you likely had one of these positions in mind before coming today, but we want to make sure you have the opportunity to rethink after the tour.

"I know most of you have another career or two to consider other than this one, but we don't want anyone to mistakenly decide The Ward is an undesirable job for them until they've considered all the options, and are given the chance to choose the best fit. I must stress, not all of the positions require you to deal directly with the subjects."

Holy crap, were they that hard up for workers down here?

"So, keeping all of that in mind, let's proceed. And once again, we hope to see you all on the other side."

Yeah, she was looking right at Lizzy when she said that.

At least she had no problem with her name and identification number by the time it was her turn to go through the last door. It was pretty much the only thing she'd said for the last hour, not counting the first botched attempt and the finger crossing incident.

The others were standing around and taking in the large reception area when she entered. Weird. Even though she'd watched the clips, she always pictured The Ward to be like a jail. In her mind it was old, rundown, grey.

Nope. White, white, white as usual. It looked more like one of the stress-reduction wave rooms, the closest thing they had to a spa on Celadon. Much better than the narrow, stifling halls they just journeyed through. No claustrophobic basement feeling in here; the vaulted ceilings were at least two-stories high.

A long white desk ran along the wall in front of them. The circular room was lined with settees and tables. The staff behind the desk and the half dozen patients sitting on the settees were all dressed just like them in, you guessed it, white jumpsuits.

The trainees were busy checking out the structure of the room and the other employees.

Lizzy's eyes went straight to the patients.

Most of them were looking away or had their heads down. Only one met her gaze – an elderly man who must have been in his 200s. What a beautiful smile. Lizzy returned it as she studied his aura.

Whoops, she shouldn't be concentrating on such things. Especially not down here. But it was too late. She couldn't not see them now.

Each patient's inner aura was muted. Blue, purple, yellow, green, the colors were all there, but they were so faint. Every last one of their outer auras was a wispy white. All but the man's.

His inner aura was a brilliant gold, much like the color of her and Henry's eyes. His outer aura was a vibrant yellow, the color of curiosity.

Maria was rolling out a standard spiel about the construction of the complex while Lizzy continued to concentrate on the occupants. The man got up from his seat and approached the group.

Lizzy was sure he was heading straight for her. Instead, he passed by her with a wink and addressed Henry.

"You have a beautiful color, son. Would this be your mother?"

Maria put her speech on pause as all eyes and ears turned to the conversation.

Henry smiled at the gentleman. "Thank you, sir. And yes, this is my mother. She's kindly offered to accompany me on my first day of field training here."

"It's a rare sort of beauty, such a distinct shade of red. Not quite pink, but soft and strong at the same time."

Henry cast a panicked look at his mother. Lizzy caught her mouth as it fell open, and clamped it shut. He wasn't delusional at all. He would have just taken the words out of her mouth if she were tasked with describing her son's inner aura.

"Albert, have you taken your waves today?" Maria asked.

Albert's face and outer aura dimmed simultaneously. Lizzy was sure hers did too. She wanted to hear more. After all these years, here he was; someone just like her.

Maria snapped her fingers and an employee appeared beside her.

Albert nodded his head and followed the man out of the reception area. They left through a door that revealed a long corridor beyond before it swooshed shut behind them.

Lizzy's heart was pounding. She could tell Henry was shaken as well.

"That's one of our oldest residents. Albert has been here for most of his life. He's a prime specimen of persistent delusional syndrome. Though waves are effective in not only controlling but curing most patients to a maintained standard, they do not work on everyone. You'll be seeing more of him if you choose to continue on in this field. We've tried hundreds of frequencies, but the waves do not seem to affect him. The ones that do, don't seem to last."

With that, she turned back to her talk on the facility's layout. Lizzy didn't hear a word until they were directed to the door her eyes had been trained on since Albert passed through it. They were going in after him.

Chapter 35

I follow Scott as he leaves his parents' home and walks through the rundown neighborhood to wait in the bus shelter for his ride. No street-sweeping in this part of the city. The wind gusts, pelting the side of the shelter with gravel and rock pellets. Is he crying?

I'd seen him throw fits, kick things and yell, but I've never seen him sob like a baby. I'm trying hard not to feel sorry for him as he uses his torn jacket as a tissue and gets up to meet the bus.

His face looks different. Vulnerable. He looks so lost. There's no evil intent in his eyes as he stares bleakly at the scenery out the window of the bus. Tears continue to leak out.

His outer aura is, for lack of a better word, despondent. It's the color of a mud puddle. It doesn't move at all. Not a twitch. Not even when a large woman takes the seat next to him, smashing him up against the glass.

He reaches up to pull the cord for the next stop as if his arm is as heavy as his soul appears to be. The woman grunts and heaves herself up to let him out. Now, there's a nasty aura if I ever saw one. Have some compassion, bitch.

Woah. Where did that come from? A few hours ago, I would have given anything for her to knock him to the ground and grind her chunky heel into his ribs.

This neighborhood is not any nicer than the one he left. I know this area. I recognize the place he ends up at. It's the same place he was crashing the last time he'd been kicked out of his house, back when we were still dating. A dilapidated apartment building that looks more like a run-down motel.

I never saw the inside except for the alcove. It was where I broke up with him. It was also where I kicked his ass with the ghostly assistance of my mother when he tried shoving me around.

Funny how he still cringes and scoots through this part of the building. That's the only rushing he does. He drags his suitcase behind him as he plods up the two flights of stairs. He stands staring at the door to his buddy's apartment for so long, I'm about to leave. Surely there are better things I could be doing with my time.

He finally opens the unlocked door, and I don't blame him for thinking twice about it. Yikes. Well, there was one smart decision I'd made in life: not going in there.

Someone's lying face down on the couch, naked but for a pair of what once must have been white boxers. The floor is littered with trash: food wrappers, beer cans and liquor bottles, drug paraphernalia, actual food. Insects skitter in and out of the mess.

Scott hefts his suitcase onto a mostly cleared off chair. Here's hoping that pizza box was empty. On the bright side, I'm not all that hungry anymore. That had been driving me nuts. Thanks for the cure, Scott.

He digs through a pile of garbage on the floor and comes up with a can of beer. He pops the tab and slugs back half of it.

When I'd known him in life, he was unmotivated, uneducated and, at the end of our relationship, violent. Yet I'm still shocked to see how much further he's sunk.

At least back then he'd been against drinking, vowing not to follow in his father's footsteps. He hadn't been a blackmailing creep set on trying to steal my children and ruining what's left of my family, either.

I leave him here, in this pitiful place, hoping he'll stay out of everyone's hair for a while. But I'm not quite sure how much I hate him anymore.

I must be sick. Yep. I almost want to stick around, not just to see what he's up to next, but to see if he's going to be okay. It's official; I need a break.

Later, Earth.

***

I need more than a break, I need therapy.

My cousin is marrying my husband, my children just said their first words, my ex-boyfriend who may be the father of said children is . . .

I don't know what he is.

I settle back into our spot, alone. Those two must have really gotten the message.

When I first heard the news that Dean and Stacey were engaged, I was furious. And the way I found out? I probably would have passed out cold, if such a thing were possible. No passing out here. No sleep, no relief.

It still baffles me how quickly their relationship came about. There's no way they could have been seeing each other on the side when I was alive. They were either at work, at school, or with me. Even when we were all together, I can't recall a single inappropriate look, comment, or touch. Not that I was all that involved or paying attention. Whenever someone was there with the babies, I normally took off to bed.

Now I'm wondering if it's really such a terrible thing after all. They clearly love each other. And I love them. Why shouldn't they be happy?

And so what if my kids call her Mom? At least they'll have a mom.

The strangest thing I'm feeling – yes, it gets stranger – is that pity. For Scott. The monster who's threatening the peace and happiness of everyone I love.

But I consider the cards life dealt him. He was born into poverty and home-schooled with no chance of seeing outside the dysfunctional, abusive environment he was raised in.

Sure, plenty of other people had risen above such circumstances and emerged victorious. But not everyone. There has to be some reason, some catalyst, to motivate someone to improve themselves and their lives. And for it to stick, that reason has to be themselves.

Take me, for example. I grew up with a loving family and never wanted for anything. Yet I struggled. I was as low as I thought I could go when Mom died. I worked hard, I changed my life, I was on the way to having it all.

And then Dad died and I completely self-destructed.

Did I just not care about myself? No. I slipped. And before I got the chance to fix what needed to be fixed, I made that final mistake. That one decision, that one act I committed.

Well, there's no coming back from that one. No second chances.

How could I have been such an idiot? Now that I'm dead, I can see everything I had and could have had. Now I'm grateful for every last person I had in my life, for all the opportunities that awaited me. I learned my lesson. I want them back.

Life is weird. It's all weird. And unfair. What is the damn point of all this soul-searching and lesson-learning if there's nothing I can do about it?

Maybe I'll figure that one out after my stint here. Of course, I doubt I'll get to remember it.

As much as I'm frustrated about all these things that don't make sense, a part of me knows they do. This part of me is also telling me to carry on and forget about overthinking them. There are some things the heart needs to know, but the mind does not.

The one thing I do know, is I'm finished with my timeout.

I don't know where Mystery Pal is, but Dad must be hanging out with Mom in her new world. Who knows how long we'll have until we're recycled, or whatever's supposed to happen next? Might as well catch up on the family time I never expected to have with them since we all died.

Yeah, that sounded bizarre to me too.

Chapter 36

The last one in line again, Lizzy recited her name and identification number over and over in her head as she waited for the others to scan through. She refused to screw up on this one. She wanted in, and she wanted in now.

"Name and identification number, please."

"Elizabeth Masters. 310TCOH7267."

She held her breath as the information was being processed. Why was it taking so long?

Voila! She was sure she was grinning like an idiot as she stepped through the doorway into the next hall lined with doors, but she didn't care. On second thought, she should probably dial it down. Way down. Just to be safe.

"Welcome, Mrs. Masters. Now that we're all here, we can carry on. This is our treatment division."

"It looks like lockups," one of the teens commented.

"Oh, no. We won't be seeing those today. These are simply the rooms in which patients receive their waves. The doors aren't even secured. A simple chip swipe will get you in and out, just like in your living quarters.

"These first twenty rooms are for regularly scheduled treatments. The ones at the end of the hall are for emergent or experimental cases."

"Experimental?" Henry asked.

"Yes, that's where your friend from the reception area was taken. When we discover patients in his situation, where the routine treatments have apparently failed, they're taken to one of those rooms where we have wave therapists standing by. It's their job to test other forms of wave treatments until they find one that corrects the problem. Albert is one of our more challenging patients."

"Is he dangerous?" the only girl trainee in the group asked, hesitant to follow as Maria started out down the hall.

"No. He's exceptionally confused, but he hasn't presented any abnormal behavior despite his obvious aberration and resistance to lasting therapies."

"How long do people usually stay here?" Henry asked.

Why was his aura so squiggly? He'd never been nervous about speaking in public before. In fact, it was one of his strengths. He'd delivered many a successful speech in front of hundreds or thousands of people in the past. This was only a group of six.

"Most of our patients are lifelong residents. The majority of them stay of their own volition. They're happy here, and feel they fit in better than they would in the upper levels. The ones that are released tend to find their way back eventually."

Whoops, time to wipe the frown off your face, Lizzy. They're looking at you again. She turned the frown upside down; toothy grin or not, it seemed to suffice as the group advanced down the hall.

"We'll be moving on to one of the social engagement rooms next. I need to go ahead and check on something else before we do. In the meantime, feel free to peer through the glass into the rooms and familiarize yourselves with the area."

Maria strode down the hall and went through yet another set of security doors, leaving them to wander the hall alone.

The group dispersed and did as she suggested. Most of them needed to stand on their toes to see through the small square windows.

Lizzy headed straight for the end rooms where Albert would have been taken. She looked in three rooms full of machinery and tables, but empty of people, until she found him in the fourth.

As far as she could see, he was alone in the room. He was just sitting on the examining pad, swinging his feet and smiling. Lizzy waved her arm in front of the glass to get his attention. It was probably one-way glass.

Without conscious thought, she swiped her chip on the panel and let herself in.

"Oh, hello. You're not the wave therapist."

Shit. What had she just done?

"No. I'm Elizabeth, people call me Lizzy. You're Albert, right?"

"Yes." He hopped off the table and extended his hand. "I'm very pleased to meet you."

Lizzy shook it, shooting a nervous look at the door behind her. It was easy enough to get in; surely she wouldn't be in that much trouble. She was just concerned Henry may be reprimanded for her actions. Also, it was crucial nobody overheard what she was about to ask.

"How did you know the color of my son's aura?"

Albert's smile widened. "You can see the colors too?"

"I can. I've never met anyone else that could. Are you the only one?"

"Who can see the colors? No, there are a few others. Well, there used to be. They've been cured now. I seem to be a troublesome patient."

His smile never faltered as he declared himself incurable, as if what he had was a disease.

"I've never heard the word aura before, though. Is that something you made up yourself? It's rather nice."

"It's a long story. I'm confused as to why you're in here. You seem so happy. Do you not want to see the auras – I mean, colors – anymore?"

"I don't mind them, but I'm not supposed to be seeing them. It's not normal. Are you here for treatment as well?"

"No, no. I'm chaperoning my son's field training."

"How strange. I was wondering about that. I don't believe I've ever seen a parent do that before."

"Yes. Strange, odd, abnormal. I'm all those things. But I don't think I belong in a place like this. I don't think you do, either. I need — I want to know more about you. Have you ever — "

"Mrs. Masters?"

Shit.

"Hi. Um, I was just talking to Albert here about wave therapy."

"I know. You'll come with me now?"

Though Maria had phrased it as a question, Lizzy wasn't fooled. She bowed her head and followed the woman from the room without looking back at Albert.

She didn't need to see his face or his aura to know he wasn't smiling or shimmering any longer.

Chapter 37

Sad, happy, happy, sad.

I'm dead, yet I exist. I have no body or brain, yet I feel and think. Why in the hell can't I at least teleport from world to world? This traveling seems so mundane compared to the other complexities of the In Between. I guess some things never change. That's probably good.

I'm right tired of thinking about Dean and Stacey, it hurts too much to think of Darren and Diedre, and why is Scott still at the front of my thoughts? Get back to thinking of him as the bad guy, Amy. It's best for everyone. Someone's going to have to stop him. Whether or not it's me, I don't need the added burden of giving a crap.

Better yet, quit thinking of Earth altogether. I'm sure even ghosts with unfinished business are entitled to a little time off. Think about something stupid, something that has nothing to do with the people I'm not thinking about.

Scott, Dean, Darren – stop it!

Maybe I can teleport. How in the hell would I know? I haven't tried. How does one try to do such a thing? Maybe put on the gas. Warp speed ahead. If anything, at least it will hurry this trip up.

Woah.

Wrapped up in my Earth and non-Earth musings, I nearly fly right past my father. He's sitting off to the side of my path, in the middle of nothing. Lucky for him. I might have plowed right through him.

He doesn't look so good.

I back up and set myself next to him, hesitant to touch him. Does he even know I'm here? His aura is dull, trembling. Is he sick? Can we get sick? I know we get tired up here. I'm still trying to catch my fake breath from that sprint, but can ghosts get ill?

I kind of poke at him and he jumps.

Settle, Dad. It's just me.

He starts moving in circles around me, like pacing. Has he gone mad?

I sit and watch him, at a loss for words. That's fine, words are useless up here. But what in the hell is he doing?

Okay, enough's enough. He's making me dizzy already.

I shoot out of the middle of his weird circle and grab him. He tries to continue, dragging me along with him. I pull back as hard as I can, and he finally goes limp. Now what am I supposed to do with him?

I start pulling him back toward Earth and our spot. So much for family time with Mom.

He's heavy for a spark.

No warp-speeding this time. Well, I wanted something to take my mind off things. Careful what you wish for, I suppose.

Damn green fog. I'm so sick of it. I bet I'm gonna hate green in my next life, if I live to see my next life. Seriously, Dad. A little help? At least some crappy wordless-feeling talk? Nothing.

Just as I'm about to join him in the marble-losing, I see Mystery Pal coming toward us. She grabs hold of him and helps haul him the rest of the way.

Yes, everything's better when you're not alone. Everything's better when she's around. Again, where have you been all my lives?

We deposit Dad in our spot, and I accept the replenishing energy she offers to us, but he doesn't. He seems to shrink as he backs away from it. What is wrong with him?

Mystery Pal doubles her efforts on me and lets him be. Trusting in her judgment, I also leave him to whatever it is he's doing.

Fully recharged, maybe overcharged, I turn my attention to him. He's still shriveled and shaking. I don't care. I tackle him and start force-feeding him strength.

Little bugger slips right out of my grip.

Not the day, Pops. I leap after him and fasten my soul to his again. He struggles but can't get loose.

I don't care if he can hear me or not. I need to do a little bitching.

You're the one who yanked yourself out of the world you're supposed to be in to come help me. Guess what? You're not helping right now.

I don't know what happened to you, but you need to snap out of it. I have enough to figure out without dealing with this crap. Plate: full.

He stops his wiggling and finally accepts the energy. Mystery Pal zooms over and adds hers.

Yeah, that's right, I'm being the grownup today. One more tantrum like that, and I'll fly you right back to that other world and dump you in there myself.

Hmm, I'm all sorts of powerful. His shaking has stopped, his color is returning, and he's not resisting at all. I loosen my grip and nudge him toward our spot. He floats on over and sits there.

I'm not sure if I should leave him be or join him. Mystery Pal seems to be having her doubts as well. She hovers beside me and we watch him together.

Funny, I've never seen her at a loss before. She always seems to have the answer. Not this time.

I make the call to leave him alone. It's what I needed earlier, and what he might need now. But I'll be keeping an eye on him.

I wonder what he saw? Did he even make it to Mom's world?

Whatever it was, I'm not sure I want to know.

But I think I need to.

Mystery Pal moves closer and plants herself just outside our spot. She knows. She'll watch him.

Kerri Davidson

With a ghostly sigh, I set out to see what's up with Mom now.

Chapter 38

Lizzy drummed her fingers on the long white desk, in the small white room she'd been sitting in for days.

No, not days. It just felt like it.

Maria had escorted her out of Albert's room and past the group of trainees including her son. She followed her through door after door, at which Lizzy didn't have to worry about swiping herself through. Maria simply announced she had a guest with her when she cleared each checkpoint.

She'd been too embarrassed to so much as look at Henry when she was paraded past them and could only imagine what he must be thinking.

A guest of The Ward. Oh, when Daniel got hold of this news, he was going to have a field day with it. He'd been against her going in the first place, correctly predicting her motivations. Her defense had been he would be getting to spend Henry's field training in dome maintenance with him. He walked away at that point, mumbling about how she needed to cut the apron strings. No aprons on Celadon, but she knew better than to correct his slip and risk opening that other can of worms.

It was getting harder to resist the urge to stick her tongue out at the mirrored glass in the door. How long were they going to leave her sitting in here? She should probably start getting her story straight. She was just trying to be friendly. Lame, but what else did she have to work with?

She didn't even know where in the basement she was at this point. Just like when she passed Henry, she'd kept her eyes glued to the floor throughout their journey. They'd taken the elevator and descended at least one level somewhere in the middle of the trip.

Small talk. She was only trying to make small talk with the gentleman. Yeah, that was a little better.

At last, the door slid open and Maria appeared. Before it shut behind her, Lizzy caught sight of two men standing outside the door. Waiting to escort her out?

Maria took her seat on the other side of the desk and activated the flashpad. She tapped away on it without looking at Lizzy for the longest time.

Okay, point made. Lizzy was sweating.

Worst of all, or best of all (she wasn't sure yet), she felt Jason there with her while she was being escorted through the complex. She didn't do anything more than turn her eyes to the ceiling, and he didn't interact with her, but she knew he was there.

He wasn't anymore. But all of a sudden, as Maria was doing her tapping, she could have sworn she felt Amy's presence. Of all the times to stop by and say hi.

Or maybe she really was crazy and belonged here after all.

"Elizabeth."

Her head shot up as Maria spoke her name. What happened to Mrs. Masters?

"Yes, ma'am?"

Maria leaned back in her chair and stretched like a cat. A cat who was getting ready to toy with a mouse.

"Would you mind explaining what you were doing in that room?"

"I was simply talking with the man. There was no one else in there, and he looked bored. I'm a bit of a people person."

What was with the toothy grins lately? She could feel her teeth poking out all over the place. She tried sucking in her cheeks to compensate, but the look on Maria's face told her she was just making it worse.

"A people person? Mm-hmm." She leaned forward and tapped some more.

"Yeah, I've always enjoyed interacting with . . . people."

Oh crap, just stop talking.

"What were you talking to this person about?"

"As you might remember, he came up to my son in the reception area and said something to him about colors. So I was talking to him about colors."

Tap, tap, tap.

"What's an aura, Lizzy?"

Had she still been living on Earth, she would have requested a lawyer. Here on Celadon, they had behavior advocates. She'd never met one herself, and wasn't sure what they exactly did. Probably not much.

"Elizabeth, are you still with us?"

"I don't know, I was just talking silly."

"But you've spoken about them before, no?"

What was she talking about? Lizzy had been careful to say not much of anything, never mind silly things as they were signing in. She'd been doing so well until the fateful visit to Albert. Unless . . .

"Yes, I've been looking over the notes from your therapist. There are a lot. I see you attend more often than the once-weekly required session."

"How did you get those? They're supposed to be confidential."

"Oh, they're confidential enough. They certainly won't leave this room."

"Well, I was under the impression they wouldn't be leaving the last room they were in."

Lizzy sat back and crossed her arms. Let them go ahead and kick her out. Her curiosity had been more than satisfied, and she would not be in a hurry to return.

"Do you want to tell me anything about Jason and Amy?"

"How far back did you read?"

Unreal. She hadn't spoken of Jason or Amy with anyone other than Henry for years.

"You're not going to cooperate, are you?" Maria asked, pushing herself away from the desk again.

"Actually, no I'm not. I'm quite ready to leave, thank you."

Maria's face settled into a smile. Great. Lizzy stood up and waited for her to do the same.

"You're not going anywhere, Elizabeth."

"Pardon me?"

"You're going to be staying with us on a ninety-hour observation and treatment hold."

"You're serious."

"I am. We'll talk more later, after we get you settled in your new quarters."

"You can't do this! I haven't done anything wrong. I was just talking to a man."

"That's not the sole reason for this hold. You must know your family is concerned about you."

"Daniel? When did you talk to him? He wouldn't request a hold."

"I talked to him just before I came in here. And while he was not the one who requested it, he does agree."

Typical.

"Well, who requested it then? I don't have any immediate family other than . . ."

Henry.

Chapter 39

Damn, things are getting thick down there.

There's nothing I can do to help her, so I pull myself away from the world and head for home. I'm pretty sure she felt me there, and that certainly wasn't going to help with the predicament she was in since it was kind of about us.

Did she just make a bad choice of worlds? They've definitely got some major control issues going on in that one. Or maybe it was because of the way she entered. A lot of her troubles seem to stem from her memories of us and the stupid color-seeing thing.

I really wish I could just yank her out of there and take her back with me. Instead, I have to leave her there to live for hundreds of years in that place.

That must have been what Dad saw. At least he missed the part about her son being the dirty rat who turned her in. I wouldn't tell him that even if I could.

As hard as it is for me to leave her there, it must have been harder for him. Still, just because she's going to be spending a few days in the loony bin, was that enough to warrant Dad's spiritual breakdown?

Maybe he'd seen something from way earlier. There's no predicting how much time could have passed since he was there. Hours, days, years. That place seemed to pause and fast forward at will.

Whatever it was he saw, I think I know what messed him up. Guilt. I'm more than familiar with this burden. He's probably feeling guilty for not making it into the world with her in the first place, blaming himself for her life falling apart because he thought he should be there with her.

Kind of how I'm feeling. Both left out and needed at the same time.

I need to get back to my world. No, it's not my world anymore. But there's something there I need to see, something I need to do, before I can move on. What would that be? I don't have a clue. I don't even know what moving on entails if I ever make it to that part. I suppose I'll find out eventually.

I'm tired, but I don't want to stop in our spot. Mystery Pal has moved closer to Dad and he looks a lot better. I send them a thumbs up they'll never see and go straight to my door.

***

What in the hell? How long was I gone for? Who had a baby?

Dean's parents' house is full of people and merriment. The living room is covered in streamers, plates of appetizers and cakes are set on every available surface. A banner stretches across the window reading, "Congratulations, it's a girl AND a boy!"

More twins?

Darren and Diedre are crawling around on the floor in the middle of it all, shrieking and clapping and calling everyone Mom, feeding off the excitement in the room. They don't look any older.

Seriously, what are they all excited about?

In addition to Stacey, Dean, and his parents, Aunt Robin and Susan are there as well. I haven't seen Susan for ages. She's sitting in the corner texting, typically unimpressed with family time, but even she's wearing a slight smile.

Dean and Stacey clink their wine glasses together and kiss. I'm not even bothered by it. The atmosphere is so uplifting, it's impossible to dwell on petty resentments.

Did she have a baby? Is she going to? Did they get married? Someone tell me something.

David lifts his glass, his red nose telling me this isn't the first time he's done this, and proposes a toast.

"To Mr. What's His Face! Whichever lawyer whose brilliance surpassed all of ours put together and suggested the test."

"Hear, hear." Aunt Robin lifts her glass. "It was probably a team of them, but let's drink to them all!"

Woah, since when does Aunt Robin drink? And what test? Heh, Susan finally perks up all the way at the mention of a toast. She hasn't changed a bit.

Eileen waits until the clinking and drinking settles before she proposes another toast of her own.

"Here's to our grandchildren. Though they always were our grandchildren, and always would have been, now they are safe and legally ours. We drink to them and their good health."

Oh, that kind of test. Dean must have done the paternity test on his own. Well, duh. Even I could have come up with that one. Yet I didn't. Apparently, it took an army of lawyers to figure it out. I suppose all that money's good for something after all.

Hmm, so he really is the father. I truly wasn't expecting that. Maybe that's why I hadn't considered him doing the test on his own. Not that I could have easily communicated such an idea, even if I'd thought of it.

I still can't see any of Dean in our kids. I am starting to see a bit of myself, though. The dark hair and eyes, for sure. But maybe their noses too.

What a weird feeling. I'm dead. Everyone down there is moving on with their lives without me, yet I'm smiling.

I bet Scott's not smiling, unless he hasn't heard the news yet. This, I've got to see.

Just as I'm about to go looking for him, something pulls me back to my kids. Their outer auras are all kinds of happy colors, but there's something else in there. Something light brown and kind of sickly looking. I hope they're not coming down with something.

Is this what I'm supposed to be doing? No, I'm not a doctor. Well, maybe a little, up here. From what I can see, I get the feeling it's a run of the mill sort of illness, if anything. Maybe a cold or a flu coming on.

Trusting them in the care of their proper family, I concentrate on Scott. I'm still not sure why I'm able to see him. What sort of connection could we have, especially now that I know he's not my babies' father? I don't even like him.

Oh, no.

Chapter 40

Henry. Her own son, the only person she truly trusted in this world, had requested she be locked up.

What had brought this on? Was it premeditated, or a spur of the moment decision he made when she was caught talking to Albert?

Neither one of those guesses made sense. He knew her secrets and shouldn't have been surprised by what she'd done. It wasn't even that big of a deal. Well, apparently it was.

If he had intended to do it before the tour, if he did in fact believe her to be crazy after all she shared with him, why hadn't she seen it in his aura? Deceptiveness on that level was not something she could have missed. Or could she have?

Whatever happened, it was ridiculous. Ninety hours, her ass. She'd been locked in this tiny white cell, with nothing but a sleeping platform and a minuscule adjoining washroom consisting of a sink and toilet, for a lot longer than that.

No mirrors, no windows, no clocks, no visitors except for whoever wordlessly pushed the nourishment packs through the slot. That was the only thing she had to go by. It had been longer than three days. Unless she'd lost count, it had been five. Five thirty-hour days.

If they were so concerned about her, why hadn't they at least started wave therapy? Her earchip, which could normally be used to make contact with her husband and the rest of the outside world if they were in her databank, was deactivated the moment she was placed in the cell.

Five days of nothing. If she wasn't mad before, she was well on her way to it now. Maybe that's what they wanted.

When she wasn't trying to figure out who was responsible for this disaster, she spent her days and nights dreaming of Jason and Amy.

She couldn't write, and she certainly wasn't about to talk out loud. No flashpad, no comms, no nothing. She paced back and forth in the small area, watching and waiting for a path to appear in the flooring. Of course, the material was practically impenetrable, and wouldn't bend under her 110 pounds no matter how long or how hard she stomped over it.

She flopped down on the sleeping surface, and the blanket dropped out of the wall to cover her.

"I'm not cold!" she yelled at it, knocking it to the ground.

The sound of her own voice, after so many days of silence, was shocking as it echoed off the walls.

So was the sound and the sight of the door opening shortly after. As if her words had been the summoning solution, Maria and her henchmen stood waiting in the hall.

Every fibre of her being demanded she get up and make a break for it. Scratch, claw, bite, do whatever she had to do to get past them.

Instead, she sat up slowly, pulling her legs into the lotus position, and stared at them.

"Elizabeth, would you like to accompany us to an interview room?"

No. But she doubted her fake cool would get her very far. She got up and went to the door, waiting for them to lead the way.

"Elizabeth, I asked you a question."

Oh, for crying out loud.

"Yes."

A fake smile from Maria, and they were on their way.

White corridor after white corridor, lined with white doors. Why were there no other people in sight? Lizzy was sure Maria had said there were only a handful of troublesome patients who needed to be locked away. Then again, a lot of people said a lot of things that weren't true around here.

And by here, she was referring to Celadon as a whole.

They landed in another white room populated with another white desk, white chairs, and . . .

"Henry?"

"Hi, Mom."

He was wearing a visitor's badge, so obviously not on field training today. Why was he here? He averted his eyes from hers, but she didn't need eye contact to see his guilt. They'd already locked her up for seeing colors, so she might as well take advantage of it.

"You two go ahead and have your visit, then we'll have our own little chat."

No response required for that one. The door was sealed by the time she looked back.

Despite everything, she almost felt sorry for her son. His aura was flashing like a disco ball. For whatever reason he did what he did, he was suffering because of it.

She took the only other seat on the far side of the table and continued to watch the light show without saying a word. She was getting good at the silence thing.

"I wasn't the one who authorized them to access your therapy notes, and I didn't give them your writing. It was Dad."

"Okay."

"You must be awfully angry with me."

"Is it you I should be angry with?"

His spinning aura looked like it was about to come undone and fly off into the ether.

"I guess so." He turned his green eyes to look into her gold ones, but only for a moment. Chin back on his chest, he started mumbling.

"I can't hear you, Henry."

He cleared his throat and began again. Louder, but his head remained hung.

"It was Dad's idea for me to keep an eye on you when we came here together, and he suggested we may want to get you checked out."

"When did he say this?"

"The night before field training, right after the Education Completion Ceremony."

"What made you go through with it?"

"I don't know. I'm still not sure it was the right thing to do. I've been worried about you for a while, and when they caught you talking to that guy, it just seemed like the easiest way to make the decision."

"You think I'm crazy?"

"You're doing it right now, Mom. There is no such word as crazy."

"Fine. You think I'm abnormal?"

"Aren't you?"

Ouch.

"Mom, I told you I'm sorry. Please don't hate me."

"I don't hate you, Henry. I could never hate you. I'm just disappointed. I thought we were closer than this."

"We were. We are! It was fun playing around and all that, but I just want you to get well."

The door whooshed open.

"Time's up for today. Henry?"

It didn't take long for him to spring out of his seat and flee to the safety of the hall.

"I love you, Mom. I'll see you soon."

The door sealed once more, leaving her to sit alone and await the interview with Maria.

She refused to let a single tear leak out, but she was crying inside. Crying for her past life, her sham of a marriage here, and for the broken bond with her son that would never be healed.

How could it be? How could any of it ever be fixed?

Chapter 41

Okay, part of me was hoping to find Scott utterly miserable. I was fully prepared to laugh and try chucking some ghostly things around to rub in his failure.

The last time I was in his buddy's place, I noticed some small change littered throughout the trash heap that was the floor. Flinging those little coins around would be easy enough, and it would have been fitting. I mean, he tried to destroy my family over something as frivolous as money.

But when I found him alone in the dark, in some crappy little closet-sized bedroom in the filthy apartment, glee was not what I felt.

He was cowering in the corner of this room, crying, and holding a bottle of liquor in one hand. His other hand held a gun.

His inner aura had changed. It was still red, but no longer fiery. It was more like my Dad's, just not as shiny. It looked like it had given up, just as he appeared to have done. His outer aura was pure black, with these strange little pockets that looked like bubbles of nothing.

All the terrible things he'd ever done to me and the people I loved didn't matter anymore. Well, they did, but they were no longer relevant. I didn't see the evil stalker ex-boyfriend, or the blackmailing coward now. I just saw a boy.

A boy who'd grown up without love, without support, without believing he had a chance.

A boy who'd been abused, both verbally and physically. A boy who'd never known any other way of living.

A boy I once cared for.

The first thing I did was to try reaching out to him. I just wanted to show him someone was there, that he wasn't alone. I wanted him to know that someone did care.

Not a good idea. The sparks flew. Apart from shocking the both of us – literally – I'd only creeped him out even more. His sobbing intensified. He hugged the gun closer.

I've been sitting with him for hours, as the moon creeps across the curtainless window. He alternates between crying and groaning. Every now and then I cringe as he bangs his head against the wall or delivers a blow to himself with the liquor bottle.

What happened, Scott? What am I missing? You didn't care about my kids, you only wanted money. That can't be what drove you to this point.

Or could it? Look at what happened to me. A bunch of rotten days all lined up in a row had ended in disaster. There was nothing out-of-the-ordinary terrible about the day I took those pills. It was all too easy to simply give up. And it happened so fast.

There was no one there to keep watch over me. No one saw what I did until it was too late. I wanted to be alone, and they left me alone.

I was wrong. I won't leave him alone. Not like this.

Just before dawn, he stops crying. He brings the gun up to his temple, finger on the trigger, and squeezes his eyes shut.

My surge of panic knocks the gun right out of his hand. More sparks, more wide-eyed terror from down below.

Did it go off?

No, it just fell to the floor.

Angry now, he picks up the gun and points again, keeping his eyes open this time.

I'm angry, too. I flick it harder, sending it skidding across the floor. For a split second, I can actually feel the metal in my fake hand.

He stares at the noncompliant gun, then turns his eyes to the ceiling.

"Amy?"

Yep, I'm here. You can't hear me, but can you see me? I wave my invisible arms at him. He squints up at me, but I still can't tell if he's looking at me or just the ceiling.

Giving his head a shake, he returns his focus to the weapon. He crawls across the floor toward it. I kick it farther away.

"Oh, come on! If that's you, leave me alone. You made it clear enough before you died that you don't care about me. And if it's some other demon or devil, just hold your horses. I'll be seeing you shortly."

He lunges at the gun, and I send it flying under the bed.

Face down on the floor, he releases a cry of frustration and goes back to weeping.

Fine, let it out. You're not getting that gun again.

"What's going on in there?"

Scott sits up and wipes his eyes. "It's nothing, I just dropped something," *he calls through the door.*

"Well keep it down, we're trying to sleep!"

Another wary glance in my direction, and he starts digging around under the bed. After a lot of stretching, he emerges victorious.

Dammit.

He leans against the bed and holds the gun tightly, but doesn't point it. He just sits and stares in my direction.

I sit and stare back.

I'm not going anywhere, Scott.

Keeping his eyes trained on the ceiling, he scoots back over to his corner and picks up the liquor bottle.

I want to knock that out of his hand as well, but it's almost empty and I should conserve my strength. It looks like we're going to be here for a while.

Chapter 42

After all these years, Lizzy had yet to adjust to the similar but inconsistent lengths and labels of time on Celadon. They had days and nights, and days of the week. The days didn't have names, just numbers. The weekends were three days long instead of two. They had years that were 365 days long, but she was currently existing in the 117-34th. Yeah, she'd never been able to wrap her head around that math.

The thirty-hour-long days were still the worst for her. God forbid she should try going to sleep early; that was not normal. She did retire as early as possible, but not in the late afternoon as she would have preferred. In her last life, she hadn't been much of a napper. In this life, she'd kill for one. But guess what? That wasn't acceptable behavior either. Napping was for infants.

Lizzy splashed cold water on her face from the sink in her new and improved washroom and checked out her reflection in the mirror. She had no more worries about the toothy grins. She couldn't remember the last time she'd smiled.

What was there to smile about?

After the long-awaited interview that turned out to be nothing more than an admission process, she'd been moved to a larger, less secure room. She could swipe in and out of it on her own, but that only released her into the corridor.

She did this every day, even though the hall was drearier than her room. Apparently stretching one's legs was another behavior unique to herself in here. She never saw or heard another resident moving about, and she didn't look in the windows to their rooms.

How did these people not need to get out and move? Had they been there so long they forgot about cardiovascular sessions? Or were they so diminished by the wave therapies that they didn't have the capacity to remember or care?

The only form of exercise provided came when she was escorted to the recreation room which was – surprise, surprise – a big white room with couches. They were given no encouragement to actually move around. In fact, she was one of the few who did. The other residents sat on the couches with slack faces, much like they had in the reception area.

Her earchip remained disabled except during her wave therapies at night. The non-effective wave therapies, in her case. But she had been given a standard flashpad.

A restricted standard flashpad. The only things she could access were therapy articles and boring memos from Maria.

The flashpad did come with a pretty little calendar, though. A calendar that told her she'd been locked up for two months and counting.

The only person who'd been to visit her was Henry. At the beginning, he came by once a week while on field training. Over the last month, it dropped to once every two weeks. He was due to come by today but had already sent word he wouldn't be able to make it. So said the memo from Maria.

Lizzy couldn't muster up the energy to be disappointed. Their visits were strained, the underlying atmosphere hostile. Henry always managed to turn their brief conversations away from himself to her progress. How were they treating her? How was she feeling? Was she getting any better?

Yep, all was good and normal.

He did tell her he had chosen his life mate. Lynette, the girl from down the hall. She thought they experienced a moment of shared happiness. A short one. The smile that tried to break through her bitter exterior evaporated, as she wondered if that too was a lie. Just an attempt to placate Lizzy and make her feel better.

She knew Henry still cared about her, and of course she still loved him. He was her son. But she didn't trust him. How could she? It had finally happened. The one thing she vowed she would never allow. They were drifting apart.

Hopefully, he was telling the truth about Lynette, because the unique bond between mother and son had officially been severed. She still wanted a good life for him. She wanted him to have a real marriage, unlike herself. She wanted to believe true love was possible in this realm.

It was a struggle.

She had all the time in the world for thinking. She wondered what was filling the void she left when she never returned from the tour of The Ward. What was Daniel doing? Had he moved Anna into their home yet? Probably not. She apparently had a husband of her own. She most likely spent some time there, though.

She pondered what the rest of her relatives thought of her being in lockup, if anyone at work missed her.

She didn't spend a lot of time with these musings. She simply didn't care enough.

The thing she thought of the most was her other life. Jason, Amy, even Belle. She remembered her parents, her sisters, her old home. And she had no one to share it with. She didn't even have the freedom to write about it anymore.

As before, the wave therapies she was given only increased her abnormalities. She remembered more from her former life and recalled it more vividly. The colors she saw were brighter, impossible to ignore.

She said nothing. It was her only form of entertainment, her only source of happiness. It was all she had left.

So, yes. As far as anyone on Celadon was concerned, she was getting better.

But she wasn't going anywhere anytime soon. She had no delusions about that. She could nod and agree and take all the therapies they recommended, but deep down inside she always had a suspicion she was destined to end up in here someday.

She'd crossed too many lines, too many times, and now they had her.

Come to think of it, why bother pretending to be normal? The only good thing she was getting down here was the wave therapy treatment, which caused her other senses to flourish. Maybe if she let herself slip up every now and then, they'd give her stronger waves, waves with more punch.

It was a fantastic idea, really. She'd pulled off a similar stunt when she was younger. She just had to make sure she found that line. The line for The Ward. The one between this level of living and being tossed back in the secure room.

Maybe a conversation with Albert wouldn't be a bad idea. She'd seen him in the recreation room a few times but hadn't dared to approach him.

So long as it didn't hurt him, she was more than willing to join him in being the borderline problem patient who was never getting out.

Because she might as well face it. She was never getting out.

Chapter 43

Another swat, another fireworks display across the veil.

Okay, now you're just playing with me. How are you still awake?

Scott had pitched the empty whiskey bottle across the room hours ago. He has both hands free to play point-the-gun-at-my-head now.

He gets up from his spot in the corner of the room and retrieves the weapon yet again. This time he stops at the dresser and looks up in my general direction.

"Okay, you win. For now." He places the gun on the dresser and rubs his face with his mercifully empty hands. "I need a break."

Finally.

He clears a pile of clothing from the bed, sweeping it onto the floor, and lies down on it. Eyes still pointed up at me, his lids begin to droop.

"Why do you even care, anyway? It's not like you loved me when you were alive. Bet you just feel sorry for me now."

He's not that far off. But I do feel something other than pity. No one deserves to go through something like this alone. No one. Not him, not me. In fact, no one should have to go through this at all. Unfortunately, I think many people do end up here, or someplace similar, at some point in their lives. I suspect a lot of people make it through and never speak of it again.

"And who are you to talk, anyhow? Or slap, or whatever it is you're doing . . . you offed yourself too."

I was wrong.

He can't hear me, but I don't care. I reach out and take his hand. Nothing stops me this time. No sparks, no rippling.

His eyes grow wide, but he's not alarmed. He smiles at me.

"How are you doing this?"

I'm spent. But I hold onto his hand for as long as I can, sending him nothing but the message he's not alone and someone cares. I care.

Maybe he gets it. He tightens his fist around my invisible hand and closes his eyes.

He's asleep.

I release his hand and pull right out of the world.

***

Dad and Mystery Pal are close beside me. I was so wrapped up in Scott, I hadn't felt them there at all. They look tired too. They must have been replenishing me as I held my vigil.

All three of us drift over to our spot to rest. No sleeping, no eating, no drinking, we can't even close our damn eyes, but we share our energy in the circle. It's kind of like a dialysis. The energy is being cleansed as it passes through each of us and then returns.

Recharged, my dad gives me an extra punch of . . . pride?

He couldn't have known what I was doing, but he must have sensed it was important. Hard. Noble?

I don't know about noble. I just know I couldn't have left him alone. Not like that.

Speaking of alone, time flies when you're rejuvenating. I've probably only been gone for a few hours, but it's hard to tell. Time to check on my new ward.

Maybe I'm supposed to be his guardian angel or something. Maybe that's why I can still see him. For all I know, he could be my unfinished business.

***

He's up already, and he's fixed himself up, too. Properly dressed, as opposed to the white undershirt and boxers he was wallowing in the night before, he's even combed his hair.

But he's standing at the dresser flicking the damn pistol around with his finger.

Just as I'm about to wallop him, he looks up with a grin.

Rat bastard. I do thump him, but gently. Not funny.

He sighs and sits down on the bed.

"I thought you were gone. I guess I can't expect you to hang around all the time, hey?"

He looks so vulnerable. So much like the old Scott when I first met him. The outsider I was drawn to and could relate to. The guy I was falling in love with before things turned sour.

"You don't have to worry about me using that. Last night was my bottom. I don't know if you saw, but I emptied the bullets and gave them to Stuart."

He snorts. "He didn't even ask why. Some friend, huh?

"Anyhow, you don't have to be concerned about me anymore. Well, maybe a little. Last night was bad, but I know I don't want to end up there again. I won't end up there again. I made some plans, just like you were always telling me to do."

He holds up a notebook, and I can't help but smile.

"I still have my construction job, but work is slow. I'm going to see if I can get enrolled in the GED program before summer, and I'm going to move in with my grandma for a while. My mom's mom. I have to get out of here, and I can't go back home where my dad is."

He pauses and fingers the notebook page.

"I didn't write this down, 'cause it's not really a plan, but I want to ask for your forgiveness. There are so many things I'm sorry for. The biggest one being the way I treated you when we were going out, especially what I did when you dumped me. I never wanted to hurt you.

"I'm sorry I did what I did to your kids and husband, and I wish I could tell them that, too. Part of me really did think they might be mine, but I wouldn't have taken them even if they were. I wouldn't know how to give them a good life. I guess I just saw a chance to get some easy money.

"And I want to say, I'm sorry about what happened to you. I couldn't believe it, at first, when I saw your obituary in the newspaper. I was sad, but after I found out what you did, I didn't feel sorry for you.

"I do now. I nearly joined you last night. I don't know if you did do it on purpose, but I see how it could happen.

"I guess what I'm trying to say is, thank you. You saved my life. I did love you and I do miss you."

He isn't lying. His aura has changed again. It's solid, calm, and the holes are disappearing right before my eyes.

"Even though I'm going to be okay, would you mind stopping by every now and then, just to say hi? I've never had a ghost friend before."

I give him one more reassuring pat and focus on my kids.

I hear his repeated, "Thank you," as I depart.

Chapter 44

Having made the decision to talk to Albert, Lizzy couldn't wait to get to the recreation room to find him.

But he wasn't there. Days, then weeks passed before she finally saw him sitting on the settee with that slight smile on his face, swinging his legs that were too short to reach the floor.

At the risk of freaking everyone out, including him, she made a few casual laps of the room before sitting at the far end of the same settee.

There were a dozen or so other patients in the room. Most of them were sitting, staring straight ahead or at the floor. The ones who were walking were moving so slowly it was hard to tell they were moving at all.

No one was talking.

The staff members situated at each of the two entrances appeared to be just as bored as the patients.

Lizzy sidled over closer to Albert, so she could speak as quietly as possible and still be heard.

"Hey, Albert. Do you remember me?"

Even though her hushed voice sounded like a bullhorn in the otherwise silent room, the guards didn't look their way. Maybe they were dosed on waves just like the rest of them.

Albert's small smile blossomed into a welcoming grin.

"Of course, I do. You're that boy's mother." A flicker of a frown. "Are you a patient now?"

"Yes."

"I hope it wasn't my fault."

"Oh, no. Of course not. I was worried I might have gotten you into more trouble."

"No need to worry about that, my dear. They're used to me by now. There's not much more trouble for me to get into. I was just happy to have met you, as brief as our meeting was."

"Albert, can you tell me what color I am?"

His smile was back.

"White."

Wow. After all this time of being able to see other people's auras and wondering about her own, there it was.

She had such mixed feelings about this discovery. In her old life, white had been her favorite color. Ironic. Living here in this world of nothing but white had put something of a tarnish on her former fondness of it.

Albert noticed her dilemma and correctly assumed the cause of it.

"But it's nothing like all this other white we live in. It's brilliantly bright. It swirls and sparkles; even your outer color is full of life and vigor. You don't see that in patients here."

"I see it in you," she told him.

"Really? Well, I'm pleased to hear that. Not bad for a 212-year-old patient of The Ward. You can't have been here that long. How are you adjusting?"

"Actually, surprisingly well. The thing I miss the most is going outside." She closed her eyes and inhaled like she used to, trying to recall the memory of the fresh air.

"Outside? Oh, my goodness! Are you one of them? Did you live outside?"

"Live outside?" Her mind was racing with questions toppling one over the other. Were there people who actually lived out there? Was there something for humans outside of the domes? Something more than scanning and documenting?

She was gearing up to begin her inquiries, when she noticed the two employees had left their stations by the doors and met in the middle of the room.

They were coming toward them, but they weren't rushing. There was still time for a question.

Albert noticed them too, and gave her the saddest little smile.

"We'll have another chance to talk, I'm sure. Go ahead, the floor's still yours for a moment."

Instead of asking all the questions she was dying to know the answers to, it suddenly hit her.

"Albert, do you want to know your color?"

Right on target. Of course, he'd never seen his own aura before. His smile glowed brighter than all the auras in the room put together.

"Yes, please!"

"It's gold."

"Like your eyes?"

"Exactly like my eyes."

***

"Well, you're quite the conversationalist, aren't you?"

"I enjoy talking to people."

Maria pushed herself away from the desk and leaned back in her seat.

"You still seem to enjoy talking about those colors. Are the therapy waves not working?"

"Oh, I think they're working fine. I suppose it wouldn't hurt to increase them if you're concerned."

Maria tilted her head as she studied Lizzy, who was sitting angelically with her hands folded in her lap.

"We'll see," she said, moving back to the flashpad.

"Before we up the frequency, tell me what it is about colors that fascinates you so."

"As I was saying to Albert, I miss the outside. My job, mostly. It's hard being down here, not being able to contribute to society."

"You're feeling unproductive then?"

"Yes." That wasn't a lie.

Maria turned to tapping on the flashpad.

"We'll see what we can do about that. For now, we'll adjust your waves."

"Can I go?"

"I'll have someone take you back to your room."

Of course she would. Recreation time was over. Probably for longer than one day.

"And in the future, Elizabeth, you may want to redirect your energies toward getting better, instead of weaving tales and bothering the other patients. Your son was scheduled to visit today, but he's chosen to cancel because of the incident."

"I didn't get Albert in trouble, did I?"

That was the last thing she wanted. Albert was the most genuine soul she'd met in this world. She hadn't even known Henry was planning on visiting. Sadly, she wasn't disappointed he decided against it.

"Albert was quite agitated as a result of your discussion with him. He needed to be taken straight to the therapy room."

"He was just happy."

"Abnormally so. You're not qualified to diagnose such a thing."

No, she certainly was not. Lizzy hung her own abnormal head and allowed a not-so-abnormal tear to fall.

Chapter 45

Why am I not more upset about this?

It's evening. Dean and Stacey are sitting in the living room of his apartment, addressing wedding invitations while my kids crawl around in the playpen.

The sound of the wind and pelting rain against the window gives me a chill. There's nothing cold about the inside of the room, though. Dean kisses his bride-to-be and gets up to add another log to the fire. Stacey never takes her eyes off him.

He refills their wine glasses when he returns. There's no need for words as they clink their glasses and kiss again. They would do well up here. Well, minus the liquor.

How different from my date nights with Dean when I was alive. I'd either stumble in late after drinking all night at the bar, or we'd sit and watch television while I was wishing I was someplace else.

He tried before and after we were married to take me out to dinner or to a movie theatre, but it had all seemed so forced. I know he was just trying to make me happy, wanted to be happy with me himself; but all I cared about was being young and free. I wanted to let my hair down and party with my friends, consequences be damned.

Yeah, those consequences . . . I sure did miss out.

Looking at the cozy scene below, I'm not jealous. I'm happy for them. I'm happy for Dean.

I'd been a terrible girlfriend to him, and an even worse wife. I never loved him like he deserved to be loved. I never had romantic feelings for him. I didn't give a thought to anyone but myself.

But I do love him. Not as a friend, something more. Not as a husband, something different. I have no doubt we're meant to be together, but marriage wasn't where we were supposed to end up. The only positive thing that came out of it was the children. At least I left him with something.

He leans over to get a stamp, and he and Stacey brush arms. That look in their eyes, now that's true love. It's heartwarming, yet it's still weird for me to see them kiss so much.

Diedre starts to wail, and Darren isn't far behind. Funny how the sound that made me see red in life is now music to my ears. I turn my attention to my kids as Stacey and Dean get up to tend to them. What I wouldn't do to be the one picking them up, holding them close.

Their auras. The sickly-looking outer auras I noticed before I went off to find Scott are unmistakable now. They're definitely not well.

"Dean, he's hot."

"Oh geez, he's got spots."

"Chicken pox?"

"I'll call the doctor."

Dean carries Deidre with him while he goes to make the call.

Better make reservations for two, pal. You don't need to see auras to know they can't do anything in ones.

"There, there, sweetie. It's going to be all right. Aunt Stacey's here."

Again, my lack of jealousy takes me by surprise. I'm thankful she's there, doing what I can never hope to do. I'm almost onboard the calling-her-Mom train.

Almost.

I wonder if I can do any ghostly healing? I'm not sure I want to try. What if I only mess them up more?

The kids have stopped crying. Darren is snuggled deep in Stacey's arms, Diedre in Dean's.

No, I think I need to let them be. Worrywart ghost-mom is probably not what they need. They just need someone to hold them and care for them. Also, playing guinea pig with my kids is just a miserable idea. If it is chicken pox, I'll have to stand by watching and fretting the same as any other parent. Except I won't be able to do anything but that.

No rubbing their backs, like Stacey is doing to Darren. No rocking them back and forth, like Dean is with Deidre while he talks on the phone. No placing cool cloths on their heads and singing them to sleep. Well, maybe I could try singing to them later.

What the —

This is new.

Something's pulling on me hard. I can't fight this force that's taking me from the living room here, and depositing me in . . .

Another living room. I feel like I've been physically picked up and tossed here. Where am I?

It's Aunt Robin's place. Why? I've never been able to see her without Dean or my children around before. What could she possibly have to do with my sick children?

She's pacing and muttering to herself. I can't understand what she's saying, but her aura screams of confusion, doubt, and is that fear? She can't know about the possible chicken pox situation unfolding where I was just yanked from. Even if she did, it wouldn't warrant this level of panic.

She jumps as the buzzer for the building door sounds. She stops pacing and stands frozen in the middle of the living room. Her outer aura could give a person a seizure. Good thing I'm not a person anymore. Still, it's playing tricks with my mind. I would look away if I could, but whatever it is that brought me here is not allowing me many options. My eyes are glued to her, just as her feet are glued to the floor.

The buzzer sounds again. She unsticks her feet and walks into the kitchen. She presses the button to allow the person entry to the building and opens the door to the apartment. She takes a seat at the kitchen table facing the door, clenching and unclenching her hands.

What is going on now? Who's about to come through that door?

Oh, I am so sorry I asked.

Chapter 46

"To what do I owe the honor of your presence?"

Lizzy stood by the door as it sealed behind her, not in a hurry to take the seat across the table from her son.

"I miss you, Mom."

"That's nice. Have you missed me all year long, or is this a new experience for you?"

Henry fidgeted in his seat. "Would you please sit down so we can talk?"

"You're the boss."

Lizzy plunked herself into the chair and continued to stare at her son. He was wearing the official worker credentials. She hadn't seen him for over a year and had no idea he'd decided on this career path.

"I'm really sorry I haven't come to visit. At first, I was nervous because it's kind of my fault you're in here."

"Yes. Kind of."

"I was only telling the truth, and I was worried about you."

"That part I remember."

"Well, after I canceled our visits a few times, I felt even worse. I guess I just took the easy way out, and stopped coming to avoid . . ."

"This?"

"Yeah. But I do miss you. Even more so now that Lynette is pregnant. I'm going to be a parent, Mom."

"I didn't even know you had secured your life mate."

"I know. We were wedded last month. I wanted to come then and tell you, but . . ."

"Oh, you didn't want your life mate to know your mother's a loon? That's a tough secret to keep."

"No. I don't keep secrets from her. She knows about you. But what's a loon?"

"Never mind."

"She's actually the one who encouraged me to come today. I always thought you were spunky, but she's something else. When she found out how long it had been since I visited, she ripped me a new one."

"Careful, now. That's not a Celadonian term."

"It's not?"

"No. It's one of my made-up ones."

He stared at her for a long time, his face and aura stone-cold serious.

"Mom, do you truly believe the things you said? The things you wrote about?"

"Nice try. Look, I know I'm never getting out of here, but I don't need any more trouble. Everything I ever said about colors and imaginary friends was only a product of my abnormal brain. None of it is real. I never thought it was."

Though she was answering her son's question, she spoke the words to the walls for the eavesdroppers.

"No one can hear us in here."

"Gotcha." She flashed him a big fat wink.

"I'm serious. This is a secure room."

"Heard you the first time."

"Mom, I used to believe what you said. I still kind of do. At least, I want to. I want to know more. I want to know there's something else out there. I want to have a reason to bring a person into the world. I want to have hope."

Why was he doing this to her? After so long, too. She wasn't causing trouble here anymore. She hadn't done anything anyone could consider wrong since she tried talking to Albert.

The one time. She hadn't seen him since that day in the recreation room. They were either keeping him away from her, or he was dead. That had been the last straw. That was when they'd broken her.

"Why are you doing this, Henry?"

"I need to know. And I need you back in my life."

"And you expect me to believe they're not listening to me?"

"I told you, it's a secure room. Do you think I would have risked saying what I just said if it wasn't? I'd be your new neighbor if they heard."

"Maybe it's a trap."

"Do you honestly think I'd do that to you?"

The look on her face was the only response he needed.

"Okay, I deserved that. But I explained why I did what I did. And you will never know how sorry I am now."

"Why now? Because you're having a baby?"

Henry looked nervously around the "secure" room and leaned over the table.

"Because I know more than anyone does about this place."

Lizzy leaned over the table as well, lowering her voice to his level. "Why are we whispering in the secure room?"

Henry sat back and raked his hands through his hair.

"Because I'm freaked out."

Lizzy sat back too. "That's another non-Celadonian term."

"Mom, no one's listening. I know because I'm the head of security here."

"Then what are you scared about?"

"Everything. Do you know what I've seen since I've been working here?"

"Of course not. You haven't been to see me."

"Ouch, again. Look, we don't have much time left today. I'll be back in a week. I'd come back sooner, but I don't want them to get suspicious."

"Suspicious of what, Henry? That you want your mother to tell you abnormal fairy tales?"

"There are things I need to ask you, but I also want to tell you things."

"You have stories of your own?" That warranted a raised eyebrow.

"Yes, I do. True stories that will curl your hair, and could potentially put us all in danger."

"Then why risk it?"

"Because we already are in danger."

Chapter 47

Uncle Ian is even uglier than I remembered. His inner aura looks like rotted mustard. His outer aura isn't much different, except for the red splotches that match what's left of his hair. That shaggy fringe around his otherwise bald head had always disgusted me.

When I was young, and after my pregnancy, I struggled with my weight. But I'd never been as obese as he is. He's got to be pushing 300 pounds. Nevertheless, he walks with perfect posture as he enters the apartment and sneers at the interior.

There must not be enough gaudy crosses and antiques in here for him.

Aunt Robin has composed herself on the outside. Her hands are relaxed and folded in her lap, but her outer aura is still a mess. Why would she have invited him over? I thought they split up.

"So, this is the hovel I'm paying for? I should have expected as much."

"Ian, you said you needed to talk to me in person, so here we are. I can't believe my home is what you wanted to discuss."

"Your home," he snorts. "Your home is with me. You've had your vacation; it's time you came to your senses."

"I came to my senses months ago when I left you. Why haven't you signed the divorce papers yet? I'm not asking for much. Only a small portion of our savings to get me by until I find a job."

"Our savings? A job? Never mind that – a divorce? You can't honestly expect me to entertain this silliness any longer. You are my wife. We were married in God's house, by a servant of the Lord. 'Til death do us part, Mrs. King."

"I no longer go by King. I've legally changed my surname back to Wilson."

"*Legally.*" Another snort. "*Do you really believe a stack of papers will dissolve the holy union we entered into?*"

Aunt Robin puts her head in her hands. She isn't crying, she's exhausted. Cripes, I'm exhausted just listening to this.

"*You've pushed me too far over the years. And don't start that holier-than-thou nonsense with me. There's no one else here. I know what you really believe. The only reason you won't sign the papers is because it will make you look bad. I'm sorry to tell you that I don't care. We'll go to court if you insist.*"

His dull brown eyes darken where he stands just inside the doorway.

"*I can assure you, you will be dreadfully sorry if you take things that far.*"

"*Then just sign the papers. We have nothing further to speak about.*"

"*Actually, we do.*"

"*You can tell it to my lawyer.*"

Aunt Robin stands up and does her best to stare him down, but the beast doesn't budge.

"*I don't think the lawyer will be interested in this, unless he will be receiving an invitation to this scam of a marriage you're backing.*"

"*Scam of a – who told you?*"

"*Susan. Apparently, she's the only one left that honors her father and this family. How dense are you? Do you really support our youngest daughter marrying into a heathenistic family?*"

Aunt Robin pulls herself to her full height, hands on her hips, eyes blazing. "*How do you suppose they are heathens?*"

"*This boy has two children. Two children he wasn't even sure belonged to him, until after his wife committed the heinous crime of taking her own life. They are all tainted and damned.*"

"*Get out.*"

"*I will not.*"

Aunt Robin turns her back to him, hands shaking now, and picks up the phone.

"*You're not calling the police.*"

"*Oh, but I am.*"

All of a sudden, Uncle Ian rushes toward her. I don't know if he's going to attack her or just take the phone, but he doesn't get the chance.

The thud his ass makes as it lands on the linoleum rocks the building. The crack of his head as it hits the floor is even sicker. Whoops. I only meant to give him a shove.

Aunt Robin had been on edge before the sonic boom. She drops the phone and covers her head, spinning around to find him flat on the ground.

"*What did you do?*" he yells.

"*Me? What are you talking about? What happened to you?*"

I've never seen such a sight. This whale of a man is scooting himself on his ass toward the door. Once there, he pulls himself up using the door frame. Man, is he sweaty. And that is one solid door frame.

"*You saw the sparks, the hell fire! I told you what would happen, and I'm finished warning you!*"

He shakes his finger at her, turns, and hurries from the apartment, his words echoing off the walls.

Aunt Robin watches his retreat until he's out of sight. He doesn't even wait for the elevator, choosing to take the stairs instead. I must have scared the shit right out of him.

Maybe I did. Aunt Robin wrinkles her nose as she closes and latches the door.

She retrieves the phone from the floor and dials a number. Not the police.

"*Dean? If you and Stacey still want help with those wedding invitations today, I've reconsidered and would like to be a part of it.*"

Chapter 48

The year before, after expressing her feeling of uselessness and her desire to contribute to society, Lizzy had been granted access to her research of old. Animals.

Even though she could no longer go out and scan them, she was allowed to work on categorizing and sorting data. It wasn't all that interesting, but it kept her busy enough to tolerate the long days without descending into actual madness.

It hadn't been helping this past week, the longest week she'd spent here including the beginning of her stay.

Henry's last visit had ended abruptly, as the door swished open right after his cryptic warning. Her first thought was the room must not be secure after all. But it had been exactly twenty minutes, their allotted time.

Henry would be coming back today. She wasn't sure when, but it would be today. She had to believe he would show up.

Lizzy tapped away at her flashpad, pretending to organize columns of data. Really, she was just making a mess of things. It was impossible to concentrate, waiting for –

"Elizabeth?"

"Yes?"

If Maria was there to tell her Henry had canceled, she was going to lose it. No question.

"Your son is here to visit with you. Would you like to come with me?"

"Yes."

Her excitement had reduced her vocabulary to one word. That was probably a good thing. They enjoyed hearing the word yes around here, and she definitely wanted to keep them happy today.

As she followed Maria down the corridors, she noticed they were taking a different route than the last time. What if it was just a regular visiting room, instead of a secure one?

"Here you go, enjoy your visit."

"Yes. I mean, thank you."

Lizzy stepped through the opening and the door sealed itself behind her.

"Don't worry, it's a secure room."

Lizzy returned her son's smile. When was the last time they smiled at each other? Hers was the first to slip away, as a troubling thought occurred to her.

"But Maria is the one who let me in. How secure can the room be if she has access to it?"

"We only have twenty minutes. I don't think you want me to spend it explaining the security process to you. Just trust me."

Lizzy sighed and took her seat. "I'm still working on that."

"I know. We'll get there."

"Can we start with you telling me what this mysterious danger is?"

"It's complicated."

"Of course it is."

"Mom, you haven't been talking to anyone about the outside, have you?"

"Outside? No. Well, not since last year when I talked to Albert."

Henry's face dropped.

"Did something happen to Albert?"

"Yes."

"Is he dead?"

Being as he was two-hundred-plus years old, it would be sad, but not earth-shattering news – or Celadon-shattering. Unless it was her fault.

"Worse. Do you know what happens to patients when repeated experimental wave therapies are ineffective on them?"

"No. Do I want to?"

"They get laser lobotomies."

"That's not what happened to Albert."

"I'm afraid it is."

"But why? He was a problem patient long before I got here. For his whole life, according to him. Did they do that just because of our talk?"

"No. That might have been what pushed it up, but he was on his way there regardless."

"I don't get it." Lizzy was fighting back the tears. It couldn't be true. It didn't make sense.

"My wife, Lynette, works in wave technology. She's the one who develops the programs strictly for The Ward."

"Congratulations?"

"No. She, like everyone else, is locked in her job forever. But she didn't know all the details of what she'd be doing when she signed up. It was only after she started working there that she found out how harmful these treatments can be. Last ditch efforts and experiments, they call them.

"She wanted to help people, not hurt them. There isn't a day that goes by that she doesn't regret her choice, that she doesn't cry because of what she has to do."

"She does the laser stuff too?"

"No. But she says the wave treatments they suggest here, the ones she's obligated to create and provide, are similar to an actual laser lobotomy."

"Oh, that's why their auras are so faint." Lizzy caught herself and whipped her head around to look behind her.

"Secure room," Henry reminded her.

"Yeah, but why don't any of the waves work on me? Why didn't they work on Albert? They only make my memories stronger, the colors brighter."

"Another abnormality."

"I'm next on the laser list, aren't I?"

"Not next, but it's been suggested."

"Why now? I haven't done anything for a year."

"Back to Lynette, actually back to the question I asked you last time. What did you say about the outside when you were talking to Albert?"

"Just that I missed it, working outside."

"That's all?"

"Oh!" She'd forgotten, since they'd been whisked away so quickly. "He asked if I lived outside at one time. He might have said there were people who did live out there. I can't remember, it's been so long. But that couldn't be true, could it?"

Henry's smile was strained, as if he heard the exact answer he didn't want to hear but needed to.

"It could be."

"Henry, you're going to need to start asking and answering quicker. We don't have much time left."

"I know. I'll give you the scoop. But understand that just by telling you this, I'm putting all of us at risk. You, me, Lynette, our baby. You can't let anything slip out."

"I understand."

"There's a group of people in our building that believe we're being controlled. They believe there's a bigger truth out there that's being hidden from us. A better, or at least another, way of living."

"Outside?"

"Yes. Outside of the domes."

"So this isn't about colors?"

"Not the kind you see."

"Are you part of this group?"

"Only by association with my wife, so far. They have to be careful, you see."

"I think I'm starting to. But what does this have to do with me?"

"I want to help you get out of here."

Chapter 49

As Aunt Robin talks to Dean on the phone, I'm being pulled out of her apartment and back to his.

I concentrate harder on her, trying to fight it, but I can't. It's not that I want to stay with Aunt Robin, I'd just like to have a say in the matter. I already have enough things that are out of my control.

Well, we can add another one.

Back at Dean's place, he's talking to my aunt with the phone cradled between his ear and neck. His hands are busy packing Darren into his raincoat.

"We appreciate the offer, Robin, and we'll take you up on it another time. We have to take the kids to the doctor. Looks like it might be chicken pox."

Grr. I can't even hear her side of the conversation. What am I, some sort of ghostly superhero on call for emergencies? I'm still looking for the emergency here.

Darren and Diedre are all bundled up and ready to go.

I love my kids, I send them get-well-soon kisses, but I'm not a fan of hospitals. It's just the chicken pox. No need for me to tag along.

Back in control of my destination for the time being, I'm off to check on Scott.

Oh, this must be his grandma's place. He's sprawled out on a bed made up with the sweetest little cabin quilt and matching pillows. The room is infinitely nicer than the last one I'd found him in.

Larger, brighter, cleaner, and the dressers and night table are covered with lace doilies. Yep, it's got to be Grandma's.

Well, I'll be. He's studying. I've never seen him look so peaceful. Textbook in one hand, a pen for making notes in the other, I hardly recognize him or his aura. Why hadn't he done this years ago?

Probably because he needed to hit rock bottom first.

I'm sure Granny isn't going to appreciate the cigarette smoke, but who am I to talk? I'd give my left arm for one right now, if I had a left arm.

I wasn't intending to disturb him, but he looks up from his work and tilts his head.

"Amy?"

How does he know I'm here? Why is our bond so strong? My own kids can't even tell I'm around unless I make an effort to connect with them.

Maybe I had, unknowingly. I purposely flick the page of his notebook and brush his shoulder on my way back. I'm getting right good at this haunting stuff.

"Thanks for coming back. I missed you. I didn't know if you'd be able to find me here or not."

Who does he think I am, Santa Claus?

"I don't know if you saw or heard or whatever, but I'm going back to school. I'm just doing some catchup over the summer, and they say I should be able to enter Grade 11 at the start of the new semester.

"It made a big difference when you forgave me. At least, it feels like you have. I know I was a rotten boyfriend, and I deserved everything that happened to me."

I give him a poke.

"No, not what almost happened with the gun. No one deserves to feel like that. No one should ever have to go through something like that alone. At least I wasn't alone. I don't think I'd be here today if it weren't for you."

Hmm, death has made me soft. I'm crying happy tears. Well, mostly happy.

"I know you did go through that alone, and it breaks my heart. For a while there, I wasn't even sure I had a heart."

He sure does now. His aura looks like that of a different person's. Both his inner and outer colors are bright and stable. I suppose he is a different person, in a way. Yes, people can change. I've made more than a few transformations myself, both in life and in death.

I only hope he can hold on to his. I can't hang around here forever to help.

"I did one more thing I don't think you know about. I registered to volunteer with a mental health support group. I can't do much to start with — just talk about what I've been through, really. But I hope to work my way up to the crisis hotline.

"I'm doing it for both of us. Partly in your honor as someone who wasn't saved, and partly because I was. Maybe I can help someone some day. Maybe more than just one person."

How could I not dive in and give him a big old hug after that?

"Woah, careful now. You don't want to spoil me," he laughs.

His face grows serious as I retract.

"I understand you can't stick around forever. I know you have to go, eventually. I don't know where to, but I hope it's someplace nice. Just know you'll be forever in my heart and my thoughts."

Another laugh.

"We've come a long way since you kicked my ass in that apartment building, haven't we? Sorry again, about that. I was in a bad place, as you know. I wish there was some way I could undo it."

I need to get going. How am I supposed to tell him that?

"Don't worry about me, you go do what you need to do. You're always welcome here, but I'm going to be okay now."

Again, how does he do that?

He settles back into his studies and I wave my invisible goodbye.

I hope to see you again, Scott.

***

Breaktime is long overdue. I limp my way to our spot to join Dad and Mystery Pal.

Busy day. Now to relax. I'm able to put everything out of my mind except for my sick kids. But I'm sure Dean and Stacey can handle a simple case of the chicken pox. No need for me to worry too much.

Funny. I keep drifting away from the circle and having to scoot back. Something's pulling on me. It's not Earth, and it doesn't feel like Mom. Dad and Mystery Pal don't seem to be having any trouble staying in one place.

I wonder what would happen if I completely relaxed and let whatever's tugging on me reel me in?

Let's find out.

As soon as I let go and allow the pull to take over, my stomach lurches. Too fast! Can I slow this down?

Yep, it appears I still can.

I assumed the other two would stay put as I stretch my proverbial legs, but Mystery Pal bounces up, excited. She catches up to me and passes me, as if she knows where I'm off to.

She very well might.

Chapter 50

After six months of weekly visits, they were getting close to her escape.

None of the other Keepers of The Ward seemed to have any suspicions about what they were up to. In fact, they seemed pleased with Lizzy. She was willing to bet she'd gone down on the lobotomy list.

She was so distracted and excited about her potential future, she didn't have to act like she was walking around in a daze any longer. Her work was trash. Instead of being reprimanded for submitting her reports late and incorrect, everyone smiled at her more. She was pretty sure she was getting extra nourishment packs as well.

The first few months of her meetings with Henry were spent getting reacquainted and sharing information. It went slowly at the beginning, but then neither one could stop talking as they grew to trust each other again.

After that, they moved into the planning stages.

Henry was putting it all on the line to save her. Maybe to save himself and future generations too. The faction his wife belonged to believed there were people living outside. They believed there was something better out there, a freer way of living.

But they had no proof. That would be her job. The only information they had stemmed from urban legends, as one would say on Earth. Lizzy found it hard to believe. She'd never heard of anything like it herself until that day with Albert, but the group was utterly convinced of it.

It could be because they found themselves in unhappy situations in their personal or professional lives. Maybe they were just curious. Maybe they were wrong. Lizzy didn't care. She had nothing to lose except a lobotomy. She was more than willing to be their guinea pig.

The plans for how she was to survive on the outside, where she would go, and how she would send word to them, were minimal to nonexistent. She would be leaving with a basic survival pack and nothing more. There was a good chance she'd never see any of them again.

Getting her out was everyone's priority. Whatever happened after that was up in the air. Her chips would be removed and she wouldn't have any tech or comms. She could only hope to survive, and one day return to a predetermined rendezvous point on a date they had yet to establish.

Henry's son was to be brought home from the incubator in two weeks' time. For such an occasion, the rare opportunity to leave The Ward on a day pass was up for grabs. Not quite normal for a soon-to-be grandmother to give that much of a crap, but apparently normal enough.

Lizzy had been cleared to attend.

They were watching her even more closely now that a day out loomed in her future, but she was still putting on a good brain-dead show with little effort on her part.

A day out, indeed . . .

Her mind was already outside, apparently; one of The Keepers of The Ward cleared his throat to get her attention. He was standing right in front of her as she daydreamed on the settee in the recreation room.

"Elizabeth, did you hear me?"

"Sorry, no."

"I said your son is here. Would you like to come with me to see him?"

"Oh, yes please."

She noticed Maria standing by one of the exits, smiling a strange smile.

Yes, smile your bloody face off you stupid –

"Elizabeth, are you coming?"

"Oh, yes."

Through the doors, down the corridors, and finally . . .

"Henry!"

"Mom!"

They'd waited until the door was secured before greeting each other and hugging.

"It won't be long now."

"I know. Are you sure we'll be ready?"

"As ready as we can be. They had something else going on last night, but I was working so I don't know how it went. I haven't had a chance to talk to anyone today, but I'm sure they would have told me if there was a problem."

Henry had become a full-fledged member of his wife's secret group not long after their initial meetings. The group so secret, it didn't even have a name.

Neither did this plan. The fewer words there were to potentially slip out, the better.

"Dad agreed to sign you out for the day. It took a lot of convincing, but he understands why it wouldn't look good if I did it since I work here. Well, I guess he doesn't understand at all. If he knew what we were going to do . . ."

"Henry, I'm still not sure about that part of it. I don't want anyone to get in trouble and potentially end up in here because of me, especially not your father."

"Yeah, well, I still think it's his fault you were put in here to begin with. He's the one who talked me into recommending an evaluation, and he's the one who shared your writing with them."

"Remember what you said about letting go of the bitterness. I suppose Anna will be taking care of my exit from the dome?"

Lizzy still struggled to keep her tone light when speaking of Daniel's mistress. Part of the unnamed group of superheroes, Lizzy had been horrified when she first found out. However, she was a member of the pack, and she worked in dome maintenance. Anna would be the key to releasing her from the dome into freedom.

"Yes. I know it's an awkward situation, but she's really nice. She certainly has nothing against you. She's risking her neck to help you, to help us. I don't know what she sees in Dad."

"And you're sure he doesn't know anything? You're certain there's no pillow talk going on there?"

Henry opened his mouth to respond, but instead of reassurance she got, "I can't wait until you see Samuel. He has the same golden eyes as you."

Lizzy turned to find the door had opened silently behind her. How did they do that? It normally made a suctioning, sweeping sound that was impossible to miss.

"Visit's over," Maria announced. Her odd smile had been replaced with a stony expression, impossible to read.

"It hasn't even been ten minutes," Henry argued.

"Let's go."

Lizzy and Henry both stood. No one would be stupid enough to continue to argue with Maria. Not with that look on her face.

"Not you."

She pointed at Henry, who froze on his way around the table.

"Come on, Elizabeth. Julius will take you back to your room."

Must be security business. Oh well, one more visit next week to get the final details ironed out, and she'd be on her way to freedom.

Chapter 51

I'm not surprised when I end up at the door halfway between Mom's new world and our old one. Mystery Pal is thrilled, dancing in circles around me as I come to a halt in front of it. I hadn't realized Dad was following until he pulls up beside us.

It's not as easy for me to stay in one place so close to the doorway. Is this the world I'm destined for next? The one with the fake me in it?

Yes, it feels like it is. Mystery Pal couldn't be clearer about her belief that this is the world for both of us. But it doesn't feel like it's time yet.

Of course I'm scared to go dropping into a new world like Mom did, and Dad almost did, to lose all my memories and be born again. But that's not all that's holding me back. There's something else I can't put my finger on, and it's not fear.

My kids are taken care of. They might have the chicken pox, but that's no excuse for me to hang around. They'll probably get a lot of illnesses, bumps, and bruises over their lifetimes. Sure, I'll want to say my farewells, but that's to be expected. Scott seems to be doing fine on his own, I gave Uncle Ian a whack for Aunt Robin . . . it can't be any of these things.

Why are Dad and Mystery Pal just sitting around me, as if they're waiting for me to do something? Dad gives me a hug. He does think I'm going!

I shove away from them and the world, and I can feel Mystery Pal's disappointment. I know we're supposed to go in there together, and we probably will, but not yet.

Dad follows me to where I sit thinking, a good distance away from the door. He's just as confused as I am. And tired? Yes, we're all tired.

What is it that's holding me back? That new world is trying hard to draw me in. As I sit back here, my perspective clears, and I come to the conclusion that maybe I should be getting prepared. Maybe I'm just supposed to stick around and wait until it's time. How about at least one more lap?

I don't know who I'm trying to bargain with. Fate, Mystery Pal, Time, myself?

Whether it's something inside of me, or a higher power that grants my request, the pull stops. Not entirely, but enough.

Is my stay here in the afterlife really coming to an end? Am I down to my last hurrahs? Might as well start with this door, then, since this is where I'll likely end up soon. And really, I can't say I'm not curious to see a little more of my potential new world.

***

Yep. There's fake me again. Oh, I got fat. No, not fat exactly. I'm pregnant.

Okay, it's definitely not me. It can't be. The closer I look, the more differences I see, but there's still no denying the resemblance.

The woman is in bed today. She's propped up on dozens of plush pillows, covered with a light, silky blanket.

Unlike me when I was pregnant, the only part of her that seems to be swollen is her oversized belly. It looks like it's ready to pop. Her face and arms are still thin and beautiful. Her hair is perfectly styled and her face fully made up, even though she's just lounging in bed.

Also unlike me, she looks so relaxed. Comfortable and happy, she plucks a chocolate out of a heart-shaped box as she flicks the remote control, skimming through the channels on the gigantic TV hanging on the wall.

Pregnant or not, I can't blame her for smiling. If I thought her closet/dressing room was something, this bedroom is beyond words.

As she browses the television, I snoop around the room. It's the size of the apartment Dad and I used to share. And talk about glamorous!

It's decorated in deep purples and reds, the walls covered with framed pictures of herself. Some of the smaller pictures have a man in them. Not the same man I saw the last time I was here, yet he's just as handsome. Her husband?

I'm eyeballing the enormous window seat, trying to see out at what is sure to be a spectacular view of the city, when I hear her chuckle.

Holy crap. She's laughing at herself. On TV.

It's a tabloid news clip with a candid shot of her that's obviously dated. She only has a baby bump in this picture. The headline reads, "Father Revealed!"

I look more closely at the pictures around the room. The biggest ones are headshots. There, on one of the dressers covered with clutter, are awards of all sorts.

She's famous.

Well, go ahead and sign me up for this next. Just imagine what it must be like to be her!

But that doesn't make sense. I wouldn't be her. She already exists.

It's not a pull, but a push toward her stomach that fills me with the craziest notion.

No, not crazy. All at once, I know.

Mystery Pal is my soulmate, the one I'm meant to travel with over all others. That, I knew. She's been waiting for me, and she's had her eye on this world for some time now. Is there room for two of us in that belly?

Oh, my God. Mystery Pal is positively vibrating, her excitement infectious.

But that would mean we'd have to go soon. Whoever's going to come out of this woman is going to be coming out before long.

I think it's time to get on with that last lap.

Chapter 52

A week passed without a visit from Henry. And then two. After the third week, Lizzy had given up on her hopes of being freed. Her previous excitement was replaced by bitterness, anger. She'd been lied to again.

Or could it be something else? Henry had nothing to gain from lying to her. She didn't have much to share with him, information-wise. It was he who was filling her ears with tales of the outside. He was the one who suggested the escape plan.

And she stopped trying to unsee auras ages ago. He'd been genuine every single time they met.

It was a month later when she was called into Maria's office. By that time, her irritation had all but disappeared. Fear had taken its place.

"You're probably wondering about your son."

No shit.

"Yes, I was so enjoying our time together before he stopped coming."

"What did you speak about during those visits?"

"It took a while to get to know each other again, so to speak," she was treading on thin ice here, "but we did reconnect. We shared memories of when he was growing up, and he told me how happy he was with his wife and career. I can only assume he's enjoying being a parent now. I was supposed to get a day pass to meet his new son. I hope everything is all right."

"He didn't mention any other activities he was involved in?"

Time to crank up the dumb and harmless act.

"You mean like therapy and exercise?" She hoped she was pulling off the look and tone she was going for. Innocent, confused, and stupid, stupid, stupid.

Maria tapped her fingers on the desk and stared at her for the longest time. Lizzy called in all her self-control, denying herself permission to leak so much as one drop of sweat.

When Maria finally spoke, her voice was seething with fury, though her blank gaze never faltered.

"You have been cleared for release."

Lizzy's mouth dropped open. "Release to where?"

"Your quarters." Maria rolled her eyes to the ceiling as Lizzy's mouth continued to hang. "Your quarters at home."

"Why?"

She was having no trouble maintaining the idiot act now.

"Your therapy seems to be working, we've had no incidents of note over the last two years, and your husband has petitioned for your release," she answered through clenched teeth.

"Daniel?"

"Were you expecting another husband?"

"No, I just . . . I wasn't expecting to be released."

Henry must have done something. He hadn't been to see her because he was working this apparent magic. She'd been a fool to question his loyalty. He hadn't let her down at all.

"Well, unless you give us a reason to reconsider, you'll be leaving at the end of the week. The board has made its decision."

She spat out the last words as if they were poison on her tongue.

She was going home! Lord only knew why Daniel wanted her there – Henry's doing no doubt – but she was going home. She could find out the hows and whys of it all later.

"Thank you. Where do I go now?"

"You'll be taken back to your room." She paused and narrowed her eyes again. "Are you not wondering about your son?"

"What about him?" Lizzy gripped the arms of the chair she'd been in the process of rising from.

"He's being held on suspicion of involvement with a group of rebels. While he hasn't been charged as of yet, he'll be staying with us for the foreseeable future."

Lizzy slumped back into the chair.

"Rebels?"

"Yes. We've detained a number of them, who have been charged and committed. One of those rebels is your son's wife."

"No."

"Again, yes. Henry and Lynette's son has been assigned to your husband, and by default, you. There will be conditions pertaining to your release, which we'll discuss in greater detail this week. You won't be working right away, you'll have a strict curfew, and you'll be continuing your therapy."

Lizzy was only half listening as she tried to absorb the news of her son and his wife. Lynette was already condemned and Henry was next in line?

"You can go now."

That, she heard. Lizzy turned and walked out the open door, where one of the Keepers waited to escort her back to her room. The sound of Maria pounding on her flashpad followed her out.

It couldn't be her fault, could it? How would she be able to live with herself if she regained her freedom only to have Henry take her place?

It was hard enough to live here as it was.

Chapter 53

Dad's still waiting for me to disappear into this new world. He's both happy and sad. Probably happy that I've found a place, sad because he'll be losing me again. No one's expecting the next rebirth to go like his and Mom's fiasco did.

Not yet, Dad. I pull on him, taking us farther away from the doorway.

Where to first? Maybe Mom's world? Yes. I think it's time for me to say goodbye to her. Again.

This all sucks. I already lost her on Earth, and I would have been happy enough to complete my second farewells to both her and Dad when they were entering their new lives together. Of course, I screwed that up for them.

How am I supposed to go through all these losses again? And why should I have to? Not fair!

Mystery Pal hovers next to me, lifting my spirits. At least I found her. My twin flame, my forever friend.

Yes, I'll be strong enough to get through this. I can handle anything so long as she's around.

Decision made, I turn to the world where Dad should already have been living. He bobs along beside me, realizing now where we're going.

Maybe this won't be so bad after all. Maybe he'll stay by her doorway and wait for her to come out. Sure, it would be lonely to sit there all by himself, but I think that's where he wants to be. It's not like he has to worry about me anymore.

Damn, Dad. I would have been fine. You should have just let things happen like they were supposed to.

As much as I wanted this chance to tie up my loose ends, I'm not looking forward to the Earth goodbyes anymore than these next ones. I don't have a clue how to say goodbye to the children I never got a chance to know. I'm thankful for the bits of supernatural time I got to spend with them, but really that's just making everything more difficult now.

That's the hardest part about being recycled for me. The finality of it all. The losses. But as much as I'm going to miss everyone, and then lose my memories of them, I know it's the way it has to be and we'll see each other again some day. It'll just be different.

I'm reminded of my earlier realization and musings.

This place I'm in right now is a place for existing, not living; and the soul must go on.

Even better that mine doesn't have to go on alone.

Mystery Pal can tell we're doing our final rounds, and floats along happily beside me and Dad. Still, she mirrors my sadness, grieves with me as we go.

Okay, Mom. Time to say goodbye.

***

She's back in that same white apartment with that guy she married. Daniel, was it? But she has a different kid.

This one is still a baby, maybe a year old. His little lime-green aura is rather dull. What happened to the other one?

"Lizzy, you're going to be late for therapy."

Mom takes her time in handing the baby over to him.

"I'm going to see Henry after therapy, so you can go ahead and eat without me."

That was the other kid's name. Henry. And this would be his dad. Why does he look so angry?

"You've been to see him twice this week already. It's not normal."

Mom's aura tells me she's fed up with him. Her mouth confirms this.

"Neither is daily therapy, or having you as my jailer, or being monitored twenty-four hours a day."

"Thirty hours a day. And it's keeper, not jailer."

"Dammit, Daniel! Why didn't you just leave me in there? It still makes no sense at all that after two years of not laying eyes on or speaking to me, you all of a sudden petitioned my release. Why?"

Two years in where? Not that asylum.

Daniel doesn't answer, so she continues with her rant.

"I thought it was because you needed help with our grandchild, but you don't even trust me to be alone with him. Then I thought maybe you were lonely since your girlfriend was locked up, but you can't stand being in the same room as me."

Daniel puts the baby in a white playpen that looks more like a packing carton and turns back to her. Finally, some color in this world; his face is flaming red.

"You really don't know why? I'll tell you why. You ruined my life. We could have had it so good if you would've just dropped your made-up stories and fantasies. We could have had a normal son, who would be taking care of his own normal kid, with his own normal wife."

"You blame me for everything?"

"I do. I've lived in this building my entire life, and I've never known someone who went to The Ward – never heard of it happening to anyone. Now the whole damn floor's been wiped out, including our son."

"And your girlfriend," Mom adds bitterly.

"The only reason I pushed for your release was to try to return some sense of normalcy to our lives."

"So it was to save face. You're not even sorry you had me committed?"

"That was Henry's doing, and no. The only thing I'm having second thoughts about is bringing you back. You're just going to mess this kid up next, and you're not even trying to fit in."

"It was not Henry's doing. You forced him to do it. And I would love to see you try fitting into a place like this after what I've been through. I can't work, and everyone knows where I've been. They don't even look at me anymore.

"And not that you've ever asked, but do you know what they've done to our son down there? His wave therapies are so strong he can barely talk."

"So why do you keep going?"

"You are hopeless. Because of love, Daniel. Love! Have you ever experienced the emotion?"

"I thought so, once. Turned out it wasn't real."

Mom shakes her head in disgust and leaves the room. She swipes her arm at the door and walks off down the hall, blending into the crowd of other people dressed all in white.

Well, that's not what we wanted to see.

***

Mystery Pal and I back away while Dad continues to watch. She's got to be thinking the same thing as me. How are we supposed to leave him here?

He came out of there to save me. Even though it wasn't necessary, it meant a lot to me and I enjoyed having him around. But now that I'm almost ready to go, I don't know what to do with him.

At the risk of running out of time for proper goodbyes on Earth, we settle in to wait for him to come up for air.

Chapter 54

"Name and identification number, please."

"Elizabeth Masters. 310TCOH7267."

"Good day, Lizzy. Please have a seat. I'm just finishing up some notes."

Dr. Artaria was the only person she looked forward to talking to anymore. Sure, every now and then she gave her a strange look over something inappropriate that slipped out, but the looks didn't feel judgemental.

"Sorry about that." Dr. Artaria pushed aside her flashpad. "How's today going, Lizzy?"

Lizzy was trying, and had so far been mostly successful, to communicate honestly with the doctor. Of course, she couldn't tell her everything, but she had no one else. This was the closest thing to a friend she had here.

Resisting the urge to mention she felt her past family's presence today, she went with the more acceptable topic of her Celadonian husband.

"It was going all right until I went to leave my living quarters."

"Another argument with Daniel?"

"Sort of. He finally came out and blamed me for everything, including our not-so-perfect marriage and son."

"Do you think those things are your fault?"

"The marriage, I'll take part responsibility for. You know I'm not the easiest person to deal with."

The two women grinned at each other.

"You're definitely a challenge some days, but in a good way. I don't know if I've ever told you this, but I look forward to our sessions. You bring a little light into this otherwise overly formal world."

She stopped talking and smiling abruptly, probably remembering their sessions were being recorded now.

"Too much, I guess. But I think I'm getting better at conforming."

Her smile returned, but fainter.

"I still can't believe you spent so much time in The Ward. I certainly wouldn't have ever recommended so much as a hold to be put on you."

The rest of Dr. Artaria's smile slipped away. They were getting too close to dangerous territory, and they both knew it. Lizzy was not about to risk ruining yet another person's life.

"I don't feel like I did anything wrong with Henry. He's not convicted of anything; he's only being held on association with his wife and their group. I think he'll be released; I just don't know when. Things run rather slowly down there."

"I can't say I know much about what goes on in The Ward. Your detainment was enough of a shock before all the others in our area. I'd never known anyone who was sent to the place until you were. As a matter of fact, I've never heard of anyone being released until you."

"Yes, the building is reeling with all the latest additions, and my release. Specifically, on the floor where my quarters are."

"They're still treating you differently?"

"Yeah, it's like I have – " Lizzy caught herself before saying the plague. No plagues here on Celadon. "It's like they're afraid of me."

"My advice is to keep on doing what you're doing. They probably just need more time. Give them a chance and they may come around. How's your new grandson?"

"He's a delight. But Daniel doesn't seem to trust me with him. We rarely get time alone, and he watches me every time I so much as pick him up."

"I sincerely hope he can get over his trepidations, as well as the others. You've got to understand, the fact you spent time in The Ward and were subsequently released is more than unusual. You just have to be patient and hope for the best."

"Patience is something I'm getting good at. I've had plenty of time to practice."

"I do think Daniel will be able to come to terms with the situation. He was the one to petition for your release."

"I'm still not sure why."

"You're his wife. Whether he knows it or not, on some level, he needs you. It's the way of our world."

"I'm not so sure."

"Well, while we're on the topic of trust and reacceptance, I'm thrilled to be the one to let you know you've been cleared to go back to work."

"Are you serious? When? Why?"

Dr. Artaria's laugh was full of sincerity.

"Lizzy, your progress has been remarkable. You're taking it all in stride, and your attitude is great despite what you're dealing with in society. And well, I do have some pull when it comes to decisions like this."

"You're recommending it?"

"Of course. I also played a large part in your release from The Ward."

"I didn't know that. Why would you do that?"

"I remember you, Lizzy. We've been seeing each other since you were only four years old, with the exception of those few years you were away. I know you, and I like you."

"Come now, you must say this to all your patients," Lizzy kidded.

"I do enjoy my job, but you've always stood out as one of my special charges."

Lizzy's smile drooped.

"No, not special in that way. Special, meaning I look forward to the time we spend together. Now, as for work, you'll be restricted to a smaller area close to the dome walls to start with. Just to start. I'm sure it won't be long before it's back to business as usual."

"Thanks, Doctor. I'm going to see Henry right after this. He's going to be so happy for me. He knows how much I love my job."

The doctor's eyes roamed the room. There was no need to voice her concern about what Lizzy had just said.

"Actually, I don't think I need to mention that today. Considering the people he's been associated with, my workplace might not be the best topic."

Doctor Artaria nodded and managed a slight smile. Not for the first time, Lizzy wondered just how much she really knew.

If she had to wager though, she'd bet it was a lot. She'd also bet the doctor really was on her side.

Chapter 55

Finally, Dad leaves his post at Mom's world and joins us. Now, how to say what I need to say without the aid of words?

Dad is the one who makes the decision, and he gets the point across by giving me a shove.

He wants us to go and leave him here.

Argh. An impossible decision. But, not really. Just a hard one.

He's done what he came out to do. As much as I say I would have been fine without him, that's not exactly true.

Both he and Mystery Pal saved me from myself just by being here. If I'd been left all alone, I may very well still be rambling through the green murk, cursing everyone and everything for my miserable life.

No, no soul can exist well on its own.

Which is what makes this all the harder. It's like releasing an animal back into the wild. You know it's for the best, and it's the right thing to do, but you love him. And he's not an animal, he's my dad.

I guess he's not going to be completely alone. The way time's flying by on that planet, Mom will be with him before too long. Providing he peeks in only on occasion.

I think. I have nothing but instinct to go on here. At least I'm pretty sure I'm already doing better, decision-making wise, than I did in my last life.

I know I said this was my final lap, but we'll probably end up detouring back here just before Mystery Pal and I enter our new lives. Maybe he'll already be gone.

I'm surprised by the excitement I feel just thinking about my next life. It's my turn to live. Surely, it must be my turn to thrive.

I press my soul against Dad's, and I feel the love. All of it.

I remember watching him get ready for work when I was younger. He looked so brave and handsome in his uniform. I remember Christmases, birthdays, and all the holidays; shiftwork or not, he'd always pop up at some point to share in the moments and be part of the family.

I remember the one and only wedding photo I ever saw of him and Mom. Just the two of them, standing in a gazebo, staring into each other's eyes. There could be no mistaking that look. Not the romance; the pure, deep love. Soulmates of the truest kind.

There's no doubt they have that connection, that universal love that can never be defined or destroyed. The only reason they aren't together right now is because of their love for me. Mom had tried to come with him, but according to her writings down there, she couldn't make it out.

Yes, he belongs here now. They've been apart for long enough. And I have another family to say farewell to.

Mystery Pal and I leave without looking back. None of these are goodbyes. In this never-ending cycle of lives and souls, we'll be together again and again. How could it be any other way?

As we pass the doorway to what I hope will be my next life, it's hard to keep going. Part of me wants to dive right in and save myself from the sorrow I'm about to experience.

Sure, no goodbyes and we'll meet again, but . . .

Mystery Pal tugs on me, encouraging me to keep going as I lag behind.

I continue on, but slower.

Why should I have to do this? What is the point of this In Between? It would have been a hell of a lot easier if I could have just woken up in my new life. Is this some sort of punishment or trial? Does everyone have to do this? It doesn't seem fair.

Well, of course it's not. None of it's fair, and none of it's easy. Just like life, most of it makes no sense at all.

So I follow Mystery Pal, and my heart, and do what I feel has to be done.

Mystery Pal settles beside the doorway to Earth as I prepare myself for . . .

***

No. Who could be prepared for this?

The last time I'd been in the hospital was for the birth of my children. Not a fan.

The time before that, I spent days in one of these rooms while my dad was hooked up to a life support machine. We all know how that ended.

Now here I am again. Another dimly-lit hospital room, another person I love lying in the bed.

I'm not sure I would have recognized him if it wasn't for his aura. His barely visible, cream-colored inner aura.

The rest of Dean's face and body is covered in blisters, his eyes swollen shut.

His outer aura is nonexistent; the other one flickers and jumps. It's like it's trying to leave his body and come up here.

Not on my watch. I'll shove the damn thing back down his throat if I need to.

Chapter 56

Dr. Artaria had been correct in predicting it wouldn't be long before things were back to normal.

As normal as they were going to get, anyhow.

The years went by. Lizzy completed her period of supervised work near the domes and returned to her previous route with her own travel pod.

The best part of her days once again revolved around taking her helmet off, breathing in the fresh air, and spending time with Belle.

But she was more attuned to the world around her now. She never stopped looking for signs of life out there. If people really did live outside, where were they? In the trees, underground, someplace far, far away?

She was loath to do any sort of real investigating. The closest she came, apart from keeping her eyes peeled outdoors, was a little snooping around other departments in the travel pod docking area.

The rumors had been sort of true. There was an entire division dedicated to searching for people on the outside. They were rather clandestine, working under the title of Theoretical Outside Organics.

The most surprising find, as a result of her limited sleuthing, was that the people working there didn't take their jobs all that seriously. They joked about another day of sailing around aimlessly, counting trees. As far as Lizzy could tell, the only ones who seemed to be concerned about outdoor people running amok were Maria and her goons in The Ward.

Lizzy forced herself to file it.

Her therapy had been reduced to twice a week instead of once a day, and she and Daniel had settled into a civil living situation. Henry was still being held in The Ward, and little Samuel was not so little anymore.

She still visited Henry once a week, even though he was fading away right before her eyes. The only thing that sometimes perked him up was news about Samuel. His eighth birthing commemoration was coming up, and Lizzy was trying to convince Daniel to petition for a day pass.

He hadn't outright refused, so that was something.

Lizzy signed into The Ward and was being escorted to a visiting room when she caught sight of Maria stomping through the white corridors. She hadn't seen her since the day of her own release. The woman walked right by her, nose in the air. She must still be miffed about having all her objections overruled.

Lizzy shivered at the memory of the time they spent together as she entered the visiting room.

"Twenty minutes," the Keeper announced, sealing the door between them.

"Good morning, Henry. You're looking well today."

That was a lie. His face was whiter than his jumpsuit, his outer aura a dull grey. His inner aura no longer glowed like a blossoming rose; it just sat there, pale and salmon-like.

"Henry? It's Mom."

He pulled his eyes up from the table to look into hers. No, he wasn't looking at her, he was looking through her. It wasn't uncommon. It broke her heart every time, but Lizzy refused to let it show, carrying on as usual.

"Can you believe that Samuel is already interested in job options? He's not at all like you were at that age, not when it comes to interests or appearance. He's almost as tall as me already. He has Lynette's dark blond hair, and his eyes are the oddest shade of green. Almost like a . . ."

She couldn't think of a safe comparison. Pistachio or avocado were not words here, and anything referring to the outdoors was a definite no-no. What had she likened it to before?

"They're just different from yours. Maybe like a combination of yours and mine."

Henry nodded but had yet to focus on her.

It wasn't the first time she'd described his son's appearance to him, but it was one of the things that sometimes got his attention. Not today.

"And you'll never guess what his top job option is so far. Nourishment pack production. It just might stick; he's always reading the labels and examining the packaging on everything."

Henry laughed and laid his head down on the table.

She took the opportunity to allow a couple of tears to leak out as she continued talking.

"Your father sends his love. We can't wait for the day you're released and can come home to us and your son."

The door opened and the Keeper announced their time was up.

Risking the guard's impatience, Lizzy took a second to wipe the drool off her son's face and give him a kiss.

"See you soon, Henry. I love you."

No response. Tears burned her eyes again as she was led back down the corridors and through the doors.

She took her time on the way back to her living quarters, allowing herself a chance to recompose. Never an easy task after spending any sort of time in that place.

Samuel arrived at the door to their place the same time she did. One at a time, they swiped and entered their home.

"How was your exercise period, Samuel?"

"The same as usual. Invigorating and beneficial."

Oh, what a different child this was. Henry had been so much fun at Samuel's age, curious about everything just like herself. Too much so, for this world. The Ward seemed to enjoy collecting people like them.

Lizzy hadn't uttered a word about her other life, and was extra careful not to slip up with her words or comments about colors in Samuel's presence. He was the reason she'd been so well-behaved over the past eight years.

Well-behaved and dull. She could only pray it would be worth it.

"I visited your father today, and he sends his love."

"Thanks. I think I'll probably want to go see him when I'm old enough."

"You won't be old enough for years. He's sure to be released by then."

Samuel shrugged and took a nourishment pack from the cooling machine, rolling the bag in his hands.

"You see, these are a prime example of how the packaging could be improved."

Lizzy tuned him out as he launched into an evaluation of the slightly pointed corners and uneven creases.

When had the lies become so easy for her? She didn't realize she was doing it half the time anymore.

No, Daniel hadn't sent his love to Henry. No, Henry hadn't sent love to Samuel. And no, she wasn't certain Henry would ever be released.

She was no better than the society she lived in, justifying her actions for the greater good. Lies to make people happy, lies to cover the painful facts and possibilities.

Lies, lies, lies.

Sure, there was no crime or disease in this world. Not on the surface. But at what price?

If she'd been born into the world properly, she may not have been aware of the hidden truths. She may not have suspected corruption and conspiracies.

But if she had come in fresh and clean and still had these suspicions of treachery, what would she have done? What if Jason had made it in with her and taken Daniel's place? How different would life be?

They would have either been foolishly happy or taken on the falsities together. If they'd become aware of them, they would have done the right thing. They would have had the courage.

She turned her attention back to Samuel and smiled as he proudly finished off his proposed solution to the great packaging problem of his generation.

Soon. Soon he'd be old enough to begin his own life. He'd find his occupation, wed, and have his own child.

She'd see his upbringing through.

And then she'd be free to take on the powers that be.

Chapter 57

Chicken pox. It's like the universe is just toying with me already. Adults don't get chicken pox. Kids do.

Mine did. They're sitting with Stacey and Aunt Robin by Dean's bed, asleep in their arms. Their faces have faint traces of the red spots, but they're fine now.

Dean's not.

If there's one thing I can safely say I'm fed up with, it's Earth life. This one, anyhow. More of my family members are dead than alive. I'm not even going to start going through the list.

Dean can't be next.

It's the chicken pox, get over it! Get up!

His inner aura jolts and rises above his body again.

No, not you!

It settles back down.

Oh, my God. This is just too absurd to be real. No, I don't believe I caused that last bit to happen, but it was freaky enough to send me into a fit of hysterical laughter that no one will ever hear.

What next?

I have got to stop saying that.

In comes Uncle Ian. Aunt Robin leaps from her seat and hands Diedre to Stacey.

Stacey busies herself with arranging the kids, avoiding her father's glare.

"What are you doing here?" Aunt Robin hisses at him.

"You have been missing for days."

"Missing? From where? My own apartment?"

"Your own — here." He shoves a stack of papers into her hands.

Aunt Robin moves toward the door as she reads the cover page.

"These aren't signed."

"No, nor will they be. The document beneath is a notice that you've hereby been served. I'm suing you for abandonment."

"You're not serious."

Of course he is, he's a nut.

"I assure you, I am. You can either return home, or you'd better hurry up and get that job you were talking about."

Uncle Ian turns and leaves her standing there, staring at the papers.

"Mom?"

Aunt Robin returns to her chair beside Stacey and rams the papers into her purse.

"I'm sorry you had to see that. I'll deal with him later."

She takes Diedre back from Stacey and turns her attention to Dean, her clenched jaw the only sign of tension in her otherwise collected exterior.

"What happened between you two? I mean, I understand why you left. But how did things get this bad?"

"I'm not about to badmouth your father in front of you, no matter what has happened between us in the past, nor what is going on now. You know what he's like, though. I never expected him to take this well."

"You don't think he'll try to hurt you, do you?"

Aunt Robin takes her time in responding. "I don't think so, but I'll be careful. Susan must have been the one to tell him where I was. You have enough to worry about, so trust me when I say I'll deal with him."

"You should at least come stay with us. Well, with me and the kids. I could use all the help I can get until . . ."

Her voice cracks, unable to finish the sentence.

"Until Dean gets better." Aunt Robin completes it for her.

A nurse comes in with a tray of IV fluids and things. An excellent time for me to stretch my soul.

You stay there, I warn Dean and his soul.

***

And you, do up your coat.

Scott is strolling down the street, wind and rain whipping his hair in every direction. He cringes and rubs his hands together, yet his jacket is hanging wide open.

Eesh. Can no one on this planet take care of themselves properly?

Weird. Why is he walking up to Dean's building? He pulls a paper out of his pocket and tries to smooth out the creases before ringing the buzzer.

He fidgets while he waits for an answer that's not going to come. He rings the buzzer again.

He's not just moving around to keep warm. He's nervous. Move the paper, let me see the paper.

Oh.

I'm not sure what I was expecting, but it wasn't a handwritten apology.

He gives the buzzer one last try. Receiving no response, he stuffs the paper back into his pocket and walks off.

Finally, in the bus stop shelter, he does up his coat.

It's not the nicest place to bid him adieu, but I don't know if I'll get a chance to come back to him.

I reach out and ruffle his hair. Not something I'd done when we were alive, but it gets his attention.

"Ames?"

I repeat the action. It's hard to do this outside. The bus shelter helps some.

"You're leaving, aren't you?"

He's still as perceptive as ever. It makes this a lot easier.

"I know I already apologized to you, but I'm doing my steps, making amends."

Ah.

"I haven't actually joined Alcoholics Anonymous, but I haven't had a drink since that night. I found the list of steps on the Internet, and realized I do have a lot of things to be sorry for. Maybe it was a bad idea to try going to your husband's house. I don't know. It's not like I can change anything."

It's an awkward hug, but I fill it full of love and forgiveness.

"I'm going to miss you. I'm so sorry for everything I did to you. And thank you for saving my life."

Best of luck, Scott. I wish you a lifetime of happiness.

I leave him to wait for his bus, and shuttle myself back to the hospital.

Chapter 58

"What should I do?"

Lizzy was stretched out on the grass, helmet-free, as the sun warmed her bones.

Belle snatched the remainder of her nourishment pack, leaving her question to hang in the air.

Getting old on Celadon was a lot different than on Earth. There were no wrinkles, no broken bones or mystery ailments that couldn't be promptly fixed by lasers or waves. The only thing that happened was your hair turned grey and you got a little shorter.

But Lizzy was tired. She was slowing down. Not on the outside, on the inside. And she'd yet to do anything of importance in this life.

Sure, she had Henry, who had Samuel, who had Bethany, who had Arthur. The list was long, and about to grow again. She didn't attend the birthing commemorations anymore. She rarely saw her offspring's offspring at all and couldn't remember the last time she'd seen Samuel.

Henry had ended up being convicted of association with the rebels and would spend the remainder of his days in The Ward. Lizzy still visited him weekly, but she didn't stay for the full twenty minutes. He didn't talk at all anymore. He hadn't for years. She didn't think he could hear her, either.

She and Daniel had grown old together in the physical space they lived in, but not emotionally. She shared that bond with Jason.

He'd shown up again just after Samuel was wedded. Right when she was ready to start up a rebel cause of her own, to hell with the consequences.

Instead, she turned to Jason. He spent days at a time with her, then disappeared for decades. But it never felt like he went far. She pictured him hovering up there, just as she had when the situation was reversed, waiting.

It was reassuring to know he was close by. It helped in aiding her comfortably normal life to pass by more quickly.

But Lizzy, previously known as Amelia, had never been one to settle for comfortable.

After Samuel set out on his own, so had she. She overrode the travel pod settings in order to see more of the world. She searched high and low, not only scouring the wild for signs of people, but also just for fun.

After each one of these escapades, she would be pulled into the travel pod regulations office and questioned about her detours. A lovely flaw in their design: the data wasn't uploaded until the day was done, or after she failed to report in at the end of her shift. It gave her plenty of time to cook up a good story.

She had fun weaving these tales on occasion, but it was usually easy enough to blame her wave therapies and claim confusion. After all, the doses she was receiving were enough to incapacitate most people.

She wasn't most people.

Years of scouring the planet and risking reincarceration in The Ward had produced nothing. Not a smoke signal, not a footprint.

She spent additional decades sniffing around her building, looking for anything suspect or shady. She zoned in on people's auras, studying them for deception. She found nothing aside from the rare glimpse of Maria's. And that was just a mess.

Wherever the secrets were hidden, they were out of her reach. She spent years being frustrated as hell about it.

Then she took a closer look at the people around her. Maybe they were being controlled, maybe they were being lied to. But with the exception of a few of The Ward occupants, they were all content.

The only one bothered by the mysteries out there was Lizzy. It suddenly dawned on her one day in exercise class, as she watched the hamsters running in their wheels. What good would it do to go chasing after a potentially imaginary injustice, risking her modicum of freedom, when no one else cared?

If there was another pack of rebels out there, she never came across them. And by now, she wasn't sure what she would do if she did. Whatever this world's purpose was, she'd come to the conclusion that it wasn't up to her to interfere with it.

Her only regret was not being able to save Henry.

A second travel pod descended from the sky and landed next to her. She scrambled to put on her helmet as Belle flew off into the setting sun.

The setting sun? How long had she been out here for?

"Good evening, Lizzy."

"Oh, Peter." She dropped the helmet back onto the ground and returned his smile. "Did I lose track of time again?"

"You did it up good today, both time and coordinates."

He removed his own helmet and walked over to join her on the grass.

"I suppose I'm in for another talking-to?"

"Of course. Don't worry, I'll be joining you today. I took the extra-scenic route myself."

"We'll never learn, will we?"

"I sure hope not."

Peter. Her last hope at having a real friend in this world. He worked for the travel pod regulations branch, and ironically ended up in the questioning offices as often as she did.

After a while, he started jumping on the tickets to go out and wrangle her, just so they could sit together and enjoy the outdoors. Helmet-free.

They talked about everything and nothing at all. Except for her past life and auras.

They simply enjoyed being together. Two free spirits pushing the lines only as far as was fun. It was as close to an affair as she would ever get. She knew his wife had another partner and he was in the same boat as she, but what was the point of taking their relationship any further than this?

Peter handed her half a brick out of his nourishment pack, and they tapped them together in a toast to the sunset.

He chewed contentedly on the bar as she studied him out of the corner of her eye. Not her type at all. His pale blond hair was nearly as white as his jumpsuit. His nose was too long. His golden eyes were set too close together.

But his auras were beautiful. His inner aura was a startling ocean blue, while his outer aura flicked from one bright color to the next. He was curious. He was fun.

And she liked him. A lot.

She stuffed her half of the bar in her mouth to stifle a laugh. She was in her hundreds, having a schoolgirl crush on this guy who was also ancient.

Daniel had long ago found another mistress, dipping again into the pond of his fellow dome maintenance workers. She'd judged him as being needy, incapable of being alone.

How foolish of her. How had she forgotten the lesson she learned during her time in the afterlife? Souls do not do well on their own. No wonder hers was so tired.

Daniel was working late tonight, code for spending time with his lady friend. Maybe there was something she could do to help the last few decades here pass by. Maybe there was some enjoyment, some happiness to be found in this world for her after all.

Maybe it was sitting right beside her.

"Hey, Peter? What are you doing tonight after our reprimands?"

Chapter 59

Three days I spent in the hospital room, watching Dean slip in and out of consciousness.

Okay, I wasn't exactly in the room, but it might have made things a bit easier.

I'm exhausted as I give his soul another push, securing it deep inside of him.

I think I'm just doing it out of habit now. I back up a little and take a good look. It's not moving anymore. I think I've been doing ghost CPR on someone who hasn't needed it for a while.

That step back allows me to take a better look at his face, too. The swelling has gone down considerably. The tone in the room has lightened. I think the worst is over.

Looking even closer at everything I was missing, I notice his outer aura is back.

All good news, but I'm still not going anywhere. I'd been fooled before. When my dad was sick, I left three times thinking he was fine, just fine, only to return to find him sicker, sicker, and then on life support.

I'll definitely refrain from squishing Dean's soul around anymore, though. It's kinda lumpy, like it was manhandled. My bad.

Stacey had been napping on the chair beside the bed. She wakes up as Aunt Robin comes in. Who's got my kids? Dean's parents are vacationing somewhere in Mexico.

"Where are the kids?" *Stacey echoes my concern.*

"They're with Susan. And I finally reached Dean's parents. They're on their way back, even though the infection is under control."

"Oh, good. I like that Susan's spending more time with them lately. I want them to be close to their other aunt. Lord knows, we can use all the family we have left."

"Isn't that the truth? She's been different since she found out what your father did with that lawsuit."

"So have I." Stacey folds her arms around herself and frowns.

"Stacey, you have to remember I don't want you getting involved in our affairs."

"How can I not? I've seen the way he treats you. I've been seeing it my whole life. Yes, we were taught to respect and honor our parents, but – "

"But nothing. You can make your own decisions and form your own opinions. But one thing I will never do is come between you and your father."

"I don't know why you continue to defend him after all these years. I understand you don't want to influence Susan and me, but I'm old enough to see him for what he is."

"He's your father."

"Sure, a father who won't even walk me down the aisle at my wedding."

Aunt Robin sighs and takes a seat beside her daughter.

"I feel terrible about that. I wish there was something I could do to fix it."

"This is not your fault, Mom. That's what I'm trying to say. I know you don't want to talk about it, but I will tell you I think the best thing you ever did was walk out on him. And if it does come down to a trial, you can't stop me from speaking in court."

Aunt Robin smiles a tired smile. "I don't think it will come down to that. He has far too much invested in the community to lose face like that. It's a bluff."

"Whatever it is, I'm telling you to be careful."

Aunt Robin's smile turns playful. "You sound like you're the mother here."

"Well, I will be, once I adopt our children."

"You'll make a great mother, and a terrific wife. You've already shown that. You convinced Dean to quit smoking and *start eating better the first week you were together, and it's obvious how much you care about the children. Do you think you and Dean will ever have children of your own?"*

"We want to, but I'll love them all the same if we do. What do you think we should tell the twins about Amy once they're old enough to understand?"

I'm all ears for the answer to this one.

"You'll know what to say when the time comes. Just be honest with them. You'll be their mother, yes, but don't ever hide the fact they once had another mother. Lies hurt everyone, even if they're backed by the best of intentions."

Stacey grins. "By the way, I love what you've done with your hair."

"What? I thought you approved of the change."

Aunt Robin grabs a spare pillow and whacks her with it, as it dawns on her that Stacey was playing with her.

I couldn't agree more. About what to tell the twins, about the lies, even about Aunt Robin's hair. Gone is the perm from the 60's. It's short and styled in a bob now; she even has highlights.

I watch them laugh and joke around with each other, and all of a sudden I'm crying.

***

Mystery Pal follows as I meander back to our spot.

I miss my mom. I never got a chance to be a mom. What I wouldn't give to be on either end of that happy moment I just saw down there. I don't get any more mom moments. Not in this existence.

Mystery Pal is pressed tightly against me. Definitely not my mother, but she lifts my spirits all the same. She's my family, and soon we'll be off to live our next lives together.

Yes, it will be our turn to live and laugh and love again. Hopefully, I'll have some better luck this time around. Not so much death and drama.

Maybe it will be a normal life. A life where I belong.

Chapter 60

Lizzy flew back to her quarters after therapy, excited for the weekend to begin. It would be the first time she and Peter were spending the entire three days together. At 180 years old, she'd never felt so young and full of life. Not in this world.

She stopped outside the door to compose herself before entering. As strange as it was, there was nothing to hide from Daniel. He'd be doing the same thing as she was this weekend. He was working overtime.

Meaning he was shacking up with his mistress whose husband would be away on business.

Still, even after all these years, it was weird. It always bothered her a little when he went off on his rendezvous. Out of respect, she wasn't going to rub his nose in the fact that she was looking forward to one of her own.

The eating and living areas were empty. Lizzy went to Daniel's door and knocked on it. No response. He'd already left. Not unusual for him, yet she felt the sting.

She returned to the living area to sit and wait for Peter. On second thought, she got back up and headed to her own chambers to fix her hair and freshen up. It didn't take long. There wasn't much to fix or freshen.

She tightened her long, blond ponytail and sighed at her reflection. Her golden eyes were the only splash of color on her otherwise white face. She missed makeup.

Yes, after one hundred and eighty years, she remembered it all like it was yesterday. Earth. Jason. Amy. Writing, eating and drinking for fun, knickknacks and mementos lying all over the place.

She still missed it. Every last bit of it. The highs, the lows, the love, the pain.

There was some of that here, but not enough. Everything was limited, regulated, lacking. And she was the only one who cared.

She left her bland chambers and sat in the living area once again. What was taking Peter so long? She wasn't in the mood to be alone. She wanted to talk to someone; anyone would do. She'd even settle for Daniel right about now.

Therapy had been a bust for the past week. Dr. Artaria was gone. Lizzy was with her when she got the call.

The call didn't come from God, or a higher being. She received the notification via her earchip in the middle of their session. The one informing her that her organs were winding down.

The doctor had merely smiled and apologized to Lizzy for having to cut the session short. The closest thing to sadness, fear, or regret came in the form of an unprecedented hug on her way out.

People weren't afraid of death here. They didn't cry or mourn when someone else died, either. It was just another one of those regular occurrences.

Well, Lizzy cared. She'd sat in the office for the remainder of her allotted time after Dr. Artaria left for the end room, trying not to feel the feelings that weren't normal here.

And as much as she yearned to be back with Jason, her soulmate, she sure was scared of dying. Any second, her own earchip could deliver the news that her time was up.

When someone was called to the room, they went alone. There were no funerals. The person would be mentioned at the annual ethereal ceremony. The end.

At least she wouldn't be going alone when she went to the room. Jason would be there. There was no doubt about that.

At last, the door alert sounded.

Peter looked as awkward as she felt when he came into the eating area. They both just stood there like teenagers on a first date.

He was the first to laugh, breaking the silence.

"Why does this feel so strange?"

"I have no idea. Am I the only one who feels like a kid again?"

"Nope. My thoughts exactly."

"Go have a seat in the living area and I'll get us some nectar."

"I'll help."

There wasn't much to do in the way of helping. The efficiently-packaged containers needed only to be pulled out of the cooling machine.

But just the act of doing something in the eating area, formerly known as the kitchen, with someone was the best therapy she could ask for.

"You know, my grandson came up with these new and improved packages."

Peter held his up to examine it, trying hard to find the new and improved bit.

Lizzy laughed and turned it sideways.

"It's the edges. They're less sharp."

"I've got to tell you, I never would have noticed. I don't make a habit out of fondling the packages."

"Neither do I. I just remember how fascinated he was with these things when he was young. Not just the nectar packages, but all the packaging."

"You remember a lot. It's all I can do to keep track of all the names of great-great-great-great grandchildren. I'd be hard pressed to recall the occupation any of them chose."

Lizzy wondered how he would react if he were to discover the full extent of her recollections. As fun as he was to be around, and as much as he enriched what was left of her life, no way was she risking that again.

Peter was open-minded. They broke the rules together time and time again. But he was still a Celadonian at heart. She was fairly certain he'd turn tail and run if she started with the real crazy talk.

No, Peter would never know the truth. The next time she spoke the absolute truth would be in the afterlife with Jason. The place where there were no words, but so much heart.

In the meantime, she and Peter took their nectar to the living area and settled in to enjoy their perfectly normal weekend together.

Chapter 61

Mystery Pal took off again hours ago. To check on our new world, I assume. She must be feeling the increase in pull just as I am.

Everything seems to be wrapping up on my old Earth. As soon as I know that Dean will be all right, it'll probably be time for Mystery Pal and I to move along.

Yet something else is telling me to stay here for a bit longer. Not in words, of course. That would be too easy.

I sit and watch the rainbow parade of souls popping in and out of the door that we don't notice when we're right on the threshold of it. They make it look so simple. Like they know what they're doing, where they're supposed to be.

I know shit.

Except . . .

I think my kids are going to be okay. As much as I hate to leave them, I already did. That's on me. I wonder if my soul will ever be able to truly forgive me for what I did. I'm not sure that's an act that can be left behind, not without leaving a scar.

Whether it follows me for eternity or not, I can only repent. There's no changing what happened.

As for what's going to happen down there, I hope my children will have a good life. A happy life. Their stories will continue without me, until we meet again one day.

I'm not jealous anymore. I've even tried to stir up those initial feelings of anger and betrayal from when I first realized Dean and Stacey were a couple.

I feel nothing but gratitude now. Two of the kindest, most loving souls I'd ever known, they will be the ones to take care of my children. They will be the ones who will guide them through life, who will give them everything I couldn't.

And I'm honestly happy for Dean and Stacey. I'd treated him terribly from start to finish. I still cringe as I recall my behavior. There are no words for the shame I feel.

Stacey had always been sort of a wallflower. She was studious and did a lot of volunteer work; the things I'd once used to label her as a nerdy, hopeless do-gooder. When someone was in need, she was the first to come running to help. She asked for nothing in return for her charity and kindness, and that's mostly what she got.

If you wanted to be petty, you could say she was unattractive with her short red hair, pinched nose, and oversized glasses that constantly needed to be pushed back into place.

But really, she's beautiful. People like her are all too rare.

And now these two souls are going to be married. Maybe that's what's keeping me here. Maybe I can stick around long enough to watch the wedding.

I'd never been one for weddings. My own was held at the town hall while I was pregnant, right after my grandfather had a massive stroke. Dean wanted to postpone it, but I just wanted to get it over with. I bitched and moaned throughout the whole thing, and fled the building while he was still paying the Justice of the Peace.

But I would love to attend this one. As an uninvited guest, of course. I'm pretty sure none of those wedding invitations have my name and address on them.

Mystery Pal comes bouncing back and settles next to me. Well, she sort of settles. She's having a hard time sitting still. It must be getting close to what I assume will be our birthdays over there.

Still, there's no doubt she'll be patient enough to wait out this last bit with me. She's been waiting for a long time. Of course, I don't know exactly how long, but it feels like it's been ages – more than just one lifetime.

She'll be okay until after the wedding.

Unless our next world calls us first. Let's see if we can find out how close we are to the nuptials.

* * *

Sweet. Dean's at home, propped up on the couch in the living room. His face is still covered in red spots; all his visible skin is. But he's awake, and he's home, and he's smiling.

He's smiling at Stacey who's modeling her wedding dress for her mother and him. The kids have pulled themselves up on the edge of their playpen, laughing as she twirls around.

No superstitious traditions here. But who cares? Look at all the love and laughter in that room. Had I ever been in such a room? My parents loved me, but every time there was merriment or cause for celebration, I'd retreated into myself.

Was there something wrong with me right from the start of that life? Something no one could fix? I know they tried. There were so many people that cared about me, that bent over backwards trying to make my life better, but I thwarted all their efforts.

I can only hope now that my soul isn't too damaged. I pray it was just a bad go-round. I have to trust that the experiences will follow me, even if I won't remember them, and guide me toward a better way of living instead of punishing me further.

I think it's true. I smile along with them as Stacey dons the veil. She looks beautiful both inside and out. She's taken the glasses off for the modeling occasion, but the glow of happiness that radiates from her is the most breathtaking sight. Her aura is pure white, blindingly happy.

The buzzer sounds, and Stacey runs over to press the button to unlock the doors below.

"Stacey, you should ask who it is first."

"Oh, Mom, it's just Dean's parents."

"You're the one who insisted I stay with you while Dean was in the hospital because you were worried about me. You should be more careful."

"I guess you're right. Even though Dad doesn't know where we live, I was still kind of worried he might show up here looking for you. He isn't bothering you anymore, is he?"

"No. I haven't heard a thing from him since they tossed that lawsuit."

"I still don't understand why he did that. And how did you get it thrown out so quickly?"

Aunt Robin only smiles at her daughter as she opens the door for David and Eileen.

"Welcome back."

"It's great to be back. Where's my boy?"

"Over here," Dean calls from the couch. "Alive and getting well."

His parents ooh and aah over Stacey's dress on their way to their grandchildren and son. Aunt Robin follows with her coat on.

"I'm going to head home. Stacey, did you want me to take the invitations to mail in the morning?"

"Yes, I'll get them together. Thanks for doing this, Mom."

Stacey holds her dress up off the ground and walks over to a small table I hadn't noticed in the corner of the room.

"It's not a bother. I'm not exactly going out of my way since I work there," Aunt Robin says.

"I meant, thanks for your support." She lowers her voice, even though little can be heard above Dean's parents fussing over him and the kids. "I know you weren't thrilled about the wedding at first."

"I admit, it took me a while to warm up to it. You're still so young."

She turns to look at the homey scene behind her.

"But I think you'll have a wonderful life together. This is a real family."

Poor Aunt Robin. This is the sort of family she should have had. Instead, she ended up with Uncle Ian.

A sample invitation sits on the corner of the table, and finally I can see the date. Shoot. It's still months away. I don't think I'll be making it to the ceremony.

Stacey has collected all the stamped and addressed envelopes. All but one. She picks it up and turns away from everyone, frowning at it.

Ew. It has her father's name and address on it. But no stamp.

"Stacey?"

Decision made, she pounds a stamp onto the envelope and tucks it in the middle of all the others.

"Sorry. Here they are."

Chapter 62

Just when she'd given up.

Lizzy had turned two hundred the week before. A milestone to be celebrated, you would think.

Not on Celadon. Two, count them, two people had shown up for her birthing commemoration. Her own mother, and her great-grandchild. Daniel hadn't said a word as he left for work.

That had been a long day, sitting in her living quarters waiting for guests who didn't appear. A long day with her mother. They didn't have a thing to talk about, so they didn't talk.

Peter had received his call to go to the end room only months before that. And how did Lizzy find out? When someone else came to retrieve her from one of her dalliances after she'd strayed too far and was out too late.

Henry got his call the year before. That, she discovered when she showed up for her weekly visit and he was already gone.

This world stunk. She could count the good times, the happy moments, the connections she thought she'd made over her life on one hand. Well, maybe both hands if you counted the ones that turned out to be false.

She went ahead and added the false ones to her list. False was the perfect word to describe Celadon.

As she was getting ready to leave the docking station for work that morning, she took another good look at everyone as they bustled about. All happy, content, and boring.

What were they so happy about? There was no joy here. No meaningful, lasting relationships. No happy birthdays or respectful funerals. There were no games, no art, no music.

No music.

Lizzy could not believe her ears as she sat hidden in the trees. After more than two hundred years, she was listening to music.

Someone was singing. It was a ghastly, discordant tune, really. But the voice behind it carried so much emotion.

It was far away and sounded as if it was coming from under the ground at times. The acoustics of the forest were deceitful. Lizzy couldn't make out any words, but she felt the delight, the carefree pleasure of the song.

Yes, just when she'd given up.

That morning she'd been pissed off. At everyone and everything.

She'd taken her travel pod and flown straight west with the intention of never stopping. She was going to see how far she could get, just because. What did she have to go back for? Nothing. She had nothing.

She'd been flying nonstop for half the day when she noticed the battery charge was at fifty percent. If she kept going, there really would be no turning back. Not on her own, anyhow.

That was also when she noticed the flash. It looked like the sun reflecting off a piece of metal.

No longer certain about flying past the point of no return, she lowered her pod near the mysterious sighting and shut it off. Every last one of the sensors had been lit up. Off course, battery warning, etc.

At least it would be a while before they got to her. In addition to the distance she'd traveled, she was no longer a priority on the list. It would be chalked up to typical Lizzy behavior. They wouldn't even be seeing any of the data until after her scheduled shift was over and it was transmitted to them.

Out of the pod, helmet off, the first thing she noticed was the air. It was thinner here. Easier to breathe.

The second thing was the singing.

She'd been listening to it for about ten minutes, afraid to move or breathe, when it suddenly stopped. She stayed where she was for another few minutes, waiting in hope of its return.

Out of patience, her curiosity compelled her forward to investigate.

She'd never been in a forest with trees so thick, and it wasn't long before she became completely disoriented.

The moss turned to tall grass, higher than her waist and difficult to move through, but Lizzy trudged on. Right into a swamp.

She grabbed at a tree branch overhead, only to have it break under her weight, landing her on her ass in the swamp. Up to her armpits in mud and water, she just sat there and laughed. They were going to have a blast reprimanding her for this one.

It was time to get back to her travel pod. She could mark the location and return another time.

Lizzy tapped her wrist monitor. Nothing. Just blackness, no matter how hard she pounded on it. She'd never had a problem with it before. It was organically powered. She was the battery.

Seeing that she wasn't going to get much dirtier, she crawled around in the muddy water, searching for the invisible bank. Her teeth were chattering by the time she found it and pulled herself up.

"Jason?" she called up to the sky. "I've got some free time if you want to stop by for a visit."

No, he'd been around just last year. He wouldn't be back for years if he stuck to his schedule. She didn't want to call any louder. She could only assume the rules were the same as when she'd been world-browsing in the In Between.

Each time she peeked in this world, it looked as if centuries had passed in her absence, when really it was only weeks in her time. If he was indeed hovering nearby, she hoped the time was flying by for him.

They were going to need to talk about where they would end up next. Wordless talk, of course. But there was definitely going to be some more thought put into picking a new life.

All right, she was chilled to the bone already, might as well get the call over with. Lizzy activated her earpiece and sent out the signal to the docking station.

Minutes passed, filled with more nothing. Not even static. What was going on? She pulled her soaking legs up to her chest and hugged herself, shaking as the cool wind found its way through the trees to her.

She was lost. There was no way she'd be able to find her way back to her pod. She had a hard enough time finding her way out of the damn water.

How long would it be before they sent someone to find her? Would they even be able to find her? It seemed as if she'd dropped off the face of the . . . Celadon.

Alone in the marsh, Lizzy did the only thing she could think of. She threw back her head and sang.

Chapter 63

Attending the wedding is out, yet I stay on. Mystery Pal has been making more frequent trips on her own. Each time she returns, her enthusiasm level is higher. I share in her excitement, but only to a point. It's not that I'm scared to leave. I know I'll be going soon, but there's still something left for me here. Something I need to do.

She's on another jaunt as I stroke the hair of my napping children. How am I supposed to leave them? I can't. It's impossible.

But really, when I think about it, I'm just happy to have these bits of time with them. I'm closer to them than I ever was in life, I love them with all my heart, yet . . .

Part of me is already leaving them. I have no delusions of staying here much longer. They will have their own lives to live, their own stories to tell. My story here is over. It's been over for a while.

Then why am I still here? What is that feeling? I've tried as hard as I can, wracking my brain, hoping to find the source. It's not just a hunch, not something I'm imagining. It's physical. As hard as my new world and my new life is pulling on me, there's an equal force holding me in place.

The people I care most about look like they're set. Everyone has recovered from the pox. Actually, Dean looks pretty good now. The illness must have shaved a solid twenty pounds off him. Shallow, maybe. But it's obvious he feels better. He's even taken to working out and watching what he eats.

They had the great debate about Dean quitting his stock boy job a week ago. The consensus was he should be concentrating on his last year of schooling and be spending more time at home with his family.

He was the only one against it, not wanting to live off my inheritances. But they were his and the children's now, soon to be Stacey's as well.

It was Aunt Robin who got the point across by starting to list everyone they'd lost. Life was short, and family was the most important thing.

She hadn't made it through the first dozen losses when they turned it right back on her, insisting she shouldn't have to be working at her age. A compromise was reached when she agreed to quit her job at the post office and accept their funding, so long as she could be their full-time nanny.

It's all coming together for them. As much as anyone can claim to believe money isn't everything, there's no denying the impact it has on Earth life. No, it's not the most important thing. There are plenty of people that are more than happy with little or none of it. But it sure can open doors.

Now that they've finally embraced their situation, the dreams are growing. I join Dean and Stacey in the living room where they're allowing themselves to give a voice to their desires, developing real plans.

"I still feel a bit guilty continuing on my way to be a psychiatrist," Stacey says. "Part of me wants to just give it up and stay at home with the children. They deserve a mother."

"You will be their mother," Dean assures her. "What they deserve is a family. A happy, supportive family. Your mother is going to be here to help – you know how much she loves them – and those kids are going to be as proud of you as I am."

"But what about having other children, growing our family? We'll have to put it on hold."

"Stacey, we'll figure it out. There's no rush. The most important thing is that we'll all be together. You can't ever feel bad for pursuing your goals, your dreams. Which reminds me of something I've been meaning to bring up for a while now. It's about my own ambitions."

"You've changed your mind about becoming a plumber?"

"No, I'll still follow through with that. I enjoy the work, the hands-on aspect of the job. But things that wouldn't have been feasible before are all of a sudden possible."

"Your writing? Oh, Dean! You're going to do it?"

"I was thinking about it. In fact, I've managed to get some words down. I don't know how good they are, but after I'm finished school and we get everything else settled, I think I'll go for it."

Stacey squeals and throws herself at him. Watch that soul, dear. It might still be a little battered.

"I always knew you'd find a way to make it happen. I can't wait to read your books!"

"Woah, it'll be a long time before that happens, if it does. But yeah, I'm excited to get started. First things first, I want to get the crisis center up and running. That will be my first creative project: naming it."

"How about The Amy Clarke-Grant Center for Mental Health Awareness and Suicide Prevention?"

"Uh, I think I'll go ahead and claim the creative rights around here." His laughter is cut short as he looks up in my direction.

"I just wish we could have had something like that before. A place that could have helped her."

"Me too." Stacey pulls her knees to her chest and looks up as well. "Even once we have it established, there are still going to be so many people who fall through the cracks. We're going to need an excellent PR team to make sure it fills its purpose and reaches out to as many people as it can."

"Absolutely. There'll be no skimping there."

Now that I approve of. Okay, not the temporary title. But maybe this was what I needed to see. Maybe I can go now?

Nope. Keep talking, guys.

"We're still on for looking at properties tomorrow?" Dean asks.

"Absolutely. The real estate agent will be here at noon. I love the idea of building on an acreage, but are you sure you don't want to stay in the city? What about winter, traveling on the highway?"

"I was thinking about that, too. Maybe we should limit our options to just a few miles out. It's not like we're buying a house, just the property. All we want is something quiet, with a big yard."

"It's going to need to be big to fit a house the size of the blueprints you were showing me. I still don't think we need a mansion like that."

"It's not a mansion, it's just a large home. We're planning on spending the rest of our lives there. Remember, our family may grow. And we'll always have plenty of space for our parents."

"You can put me down for one parent," Stacey grumbles.

"Sorry. You never know, he may come around yet. Oh, and don't forget the puppies."

"Yes! I've got to show you the ones I found at the shelter." Stacey jumps up to get her phone and scrolls through her pictures. "They're hypo-allergenic, and great with kids. These two aren't exactly puppies, but they're still young . . ."

I leave them to their dog-hunting and return to my children who are still fast asleep.

So there it is. Happy, healthy loved ones, a crisis center being set up in my memory to help the world, an upcoming wedding and new home for the new family.

Even Scott is continuing to do well. He's begun his classroom schooling, and the last time I checked on him he was still wandering around with his lists of apologies.

I was careful to tiptoe, so to speak, through my peeks into his life. We already said our goodbyes. There's no need for me to interfere any further.

This would be the best time for me to leave. But even after everything I just saw and heard, I can't ignore that annoying little itch in the back of my mind. I'm missing something.

I pull back from my children and let my mind go blank one more time. Show me the answer, Universe.

My view leaves the children's room and leads me . . .

Right into Aunt Robin's kitchen where she's making dinner, contentedly humming the tune of "Somewhere Over the Rainbow."

You're not really helping me here, Universe.

Chapter 64

Lizzy was on her fourth round of "Somewhere Over the Rainbow" (the parts she could remember after so long) when someone came up behind her and shoved a sack over her head.

The only thing she saw before it was tightened and her hands were secured was the color of the bag. Not white. A bright, emerald green.

She didn't put up a fight, didn't say a word. She just sat and listened.

People, at least three of them, were whispering to each other. Their voices were too low for her to make out what they were saying, but it sounded like two males and a female. They were definitely arguing about something. Probably her.

Then silence, followed by more footsteps arriving. Lizzy was too curious to be scared. The only thing she knew for sure was these were not people from the domes. Not her dome, anyway. The workers that came to fetch her when she ran amok certainly didn't operate like this.

The biggest giveaway was the sack. The colored sack.

They may very well be getting ready to club her over the head and dump her back into the water or commit any number of other atrocities. She didn't know, and she didn't care as much as she probably should.

There was nothing she could do but sit and wait.

"Who are you?" a male voice demanded from her left.

"Amelia – sorry, Elizabeth Masters."

"You don't even know your own name?"

"It's a long story. I'm from Dome 80."

"Why were you singing?"

That was a female voice.

"I heard someone else singing earlier, and I like to sing too."

263

"You said you're from the domes." The male had taken back control.

"You're not?"

"Never said that. People from the domes don't sing."

"Maybe some of them do."

"Look, lady – "

"I can't. My eyes are covered," she sang merrily.

More silence. They were probably wondering what was wrong with her. Hell, she wasn't sure herself. If they could only see the huge smile she was wearing underneath the sack.

A new voice rang out loud and clear. An authoritative voice.

"How did you end up here? This is a dead zone for your technologies."

"We must be close to the edge of it because my travel pod is parked not that far away. I think. Needless to say, I got a bit turned around."

They weren't whispering anymore, but now Lizzy couldn't make out a word over all the yelling.

"Stop!" The newest voice commanded. "You brought a travel pod? Where did you leave it?"

"I told you, I'm lost. I don't know."

"We have to find it before it's spotted. I want the five of you to head east to the edge of the dead zone. Spread out when you get there, and don't come back until you've located and taken care of it."

"Um, am I staying here then?" Lizzy asked through the sack.

"I don't know what we're going to do with you."

"I'm okay with talking. I haven't had anyone to talk to in ages."

"You're not normal, are you?"

Lizzy couldn't help but laugh. "I will take that as a compliment, sir."

Chapter 65

I know, I know.

I allow Mystery Pal to guide me to our spot. I've been glued to that doorway for days, haunting Aunt Robin.

There's nothing wrong with her. As far as I can tell, there's nothing wrong with anyone. Aunt Robin is happy, spending the days with my kids while Dean and Stacey are in school. She gets along well with Dean's parents, who are frequent visitors. Susan comes by often, and they've done nothing but live, laugh, and be merry.

Maybe I got the hint from the universe wrong. Maybe it was just trying to shove me on my way. Maybe there's no reason for me to stay.

Except I know there is. And I know it has something to do with Aunt Robin.

Mystery Pal and I huddle close together, sharing our energy. I was so obsessed with my door I hadn't realized how low I was running. I also hadn't been paying attention to the tug from our new world. It's massive, now that I'm out here away from my old one.

Think, think, think: what am I missing? Maybe Aunt Robin's going to be next in line for a mystery illness like the pox. Maybe a heart attack or a car crash. What am I supposed to do about any of that? Sit around jabbing at her soul like I had with Dean? No. I'm sure Dean would have been fine without my "help."

Maybe better off. I still think his inner aura looks slightly mashed.

The more energy that flows between us, the clearer my mind becomes.

I'll just have to trust in the fact I'll know what to do when the time comes. If I have to go to my new life, I'll go. But until then . . .

Back to it. Mystery Pal doesn't move, nor does she seem surprised as I take off back to Earth. I'm pretty sure she's eye rolling, though.

***

Holy crap.

It must be the weekend. Dean and Stacey are both at home, positioned on either side of the living room watching my kid take his first steps.

"That's it, Darren! You're walking! Stacey, are you getting the video?"

She nods behind the phone that's trained on Dean and Darren. Diedre is sitting to the side, taking it all in.

"Mom!" Darren yells, tumbling the last few feet into Dean's arms.

"Oh, that was perfect." Stacey puts down the phone and collects Diedre to join in the group hug, which ends up turning into a tickle fight.

Why do I feel like an intruder here?

Because this isn't my family anymore.

I leave them to roll around on the floor, their laughter following me as I search out Aunt Robin.

She's at her own apartment. Still in her housecoat, curled up in the living room chair, she's reading a book with a steaming cup of tea sitting beside her. The epitome of contentment.

Inner aura, solid. Outer aura, check. Happy, relaxed, doesn't have a care in the world.

Well, I'm not relaxed. I'm not happy. And I do have a care in this world. I just can't figure out what it is.

Try again, Amy. Don't think, just feel.

I let my consciousness drift the best I can, release any resistance I may have, and . . .

Nothing. I'm still watching Aunt Robin sip her tea and turn the pages of her book.

This is driving me nuts.

I'm bored, and a pretty skilled haunter. I might as well have a little fun while I wait.

Whoops. Maybe not so skilled after all. I only meant to flip the page of her book, kind of give her a ghostly hello. Instead, I shattered her teacup.

She jumps up as if she's been burned, even though the cup cracked on the table. Its scalding contents are pouring onto the floor, not her.

"What in the world?"

My thoughts exactly.

She hurries off to the kitchen to get something to soak up the liquid. Of course, I go with her. Paper towel for the tea and a trash bag for the glass gathered, we return to the living room.

Whoops again. That was a nice throw rug. Sorry, Aunt Robin.

"Ouch."

Oh my God, is this how it's going to go down? She pricks herself with a piece of broken teacup, develops an infection, and –

Yeah, I'm going to head back to my kids. I'm losing my marbles.

Darren is pulling himself up by the edge the coffee table, eager to keep walking now that he's had a taste of it.

"Hang on, pal. Let's give Diedre a chance," Dean tells him.

Stacey moves over to Darren, who looks like he's about to wind up and whack her. That's all the motivation Diedre needs to push away from Dean and take her first clumsy strides toward her brother.

Dean's right behind her and helps her the rest of the way when she loses her footing.

Another family celebration. They really like to roll around on the floor.

Just watching this is making me tired. All of it is making me tired. Maybe I should go back for some more energy replenishment with Mystery Pal.

In a minute. There's something else I need to try first.

There we go, a nice big stack of bridal magazines on the other side of the room, away from the cuddle-fest.

Yeah, I thought that might happen.

My attempt to nudge the stack off the table ends up pushing the loveseat a foot away from the wall, and not gently, either.

The family doesn't notice, and I'm definitely out of here.

It's not just energy drain. I've lost my control.

Chapter 66

After another round of incomprehensible muttering, Lizzy was ordered to stand up. She did so gladly. She'd been sitting in the swamp with the bag over her head for what must have been hours.

"Where are we going?" she asked, not expecting an answer.

She didn't get one, unless you counted the poke in the back prompting her to move forward.

She followed this wordless instruction just as happily. The hiking was exactly what she needed to warm up.

Someone noticed her shivering while she was sitting on the bank and had draped a blanket or something around her shoulders. Probably not a white one. She amused herself for the longest time, running through the images of what it might look like, imagining what color it might be.

The best part was the smell. A floral scent, laced with something like vanilla. No perfumes on Celadon.

Not until today, that is.

Weird, how they stopped every so often to spin her around.

She didn't understand the need to disorient her further. She was as lost as she was going to get when they found her.

And really, she assumed they were going to kill her.

There was no disguising the downward slope they took next. The air became warmer, and another scent grew stronger.

Food. Not nourishment packs. There were only about a dozen different flavors of those, and they all had the underlying stench of plastic.

This smelled like Earth food. Stew. Homemade bread. Real food.

Her stomach growled like it had never growled in this world. Even though she was dehydrated, her mouth watered.

She was hoping like mad they were going to feed her before they whacked her. Oh, maybe they would have wine or beer!

A tug on her bound arms indicated it was time to stop.

The group paused for another whispering session, but there was something else to be heard. Music.

The faint melody was cut off as someone clamped their hands over her ears and already covered head.

Her time must be up. Strange, how her last thoughts were of how badly she wanted to eat and drink, instead of how she would miss anyone from this world.

A rush of warmer air came from in front of her. Were they going to burn her at the stake?

Lizzy finally started to struggle as the adrenaline coursed through her veins. More sets of hands took hold of her and she fought all the harder.

Someone pushed her up against something solid and she was held in place there, ears still covered. Maybe the end room wouldn't have been so bad after all.

She was preparing to call Jason, really call him, to come be with her while she made the journey to join him. Just as she was about to holler his name, the hands released her.

Before she could decide whether to run away from the heat or take a kick at someone, she was pushed forward again.

And halted. There was a low rumbling and the ground vibrated beneath her.

The sack was removed and the hands released her, leaving her free to walk through the opening in the rock.

She was in a cave. An actual cave with torches on the walls.

Standing in the middle of the large circular room with tunnels branching off it, her legs finally went limp. The hands reappeared to catch her as she sank to the ground.

She couldn't believe her eyes. There were wooden tables, a cauldron over a fire, crude dishes, artwork. The walls were covered in paintings, tapestries, colors.

Of course, the most astounding sight of all was the people. Dozens of them, staring wide-eyed at her in her mud-covered white jumpsuit.

Their clothes didn't look all that much cleaner, but they were beautiful. The garments were all shades of browns, greens, pinks, and blues, and they had patterns. The people wore scarves, hair ribbons, and strands of beads around their necks.

Their skin was tanned and their hair long, even the men's.

They were breathtaking. And they were confused.

The expressions on their faces would be enough to indicate this, but their auras provided even more insight.

Every last outer aura in the room was flickering and jumping from one color to the next. She did her best to ignore them and compose herself.

Whatever happened to her next, this was what she'd been looking for all these years. Something else. Real people. A real way of living.

She struggled to get to her feet with her arms still behind her, aided again by the hands.

Smiling, she said, "Hi, I'm Lizzy. I'd shake your hand but, you know."

Despite the tension in the room, and the uncertainty of everything, they all laughed. Herself included. More music to her ears.

Chapter 67

I feel as if I'm fading away.

The call from my next world is constant and growing stronger by the day.

The sense of urgency and doom coming from Earth is just as strong, increasing at the same rate.

Mystery Pal is worried. She can tell there's something going on in my old world, and we spend half our time energy-sharing. She's giving it her all too. I'm taking more in than I'm putting out.

The other half of my time is spent practice-haunting.

I try to be careful, but being as how Aunt Robin is caring for my kids most days, she's the one who usually has to bear the brunt of my blunders. She's been good and spooked on more than one occasion.

Just yesterday, my attempt at rearranging the flower vase resulted in a pillow flying across the room and whacking her in the back of her head. At least it wasn't the other way around.

Never mind my accuracy being gone, everything I do has too much power behind it. My former nudges are now eruptions.

I dropped in on Scott a few times to do some training there, but that went even worse. The unintended effects were only amplified around him.

He wasn't necessarily spooked, but he was worried. He asked more than once if I was okay. I didn't dare try responding with an assurance. He's doing so well despite my unnerving interruptions. No way am I going to risk blowing up my former nemesis turned friend.

No, Aunt Robin will have to bear with me while I do my drills around her. She is the reason I'm doing it, after all. I think.

I also think the presence of my children dampens the severity of my power. Part of me is able to hold back the full magnitude of it for their safety. Cheers to belated maternal bonding.

***

Ready to get back at it today, the first thing I notice is the shiny cross hanging on the wall in Dean's apartment.

Yeah, I'm pretty sure that was put there for me.

Aunt Robin has the kids' playpen in the kitchen, where she's cutting vegetables for a salad.

Chop, chop, chop. The knife gets washed and put back in the block while she adds the veggies to the bowl and washes the next batch.

We'll go ahead and cancel practice for today. Knives, babies, creeped out aunt. Not an ideal arena.

I might as well go back and see if we can pump some more healing energy into me.

But wait, my sight is being directed elsewhere. Not far, just outside the building. Scott is coming up the walkway. Oh, he's probably still trying to deliver that apology.

Why isn't he in school?

Holy shit. Never mind that. Why is Uncle Ian already standing at the doors by the keypad as he arrives?

What in the world could these two have in common? Evil uncle and previously, but now reformed, crappy ex-boyfriend. They'd never met, as far as I knew.

I've never seen Uncle Ian's outer aura look so bland. Not bland, exactly. It's still a fiery red, but it's not behaving like it normally does, swirling and shooting sparks. It sits around him like a puddle of blood.

Wait, what did I miss while I was studying his aura?

Scott has stopped at the bottom of the three steps leading up to the doors. His outer aura is a flashing a neon sign of fear. Uncle Ian hasn't noticed him. Scott slips around the stairs to hide behind a tree, his back pressed to the wall of the building.

They're not together after all.

But what did he see to make him retreat and feel it necessary to hide?

Uncle Ian turns to scan the street. Satisfied he's alone at the entrance, he swipes his hand over almost all of the call buttons.

Voices are talking over each other.

"Who's there?" "Yes?" "Hello?"

Scott takes out his phone and dials 9-1, watching and waiting to dial the last 1.

Of course, one or more people end up simply pressing the button to unlock the doors, without bothering to find out who it is.

Uncle Ian seizes the door handle and lets himself in.

Scott is out of the bushes in a flash, racing up the steps to grab the door just before it falls shut.

He dials the last 1.

Chapter 68

Lizzy was in heaven. No, she hadn't died. Not yet.

She was basking in a warm bath, eyeing the outfit that had been laid out for her.

The clothing wouldn't have been considered at all desirable back on Earth. The pair of ratty grey slacks and light-blue long-sleeved shirt, along with a blue and yellow checkered shawl, would be something you might find at a second-hand store. In the 1960s.

No underwear, no shoes, but the fuzzy blue socks and matching hair ribbon were the things she was looking forward to the most.

The simple pleasures. When was the last time she'd felt anything but synthetic spandex or functional foam coverings on her skin?

Not in this life.

She wanted nothing more than to sink deeper into the tub and just fall asleep, but she'd already been lounging for too long.

She got out and dried herself. Just coming across this green towel alone would have made her day.

She dressed as quickly as she could, delighting in the texture and warmth of the garments.

After hanging the exquisite towel on a peg, she exited through the opening in the rock and made her way through the tunnels back to the main room.

They were already at work preparing the next meal. Most of the faces turned to smile at her, and a few people greeted her by name. She was about to grab an apron and pitch in, when the sight of her laundered jumpsuit and clean sneakers sitting on a chair by the table stopped her in her tracks.

She had a decision to make. And she needed to make it soon.

Turning away from the happy chatter and camaraderie around the food, she walked back to the table and picked up her jumpsuit. She ran her fingers over the cold, white material, as she thought about the offer that had been presented to her only an hour ago.

The team that went out to locate and take care of her travel pod had located it. But they hadn't destroyed it.

The bearded man who had been in charge of ordering her and everyone else about earlier was, in fact, in charge.

Mario appeared to be a terrifying beast at first sight. His height, his muscular body, his thick beard, and black eyes hidden beneath bushy brows, did not represent approachability.

Until he smiled. Those black eyes lit up with compassion, kindness. They felt like home.

His gruff voice remained, but his words erased her fears.

Only one family in the settlement had come from the domes. Eric, Mario's great-great-great-grandfather, along with his wife and a handful of orphaned children. Everyone else had been born here.

As far as they knew, they were the only ones who'd ever escaped the domes, and their reasonings and intentions were exactly as Lizzy's had been.

They wanted to live free, and on their own terms.

Eric would have been about Lizzy's age, had he stayed in the domes. But he didn't live to be half as old as she. Without the waves and lasers, the average life expectancy out here was about eighty years. Not one of these citizens believed it wasn't worth the price.

She looked around the room again at the aging people. The oldest ones had wrinkles and infirmities that caused them to hunch over, rubbing their aches and pains as they worked. But they didn't complain. They were nothing but happy. Real happiness, not robo-happiness.

The only complaints about being tired and sore were voiced with laughter and acceptance. They were happy to be growing old, and thankful to be growing old together.

Eric worked for the travel-tech department before leaving the dome. He left handwritten documents of his experience of dome-life behind for his new family.

He also left a non-trackable flashpad, containing the most crucial of technical skills they would need to ensure their security out here. Stored in one of the recesses of the mountain was his original travel pod, which each generation studied to learn its ways inside and out.

The documents were the textbooks of the tribe, to be passed on from generation to generation. And while they were not printed and bound, Lizzy had been more than thrilled to lay eyes on the stacks of handwritten stories and lessons. Books, at long last.

The other lessons were learned on the flashpad, which had to be taken outside of the dead zone to operate. Mario's ancestors diligently passed on Eric's knowledge through the ages. They were capable of creating this dead zone where dome technology was unable to function. It didn't extend much higher than the treetops, so travel pods flying over would be unaware of it.

They also knew how to erase, override, and overwrite travel pod data.

Lizzy dropped her jumpsuit, spinning around as Mario cleared his throat.

He didn't have to say anything; she knew it was time to decide. It was past time. The longer she waited, the more danger she was putting them all in.

Her own travel pod sat waiting at the edge of the dead zone. It wouldn't be long before her shift was over. Her data would be summoned, and someone would be sent to retrieve the pod and her.

Despite having seen them and learning something about where they came from and their culture, they were willing to let her go. Their first visitor from the domes, they'd been rightly scared and confused about how to handle the situation.

But there wasn't a soul in the group that would actually consider killing her.

They were kind and peaceful humans. Apart from risking their lives by letting this stranger go (and she was sure she presented as strange, even to people much more like herself) they presented her with an additional consideration. One that could threaten their very lives and civilization. One that she was making riskier the longer she stood there thinking.

They could reprogram her travel pod with false back-data and send it to fly away on its own. They were offering her a life here.

A different, better life. But a shorter one.

At Lizzy's age, without wave therapy and laser treatments, she was long past her expiration date. She would age rapidly, and they had no high-tech pain solutions.

There was no end room here. Only basic herbal and palliative care when the time came.

Lizzy had wasted enough time thinking things through. What other answer could she possibly give?

"I want to stay."

Mario beamed, his black eyes sparkling with happiness. Then he was all business, barking out orders at the men to finish the job of reprogramming and disposing of her travel pod.

As the others dragged the boulder-like door of the cave open, he turned once more to her.

"You are certain?"

Her smile was the only answer he needed.

Chapter 69

No.

Scott stands frozen in the lobby of Dean's apartment, his 9-1-1 call abandoned.

Waiting out in the cold rain, preparing to dial the final digit, his phone had died. Maybe it hadn't been fully charged. Maybe the elements outside sucked the last of the life from it. Hell, maybe it was me. I may never know.

I don't need to. What I need is to find out what he saw to prompt him to try calling for help in the first place.

Uncle Ian has already entered the elevator, but I can't follow him.

I pop back and forth between Aunt Robin and her meticulous salad making, and Scott sweating bullets in the lobby.

Shit. He keeps looking from one set of doors to the other, probably trying to decide whether to go for help or follow the man.

I know which way I'm going.

Aunt Robin is picking up the twins from their playpen in the kitchen.

Dammit. The door isn't locked. Didn't she just finish giving Stacey crap for lax security? Of course, now she's also left the knife on the counter. Just leave me here so I can try locking it.

Through the living room and down the short hall we go. She puts the sleepy kids in their crib and tucks them in.

It's only Uncle Ian. Maybe he's coming to tell her he's suing her again.

She waits in the doorway to see if they'll stay asleep or need to be settled.

What did Scott see?

Diedre and Darren are out cold. She closes the door part way and takes the baby monitor from the living room back to the kitchen.

Uncle Ian is sitting at the table waiting for her.

"Holy — Ian!" Aunt Robin stops dead in the doorway, clutching the monitor to her chest. "How did you get in here?"

He points at the door.

Aunt Robin's eyes flick from the closed but still unlocked door to him, and back to the door.

He produces a gun and a letter from his coat pocket and lays them on the table.

"Happy Anniversary. Come, sit. We have so much to talk about."

Chapter 70

It was well after sunset. The group of men who set out to scrub and dispose of Lizzy's travel pod had yet to return.

She was perched on a ledge high above the mountain the tribe lived under, her shawl wrapped tightly around her, as all the worst-case scenarios flashed through her mind.

What if they hadn't been able to overwrite the data? Her shift had ended hours ago. If they hadn't done at least that much by now, workers from the dome would be on their way to get her. Instead of her, they'd find them.

Oh, God. They'd find them, and then they would find the dead zone, and eventually the rest of the tribe. What had she done? She couldn't live with herself if her selfish decision resulted in the downfall of the only real people she'd come across in this world.

Lizzy was utterly convinced Maria herself would be leading the search and capture party dedicated to finding her when the torches finally appeared.

She spit out one of the fingernails she'd gnawed off and scrambled down the side of the rocky cliff.

"Did you get rid of it?"

Mario nodded and stepped to the side, allowing the others to open the boulder-door and enter first.

"It was a bit trickier than I expected, but we got your data erased and entered the false history easily enough. Getting it to fly on its own was what took so long."

"Here, let me take something."

Lizzy lifted the heavy sack filled with blueprints and tools off his arm so he could better hold the torch.

"Thanks. By the way, you're currently continuing on your trip to the west, and you have no intention of stopping anytime soon."

His grin faltered when she didn't respond.

"Are you sorry you chose to stay? I'm afraid there's nothing we can do about it now."

"Oh, no. I was just wishing I found you, this place, earlier."

"Better late than never. Let's go inside."

Smiles back on, they entered the cave where the final preparations were being made for the evening meal.

Lizzy's smile widened at the sight of her new family, singing and laughing and setting the table together. This was living. This was real.

Just hours before, she was certain she was going to be slaughtered by these people. Now, she walked over to them with a warmth in her heart she hadn't felt for centuries. Someone handed her a bowl, which she took over to the dining table.

There were quite a few curious looks still being directed her way, but there was no malice, no suspicion in them. No doubt they'd never seen a two-hundred-year-old person before. Hell, they'd never seen anyone from the domes.

As with the last meal she'd taken there, Mario proposed the toast before they dug in.

"To Lizzy, our dome refugee, our friend, and now part of our family."

All glasses were raised, including hers. There were cheers and welcomes, thumbs up and applause.

"We look forward to hearing all about dome life and learning more about you. Think you'd be up to leading storytelling this evening?"

The strong brew came flying out of Lizzy's mouth and nose.

"I'm so sorry," she choked, her smile as big as it could get. "I would be honored to lead the storytelling. It's just, I've got a lot more than dome stories to share with you."

Chapter 71

Aunt Robin seats herself in the chair farthest away from her husband and the weapon, closer to the living room and my children that lie sleeping beyond it.

Dammit. I can't trust my wonky aim to send the gun flying, but it's so tempting. He's not even holding it.

Scott. Where's Scott?

Woah. He's in the hall, right on the other side of the door, ear pressed against it.

I try tapping him on the shoulder and a painting flies off the wall, whacking him in the back.

He jumps away from the door, looks down at the picture on the ground, and then up to me.

"Amy?" he whispers.

Good thing I'd left the gun alone. But now that I have his attention, I don't know what to do with it. I can't talk to him, and I can't seem to do anything else without chaos ensuing.

He smiles and leans his head against the door.

Crap. I shouldn't have done anything. He probably feels like his guardian angel is here to protect him in his time of need.

Cancel, redact, undo! No can do.

Back to the kitchen.

Aunt Robin sits posture perfect, her face as blank as Uncle Ian's. Her aura isn't blank. It's freaking right out.

"I'm going to guess you haven't come to deliver the signed divorce papers."

Her voice doesn't reveal her fear. The only physical sign of nerves is shown by how tightly she clutches the baby monitor.

If Uncle Ian notices, I can't tell. His outer aura hasn't changed since I saw him downstairs. It's still creepily calm, settled.

"No. I believe you know there will be no divorce."

283

Aunt Robin says nothing.

"You shouldn't have pulled that move with the courts."

"I only told the truth. You gave me no other option."

"I gave you plenty of other options. You could have come home. You could have apologized for running out on me and breaking our holy bond. You could have not accused me of abuse."

Aunt Robin's face is red now. She opens her mouth, then closes it, holding the monitor even tighter.

Instead of the outburst I was expecting, she speaks in a low and even tone.

"You know what I said was true. I was willing to walk away. I would have let all the years of verbal and physical mistreatments remain forever buried, if you hadn't pushed me with that lawsuit."

"Verbal and physical mistreatments? Do you realize how hard I tried to keep you in line all those years, how much of a handful you were? You're lucky you got off so easily. The Lord will be the keeper of you, and He will judge you for your sins from now on."

His hand inches toward the gun.

"There's no one else around, Ian. No need to put on your act."

"It's not an act." His hand pauses mid-creep. "It used to be. I used to care what other people thought, more than the Lord or my own salvation. That has since changed. My eyes have been opened. I know what I need to do."

His hand completes the trip and sits atop the gun.

"How did you find me here?"

His other hand comes up and he pushes the envelope across the table to her.

The wedding invitation Stacey had sent at the last minute, complete with return address, of course.

"Your other daughter told me you were living off the dead girl's money, posing as a nursemaid for her children.

You don't seem to spend much time at your own place, and I must say the security is a bit tighter there."

Aunt Robin's eyes fill with tears as she fingers the envelope.

"Finding the address would have been easy enough, but thanks to that thoughtful invitation, there was no need."

Aunt Robin keeps her voice low, although it's no longer steady. Her lips tremble and tears fall from her eyes as she begins her final plea.

"The children." She holds out the monitor. "I ask you not to harm these innocent children."

"I have no interest in them. I'm here for you."

She tears her eyes from the envelope to look into his.

"You were so worried about what people would think when it was just a matter of divorce and possible abuse. What do you think will happen when everyone finds out you murdered your wife?"

"I don't know. And I won't know. I told you, you're not going anywhere without me."

Chapter 72

"Grandma Lizzy?"

"Hmm? Oh, Destiny. What can I do for you?"

Lizzy put down her pencil and paper and turned to the girl.

"Nothing. Here."

"A rose." She closed her eyes and breathed in the delightful fragrance. "How did you know it was my favorite flower?"

The young girl climbed carefully onto her lap, having been warned about Grandma Lizzy's old bones.

"It's most people's favorite. I like that you call it a rose."

"Well, thank you for giving it to me."

She put her arm around Destiny and turned back to her writing.

She'd been known as Grandma Lizzy ever since the first week of coming to live with the tribe.

A lot of things happened that week. She noticed her first wrinkles. Her light grey hair, which had been practically white, grew dark. Her joints ached, her head ached, every last bit of her ached. And she loved it.

"Grandma Lizzy?"

"Yes, dear?"

"Would you tell me a story?"

She laughed and abandoned her papers. "Of course. Which one would you like to hear?"

"The one about little Amy, please."

After telling the people all about her dome life, she went ahead and told them all the rest. She told them about her previous life, about the auras she saw, even the stories she wrote in her past life as an author.

Needless to say, she dominated the nightly storytelling hour. And funnily enough, no one threatened to lock her up.

She also found a place in the children's education system. For the past eight years, she'd been teaching creative writing. More than a few adults attended the lessons along with the younger students.

Destiny had heard all of her stories more than once, but she clung to every word as she retold the tale of four-year-old Amy sitting on the floor by her mother's writing desk with a pencil and paper of her own.

"You missed a part."

"I did? Which one?"

"The part where you teach her how to write like you."

"Oh, I didn't have to teach her much. She was very smart and learned mostly by watching what I did."

"Do you think I'm smart enough to write like you?"

"Absolutely. Now, shouldn't you be getting off to bed?"

"Yes, Grandma Lizzy."

Destiny kissed her on the cheek before climbing off her lap.

After she left, Lizzy sat holding the rose, too tired to return to her work.

The last eight years here had gone by faster than the two centuries she spent in the dome. And they were a thousand times more rewarding.

She had no regrets as she tidied up her desk and prepared for bed.

Jason.

"Bet you didn't expect to find me here, did you?"

She could feel his surprise and happiness through the veil that separated them. The veil that was growing thin.

"It won't be long now. We'll be together again soon."

Lizzy put the rose in her water glass on her bedside table.

"Maybe sooner than I thought." She sat on the bed and put a hand over her fluttering heart.

"No more mistakes," she warned him. "Next time, we do this together."

Jason was so close, in the very room with her, as she pulled back the covers and crawled into bed.

"I often wonder about Amy. I bet she's lived a life or two without us by now."

Lizzy slipped a letter out of her nightstand and placed it beside the rose.

"I think about Henry as well. I hope he's found a better place. I know I did. These last few years with these people made the whole thing worth it. I'm so thankful I was able to become a part of this family and make an impact.

"To think, because of me they'll continue to add stories, even books, to their arts."

She closed her eyes and felt his arms around her.

"Thanks for coming. I know how long you've been waiting."

Chapter 73

"Ian, you don't want to do this. You know it's not God's will."

He laughs a dry laugh and shakes his head as he flicks off the safety. Aunt Robin leaps from her chair and so does he, positioning himself between her and the front door.

"Now you want to talk about God, do you? It's too late for that."

"Relax, I wasn't going to run. You just scared me."

Aunt Robin remains standing in the entry to the living room, holding the monitor. Behind Uncle Ian, the doorknob turns.

"What is it that you want? Whatever it is, I'll give it to you."

"I want two things."

"Tell me and I'll do them."

The door is inching open.

"First, I want an apology."

"Of course, I'm sorry."

"What are you sorry for?"

"Everything. I'm sorry for leaving you and betraying your trust."

Aunt Robin's eyes widen as she notices the moving door. She forces them back to her husband and keeps talking.

"I'll come home. I was wrong. I'll be a better wife and mother to our children instead of these ones."

She places the baby monitor on the chair and takes a step toward him.

He brings up the gun and aims it at her.

"Ian, I said I'll come home!"

"I heard you. That wasn't the other thing I want."

Scott's head pokes around the door.

"What is the other thing? I told you I'll do it."

"I want you to die."

Time's up. I summon all my energy and direct it at Uncle Ian.

He remains unscathed, but the rest of the kitchen doesn't do so well. The counter clears itself in an explosion of dishes, salad bits, knives, and the cat-shaped cookie jar.

It's the cookie jar that lands closest to him, smashing at his feet. That's where his attention is focused when Scott leaps through the air and tackles him.

Aunt Robin screams and backs around the corner into the living room as the kids begin to wail.

Scott clings to Uncle Ian piggyback-style with one arm, using his other to dig his fingers into his eyes.

Uncle Ian flails and swats blindly as he discharges the firearm.

Aunt Robin is crouched behind the wall that separates them, screaming into the phone.

"I need the police. I think someone's been shot and he still has a gun."

She drops the phone and peeks her head around the corner.

No one's been shot, but she's right about the gun. He fires again, this time hitting the ceiling, instead of the door where the first shot had gone.

His angry roar is as loud as the gunshots and must be audible throughout the building. Aunt Robin ducks back behind the wall as Scott digs his fingers in deeper.

The hand holding the gun comes back and finds the side of Scott's head. Stunned, he slips off Uncle Ian onto the floor.

Uncle Ian holds his head in his hands and continues to bellow.

"Robin!"

He fires another blind shot that zings into the living room, ricocheting off the stone fireplace and landing near Aunt Robin.

I take another swipe at him as he dabs at his eyes, trying to regain his vision.

Shit.

A chair shoots away from the table, knocking him in the gut.

He drops the gun but topples over and lands right on top of Scott.

Uncle Ian grabs hold of his neck. He's going to choke him to death.

I pause in mid-attack as Aunt Robin appears and kicks him in the side.

He rolls off Scott and is about to jump up but stops as Aunt Robin presses the gun to his forehead.

Scott scrambles out of his reach and slumps against the counter, dazed.

Uncle Ian presses up against the gun.

"You won't shoot me."

"I will."

Calling her bluff, his hand springs up from his side and reclaims the gun. She cries out and backs away toward the living room.

He fumbles to turn the gun around, squinting through his damaged eyes.

On hands and knees, he crawls after Aunt Robin, who has disappeared around the corner.

He raises the gun. There will be no missing this time. She's crouched behind the wall, just feet away.

The gun is pointed right at her. What am I supposed to do?

Nothing. His arm goes limp, blood splattering all over Aunt Robin and the wall. Scott kicks the gun behind him into the kitchen and sits atop the howling man, blood-drenched knife poised above his heart.

"Move and you're dead."

Chapter 74

Uncle Ian obeys the no moving order, except for his mouth.

My goodness, I had no idea he knew so many curse words. Just a few years ago, he was admonishing my dad for saying the word hell in his home.

It turns out some clawed-up eyes and a knife through the arm can motivate a person to blaspheme everything and everyone they've ever heard of.

Finally, the police arrive. Guns drawn, they enter from the kitchen. With the limited information Aunt Robin provided over the phone, they assess the situation and point their weapons at Scott.

"Put down the knife!"

He does, and a police officer kicks it into the kitchen.

"It's not him, it's the fat guy under him," Aunt Robin squeaks from her corner.

A gun is trained on her as one of the cops notices her.

"Come out of the corner and get on the ground!"

She does, crawling away from the two men toward the children's room.

"Who's in there?"

"Just babies."

A policewoman begins to frisk Aunt Robin, who is lying prone on the ground with her hands behind her head.

Scott is also face down being searched as they approach the blood fountain that is Uncle Ian.

"Where's the gun?"

"In the kitchen," Aunt Robin tells them.

"Are there any other weapons?"

"No. I mean, I don't think so. I only saw the gun. He might have more in his jacket. Not the skinny one, the fat one," she reminds them.

"Who called 9-1-1?"

"I did. This is my home."

The woman officer speaks into the radio clipped to her vest. "Send up the paramedics." She steps back from Aunt Robin. "You can get up."

Aunt Robin gets to her feet and is led over to the other side of the room by the window.

"What's your name?"

"Robin Wilson. That's my ex-husband. Well, soon to be." She points at Uncle Ian, still cursing and muttering as another officer tries to stop the bleeding from his arm. *"He showed up here with the gun, and said he was going to kill me and then himself."*

"His name?"

"Ian King." She spits out the name like a curse.

"Who's the kid?"

Aunt Robin looks at Scott. The paramedics have arrived and are splitting up to tend to Scott's head and Uncle Ian's arm.

"I honestly don't know."

Cripes. Would someone please cuff the bad guy, tend to my screaming kids, and give Scott a raise already?

***

Mystery Pal yanks me back to the In Between. Is it time to go?

Oh, Mom!

There are so many lights bouncing around, but I fly straight to her.

Everything ceases to exist. Thoughts of my imminent next life, my kids, what just happened down there, the very In Between itself. They all disappear as my mom wraps her soul around mine.

I see her as she used to be on Earth, I smell her, I feel her. I never thought we'd meet again before I had to go.

As we separate, I'm reluctant to let go entirely. This is my mom. I lost her twice, I mourned, I said my goodbyes. But she's here. She's back.

So is Dad. He joins in the group hug.

Who's the other dude with them? He looks kind of like dad, aura-wise. Oh, that's Mom's kid from the other world, Henry.

Mom breaks from our trio and goes to embrace Mystery Pal. This is one messed-up family reunion. I might as well go over and meet the new guy.

Yeah, it's kind of awkward, but he's definitely part of our pack.

I grab him, encouraging him to come with me, and float back to the edge of the action. What a scene. The love, the joy, the connections. How different, and yet the same as the interactions we have in life. If I could have seen something like this dazzling light show when I was alive, I doubt it would have made any sense.

Right here, right now, it's the only thing that does.

Mom hasn't had her fill of me (can't say I have either) and whisks me back into the melee.

Once the festivities settle, I become aware of the pull coming from my new world. Mystery Pal and I are both drifting that way.

But Mom is at the door to Earth. Can she see my kids?

Mystery Pal is practically foot-tapping already, but I need just one more mom-hug.

Actually, make that three.

Chapter 75

Mom is with me as I watch Darren and Diedre slumber. I don't think she can see them, but she can feel my love. And my pain. She presses close to me, with Mystery Pal on the other side. Dad is there behind us.

There will be no last caress. I haven't regained control, and have no desire to blow up my children.

I leave them in the makeshift pillow-crib in Aunt Robin's room and follow the voices out to the kitchen. Must be too messy back at Dean's place. Uncle Ian sure had spouted a lot of blood.

Dean, Stacey, Aunt Robin, and Scott are clearing the table after a late meal. Now, there's a scene I never thought I'd see.

"Thanks again for inviting me. I should be going."

"Oh no, we're not finished here yet."

Dean takes Scott's coat from him and hangs it on the back of a chair.

"Have a seat."

They all sit around the table, and Dean produces a check from his pocket.

"I told you, I'm not taking your money."

"Scott, you saved my life." Aunt Robin takes the check and pushes it closer to him.

"I didn't do it so you would pay me. I was only there to apologize for what I did before."

"And we forgave you. It wasn't just my mom you saved; you protected our children as well." Stacey smiles and gives the check another nudge.

Scott hesitates. I would too. That check is for ten thousand dollars.

"No. I just did what was right. And I'm going to keep doing what's right. I'm going to make something of myself, and I'm going to make Amy proud."

"And you know Amy would want you to have this to help you on your way. It was hers." Dean pushes the check all the way to the edge of the table.

Scott looks to the ceiling. "Ames?"

Risky, but all eyes are looking up at me now.

I tap the back of Scott's chair.

The floor in the kitchen shakes, and he and the chair lift ever so slightly off the ground.

The chair lands safely back on its legs, and the check flutters onto Scott's lap.

Okay, that was worth it.

The room is dead silent as they all sit staring at Scott and the check.

Dean is the first to start laughing. It's contagious. They laugh until they cry, and then some.

"See," Dean says between his howls, "Amy has spoken."

Yes, I have.

***

Okay, guys. This is it.

Darren and Diedre are stirring, but their eyes are still closed as they suck on each other's thumbs.

I wish I could hold you one more time. I wish I didn't have to go, but I do. I'm sorry I wasn't strong enough to be your mom. I can only hope you'll have a good life, and be everything I couldn't be.

Take care of each other, and your mom and dad. Always remember to be kind. Not just to your family, but to everyone. The weird kid in school, the person with the angry face who's really just sad. And know I love you.

You're going to have a beautiful home and all the opportunities in the world, but none of that matters without love and kindness.

They open their eyes as one, focusing directly on me. Can they see me?

296

Diedre coos and Darren points. I put all the love of that last hug I can't give them into my smile.

It's time to go.

I pull back from Earth, but it's not letting me go.

I'm trapped here on the edge of the world, as my view shifts from my children to a hospital room.

Chapter 76

What in the world?

Seriously, which world am I in? I didn't go anywhere, yet here I am looking at the lady from the other doorway. The doorway Mystery Pal and I were supposed to be off to next.

Yikes. She's about to give birth.

I can't see the others around me, but I can feel them. Mystery Pal is vibrating with excitement. Mom and Dad seem curious. Can they see this too?

But this is still Earth. How can she be here? She's supposed to be on Other-Earth.

Maybe the two Earths are one now?

My nonexistent stomach lurches at the sudden pull. Whichever dimension of whatever doorway we're on the threshold of, it doesn't matter anymore.

Time's up.

The scene in the hospital dissolves, and I'm looking at the planet. Definitely Earth.

I want to say my last goodbyes to Mom and Dad, but I'm already floating down. I've entered the world with Mystery Pal holding tightly to me, but I can still feel the rest of them. It's as if they're right beside me.

They are right beside me. We're all drifting down together. Even that Henry kid. Well, he looks ancient now, like a little old man, but he smiles and waves. I wave back, my heart filled with joy.

Mom and Dad look exactly like they did in our last Earth life. Their eyes are locked, hands clasped as they descend. No more Lizzy from space-world, she's taken on the form I remember and love. The one Dad obviously remembers and loves, too.

I wonder what I look like.

Finally, Mystery Pal is no longer a mystery. And she's not a girl, either. She's the cutest little boy, with features much like mine. As strange as it all is, I've never felt closer to a person in all my lives. This is my soulmate.

And we're all on our way to Earth. My children, they're down there somewhere.

The human shapes melt away, until only the colors of the souls remain.

There's nothing but love, and the blissful sensation of euphoria.

And then peace.

So, no goodbyes. No tears. No endings.

I'm going home. With my family.

About the Author

Kerri Davidson currently lives in Elbow, Saskatchewan with her husband Travis. She moves a lot, so you never know when she may pop up in a town near you.

Born in Weyburn Saskatchewan, she has lived in other Saskatchewan communities including Carlyle, Moosomin, Porcupine Plain, Saskatoon, Moose Jaw, and Regina. She spent eleven years in Manitoba residing in Oxford House, Gilbert Plains, Dauphin, Fisher Branch, and Russell.

A reluctant vegetarian, she loves vodka, potato chips, all animals, and some people.

In addition to writing paranormal fiction with heart, she is the author of The Chronicles of Henny: a series of graphic novels for grownups, featuring a drunken chicken and a cop.

Find out more at Bagoflettuce.com.